MW00940877

CYNTHIA HICKEY

DEADLY NEIGHBORS
A River Valley Mystery

By Cynthia Hickey

DEDICATION

Thank you to all my readers who clamored for another mystery series. I hope you enjoy the River Valley series..

1

Hearing voices when no one is with you is not a good thing, even when you're thirty-four years old. Some people call it women's intuition.

Regardless, I heard a distinct voice inside my head and not for the first time in my life. At that moment, the phantom whisper clearly told me not to take the last glazed, jelly-filled doughnut.

"What are you doing?" Lynn, my best friend and virtual sandpaper, entered the store and reached for the pastry.

"I was about to eat that and was afraid of the repercussions. I went shopping last week for a bathing suit and it was not a pretty sight." Images of misshapen dough rose to mind.

"Oh." Her hand fell to her side, and she stepped back like the doughnut would bite her.

The store door swung open, a bell jangling a pretty tinkle, and Sharon Weiss, my current nemesis, sailed into Gifts from Country Heaven, snagged the pastry from the plate, and shoved it between puffer-fish lips. The product of this year's latest bit of collagen injections.

The summer before she'd had liposuction and, to be honest, after seeing the cute clothes she wore, the thought occurred to me to get the procedure for myself. She could eat all the sweet stuff she wanted and have it sucked back out.

"Do you have those handkerchief dolls I ordered? I've got an errand to run right now, but if you could have your daughter bring them by my house in. . ." She glanced at her watch, a gold piece outlined with diamonds, and made sure to turn it so I could see every bit of its finery.

"About an hour? I need them for my women's breakfast in the morning. They're door prizes. Did y'all hear about Anderson's sister?" My eyes followed the last of the jelly-filled delight to her mouth. "Missing."

"What?" My attention jerked from her brightly-painted mouth to her heavily mascara-covered, false-eyelashed eyes. The lids seemed to droop with the weight.

"Mis-sing." Sharon enunciated so my slow brain could catch up.

"Where did she go?"

Mouth stuffed with temptation, Sharon threw her hands in the air as if to say, "Duh." She swallowed then leaned forward, her glittering eyes focused on me. "She wouldn't be missing, Marsha, if people knew where she was."

"I understand that." I planted my fists on hips, too round in my opinion, and stared her down. My mother said I had curves in all the right places, and that men didn't like stick figures for marriage partners.

They wanted someone soft and cuddly to warm their bed. God paid mothers to complement their daughters, didn't He? Maybe He put an extra jewel in their crown if they built up their children's self-esteem?

Besides, I didn't have anyone waiting in the wings to marry me anytime soon, anyway, so why give up on the good stuff. Like food. "When someone goes missing, you usually begin looking for them at the last place they were seen."

"Right. Since when did you become so criminally savvy?"

"I watch a lot of crime scene television."

"Whatever." Sharon drummed Scarlett-colored manicured nails against the countertop. "When you have a chance, get a load of the new high school football coach. Really hot. I met him this summer at the city pool." She winked. "I'd just bought a new swimsuit. Red and sizzling. Now, I've got to figure out how to get him to ask me to dinner."

"I bet." I glared at her back as she sashayed out the door. "Have you ever met anyone more interested in men, looks, or gossip? And maybe Lindsey doesn't want to spend a half-hour out of a summer afternoon to deliver anything to Sharon."

"Oh, stop. You know you're going to tell her to. Sharon sends a lot of business to this store. From here *and* surrounding towns." Lynn clapped a hand on my shoulder and leaned closer. "And, we're gossiping about her right now. Here's a secret, I like men too." She stared intensely at me. "I've seen the coach. He'll stop your heart, Marsha. Prepare yourself. Gotta go. See you later."

I grimaced. What did she mean "stop my heart?" How could Lynn leave out such valuable information? I'd seen good-looking men before and not one of them put me at a risk for a heart attack.

I glanced out the store window. Lindsey swept the sidewalk with all the enthusiasm of a child on punishment. She wouldn't be happy about making a delivery to Sharon. Why I did the extra work for the woman, who felt like a burr in my bobby sock, was a mystery. Oh, well. Customer service brought the people back day after day. That and the free coffee and pastries. I headed to the storeroom to grab the miniature dolls.

The bell over the front door jingled, and with arms loaded, I stepped behind the counter and caught a glimpse of the man who entered the store. The wrapped dolls fell to the floor. I ducked behind the counter. *Please, don't see me*. My heart leaped into my throat and beat with all the power of a marching band.

Duane Steele, the last person I expected to see waltz into my shop, stared into the display case above my head. Maybe he hadn't recognized me. Ten years had passed after all. I stalled, remaining crouched on the floor.

"Mars Bars?"

Darn! I cringed. Duane had been the only one with the guts to call me by that despised nickname. "Let me help you." He moved around the counter and knelt beside me.

Glancing over, I fell into the darkest blue eyes known to humankind. Like a midnight summer sky. I'd almost forgotten. His biceps bulged as he shifted the wrapped gifts into a pile.

"Duane." The word rushed from my mouth in a whisper. Trying again, I spoke louder. "Let me get those." In my haste to rise, the top of my head collided with his mouth, knocking him backward.

"I'm sorry. I'm sorry." My foot slipped on a doll's dress, and I landed in a heap beside him.

In spite of a bloody lip, Duane laughed. Clutching his stomach, he rolled to his side. "God help me, woman, you haven't changed a bit."

"*Somebody* needs to help you." I punched his arm, surprised at how quickly I could revert back to snappy teenage remarks and juvenile behavior around him. Using the counter as support, I pulled to my feet.

Duane re-gathered the scattered dolls and handed them to me. I tossed him a nearby napkin. "Your lip is bleeding."

He dabbed his lip. "Wow, it didn't take long for you to put me in my place. You've probably been waiting a long time to clobber me."

If he only knew. "What brings you back to River Valley, Duane? I thought you hated this small town."

He shrugged. "I thought I did too. Sowed my wild oats and came home. I'm the new high school coach."

"You are?" Why didn't Lynn warn me? What kind of game was she playing? Oh, stop my heart, indeed. I would so get her back for this. "You didn't say anything about getting a degree when we spoke at Robert's funeral." Of course, we'd avoided each other then, but that was beside the point. Suddenly, the dust on the counter screamed to be cleaned, and I grabbed a rag from the pocket of my apron.

Duane placed his hands over mine to still them. "There wasn't anything to say, Marsha. You'd just become my brother's widow. You had a small child." I glanced into eyes shadowed with pain. "It was too late for me to say anything."

I yanked free. "It's never too late." I wasn't ready to revisit my prior feelings for Duane. No matter how much time had passed. Make that present feelings, since his arrival brought everything rushing back.

His sad smile lured me like a lover's gesture, tugging at the part of me that brought home strays and gave money to a dirty man on a street corner. I was lost the moment Duane strolled through the door.

My daughter Lindsey barged through the front door and skidded to a stop. Her gaze fell on my visitor. "Uncle Duane?"

A grin split his face, and he turned to me. "You've told her about me?"

"There's a picture of you and Robert on our bookshelf. Plus, she was five when you left. That's old enough to remember someone who gave her piggy-back rides." I grabbed a bag and shoved Sharon's purchase inside. "Lindsey, can you take this to Ms. Weiss, please?"

Lindsey groaned. "She's a horrible tipper. Oh, and here's your sign."

"Tape it to the window, please." I pushed the box into her hands. "I know she isn't generous, but you're the delivery gal, at least for now."

Lindsey taped the sign in the window and dashed out the door.

"She's beautiful." Duane watched her go. "Looks like you, with Robert's eyes."

Your eyes, I almost said, considering the two brothers could've been twins. "She's a good kid. Smart. I'm lucky."

Duane put a strong, warm hand on my arm. "I'd like to spend some time with you and Lindsey. Get to know my niece."

My heart stopped. We'd seen plenty of each other before he'd split town. More than I cared for my mother to find out. "We'll see. Glad to have you back." I grabbed a broom from around the corner. "Excuse me. I've got work to do."

"Okay." I didn't have to look to know his face radiated hurt. What did he think? That he could just two-step back into my life in his cowboy boots and faded jeans that fit like they were custom made, make my heart stutter, and I'd forgive everything? Not likely.

I shoved the broom across the scuffed wooden floor with enough force to almost throw my shoulder out of socket. After a moment of hesitation, Duane clomped away and out the door. My shoulders sagged. *I'm not strong enough to resist him again.*

The man I truly loved waltzed back into town while I worked in my mother's business. I shook my head. Yep, I was a real success story. My gaze roamed the country store, taking in the homey atmosphere and cuddly crafts. We even had a small bakery in one corner where we served pastries and flavored teas and coffees. At least this was something I could do. I was good with people and good with my hands.

The phone rang. Relieved by the distraction, I grabbed the handset. "Gifts from Country Heaven, how may I help you?"

"I appreciate the cookies, Marsha. But I didn't order them, and I'm not paying extra." Sharon's nasal tone resonated against my eardrums. "And your quality is definitely slacking. You need to speak with your supplier. That last cookie tasted different. Plus, tell your daughter not to enter my home without me letting her in. I mean I appreciate the delivery, but still. . . I've got to go. I feel ill."

Cookies? Entering uninvited?

The line went dead, leaving me staring at the silent receiver.

2

"Mom? I'm home."

"In here, Marsha."

I dropped my purse and car keys on the marble-topped table in the foyer. The aroma of pot roast greeted me at the door of the kitchen. Lindsey glanced up from the book she read at the kitchen table, and smiled. I ran my hand along her back before going to greet my mother.

"Smells good." I gave Mom a one-armed hug.

"How was work?" She leaned into me.

"Fine. The people of River Valley, Arkansas, do love the doughnuts, cookies, and coffee. Good thing or we might be out of business."

Mom shook her head. "Never. They don't come just for the doughnuts. We're a community icon. Like the Dairy Queen, or that stuffed cow at Wanda's Cafe."

Not likely. I glanced back at Lindsey. "How'd the delivery to Ms. Weiss go? She said I gave her cookies and that you entered her house uninvited."

My daughter's eyes narrowed. "She only gave me a dollar for delivery and had crumbs hanging off her chin, but she didn't get them from our bag. Gross. She looked like I woke her up. Unless she has a twin we don't know about, she answered the door."

"Huh. She said the cookies made her ill. Maybe she's thinking of the stale doughnut she ate at the store."

"We don't serve stale doughnuts." Mom lifted the Dutch oven pan and poured out the meat juices. "If she started in on cookies after a jelly-filled, it's no wonder she got sick. You know what they say about gluttons."

I smiled at Lindsey who rolled her eyes. "Are you coming in to help me tomorrow, Mom?"

"Most likely." Her gaze searched mine, and her voice lowered. "How are you doing, really? I heard who just got back to town."

I reached in the cabinet above her head for my bag of dark chocolate M & M's. My sure-fired feel good in the moment and be riddled with guilt later method of dealing with stress.

"The fact you're reaching for those tells me all I need to know." Mom turned back to her roast. "Lindsey, set the table, please."

"He wants to get to know his niece," I said around a mouthful of candy.

"Don't talk with your mouth full. The man wants to get reacquainted with you." Mom raised her eyebrows. "Don't tell me anything different." She waved a wooden spoon at me. "I know there was some hanky-panky going on between the two of you. Once upon a time. Things no mother wants to know about her baby girl. If you want me to go into detail—"

"Stop please." I ripped the bag down the side trying to grab another handful of heaven and colorful discs scattered across the faded linoleum. "No one's heard from him in ten years. He's barking up the wrong tree."

"Yep, sure he is. You keep telling yourself that." Mom tossed a couple of potholders onto the table, then hefted the pan. "Put the candy away, and sweep the floor, then let's eat. You can have him over for dinner tomorrow."

I choked on an M&M. "I don't want him over." Lindsey pounded my back on her way to the cabinet for plates.

"Uh-huh." Mom planted fists on ample hips. "I know my little girl. And you ain't over that boy. Doubt you ever will be. We only get one true love in this lifetime. One soul mate, and I think Duane is it for you."

"Mom's got a thing for Uncle Duane? Ewww. That's like dating your brother or something." A wicked grin split my pretty daughter's face as giggles erupted.

I scowled. "I do not have a *thing* for Uncle Duane. It was during high school. Your grandmother's insane. I'm committing her to the funny farm first thing tomorrow." Gritting my teeth, I shot my mother a warning look.

She flung her arms wide then pulled out her chair. "Fine. I won't say another word."

Not talking or giving her opinion is impossible for my mother, despite her intentions. I doubt she could not say anything if her life depended on it.

After serving dinner, she stabbed a piece of meat then shook her fork at me. "Mark my words, if your father were still alive . . ."

"Mother!"

"Sorry. I'll eat now."

Lindsey watched our exchange, interested cobalt eyes glued to Mom and then to me. *Don't say anything, don't say anything.*

Forcing my lips into what I hoped resembled a smile and not a shark's grimace, I transferred my attention to the food in front of me. I'd lost my appetite, and the handful of candy I'd eaten had nothing to do with it. Feelings for Duane? God, help me, but yes, I'd never gotten over the immature jerk who had ditched me after graduation and fled the state, taking my innocence, and my heart, with him.

Then, I'd rebounded into the arms of his look-alike younger brother. The result of that union sat across the table from me. Although I hadn't loved Robert the way I should have, I wouldn't give up my daughter for anything. I forced myself to take a bite of food. Why had Duane taken the coaching job here? He could've gone anywhere. Sometimes

I thought God got a perverse pleasure out of shaking up my life.

When we finished, I shoved back my chair and stacked dirty plates on top of each other. The phone rang, and Lindsey bolted to answer it.

"Mom, it's for you. It's a guy!" She mumbled something. "I think it's Uncle Duane."

My shoulders slumped even as my heart rate accelerated. Lindsey handed me the phone and hovered. I placed a hand over the phone's mouthpiece. "Go away," I hissed.

"Why? You listen to all my phone conversations."

"Go." I waited until she flounced out of sight before turning to the phone call. "Hello."

"I'm free tomorrow or the next night. I'll bring dessert."

"Get right to the point, Duane." Nothing like inviting himself over. I leaned against the wall. "Why is it so important for you to come over here?"

"I want to make things up to you. There's a big hole in my life, and I think you're the one to fill it."

I gasped, spun, lost my footing, and slid down the wall, landing hard on my more than sufficiently cushioned bottom. "You're rather presumptuous." My mom stuck her head around the corner, spotted me slumped to the floor, and shook her head before withdrawing. Amazing how one look from my mother can leave me feeling like an awkward thirteen-year-old.

"I want to get to know my niece."

"You've said that. Maybe she doesn't want to get to know you."

"Have you asked her?"

"No."

"Okay, then."

"Fine." I studied my ragged cuticles and wished for my bag of M & M's. Here we were, thirty-four-years-old, listening to each other breathe over the phone like we did in high school. Not to mention our anything but mature verbal sparring.

Duane's heavy sigh drifted across the airwaves and sent a shiver down my spine. His deep voice still melted me, despite my attempts at standing firm against his charm. "Mars Bar, I'm a changed man. Give me a chance."

"Tomorrow night. Five o'clock." Using my thigh muscles, which hated me for the effort, I pushed against the wall and got to my feet. "Don't be late, and bring something chocolate."

"I wouldn't dream of being late."

He was about ten years too late, but who's counting? Why'd I cave beneath the pressure? I have no willpower. I marched into the kitchen and made a beeline for a new bag of candy-coated support.

"Well?" Mom stacked the last plate in the cabinet.

"He'll be here for dinner tomorrow."

"What are you making?"

"Me?" My hand with the red piece of candy paused on its journey to my lips. "It was your idea."

"He isn't coming to see me."

"But I'm working."

She hung the dishtowel over the oven rack. "I said I'd be in to help. Speaking of which, I'd better get to bed if I've got to get up with the birds. I'd like to get some more of those stuffed bunnies sewed, and I found a new pattern for International Time-Out Babies."

I popped the candy in my mouth and crunched off the outer shell before letting the chocolate melt on my tongue. Life was spiraling out of control with the ferocity of a tornado. I'd have to head to the store tomorrow to stock up on my number one stress reliever. Especially with Duane back in town.

Lindsey leaned against the doorframe. "Why don't you like Uncle Duane?"

"Who said I didn't like him?"

"You did, in so many words." She crossed one ankle over the other, her tanned legs stretched out in front of her. Had I ever looked so young, so thin, so sure of myself? If only time stood still.

"You know me."

"Yeah, the icebox of River Valley." Lindsey marched past me and grabbed a soda from the refrigerator. "That's what everyone says. The kids at school are always asking why you don't date. You're pretty enough, and not *that* old."

Gee, thanks. I opened my mouth to scold her for drinking a soda after seven o'clock. The doorbell rang, which curtailed my nagging. I glanced at Lindsey, who shrugged before she chugged from the can. I set the bag on the counter and went to answer the bell.

River Valley's very own Barney Fife stood on the other side of our front door, one hand on his can of mace, the other poised to knock. He glanced over his shoulder. His five-foot-five frame, and all of one hundred and thirty pounds, quivered with suppressed energy. His nose twitched above a newly grown mustache, reminding me of an anxious rodent.

I grinned and opened the door. "Bruce, what brings you here? Is there someone following you?"

"What? No, no, you just can't be too careful, you know."

"In this town?" I held the door wider and waved him in. "When was the last time anything happened here?"

"Oh," he dragged out the word. "We're getting busy. What with Anderson's sister disappearing and all. The man's about out of his mind with worry. Is Lindsey here?"

"Yes." I frowned. A pile of boulders settled in my stomach. "What's this about, Bruce? This isn't a casual visit, is it?"

"Afraid I'm here on business, Marsha. Can you call your daughter?"

"Lindsey!"

"I'm here." She padded on bare feet to stand beside me. "Mr. Barnett?"

"Lindsey, did you deliver some things to Ms. Weiss today?"

"Yes, sir. About two or two-thirty." She glanced at me for confirmation.

I nodded. "That sounds about right."

Bruce whipped a small notebook from his pocket. "Did you happen to notice whether Ms. Weiss wore a necklace?"

"Yeah. A big, gaudy, red thing. She kept playing with it."

"Well, it's missing, and she says you were the last one she saw before noticing it was gone."

3

"Are you suggesting Lindsey had something to do with the disappearance of that necklace?"

Bruce stepped back, probably from the intensity of my glare. "A wallet disappeared from another house around the same time. I'm just asking whether Lindsey can verify where she was."

Lindsey stepped beside me. "I stopped at my friend's house after going to Ms. Weiss. Maybe around three?"

Barney's pencil scratched across the notepad. "Were you carrying a backpack or a purse?"

"Now, wait just a minute!" I stepped forward. "Lindsey is a minor, Bruce. You can't just waltz in here and make accusations."

He held up a hand to stop me. "Don't make me get a warrant. This is for Lindsey's protection too. Ms. Weiss is fit to be tied. I've got to do something, and Lindsey was seen leaving the woman's house."

"Because she made a de-li-ve-ry." I folded my arms. "She makes them all the time. Especially during the summer."

Lindsey yanked open the closet door, banging me in the side with the door handle. That'll leave a bruise. "Sorry. Here. I carried this with me. I take it everywhere."

Bruce took the small green backpack purse covered with white polka dots and peered inside. "Don't see anything. I don't suppose you hid it somewhere?"

I grabbed the bag from him. "That's enough. You've known Lindsey since she was born. Unless you can prove her guilty, I'm going to have to ask you to leave." I tossed the pack in the closet, closed the door, and held my left arm tightly to my aching side.

"Fine." He pursed his lips. "But you're speaking to an officer of the law here, Marsha."

"Puh-leese!" I nodded toward the outside. "You may leave now, *Officer*."

"No need to get pushy." Bruce stepped onto the porch. His eyes glittered beneath the porch light. "By the way, did you know Duane's back in town?"

I gave him a thin-lipped smile and slammed the door hard enough to rattle a couple of picture frames. What I really wanted to do was give him a shove down the steps, but since I didn't relish going to jail, I thought it better to keep control.

"Am I in trouble?" Lindsey lunged at me, wrapping her arms around my waist. "I didn't even go in her house. Ms. Weiss met me on the porch. She was wearing the necklace when I left. I swear."

"I'll get it straightened out." I hoped. I patted her between her shoulder blades then held her at arm's length so I could search her eyes. "We'll get this cleared up. If you didn't do anything wrong, you have nothing to worry about. Truth always wins out."

"What's going on? Who was at the door?" Mom scurried down the hall, pulling a fluorescent pink fuzzy bathrobe tight around her. Curlers sprang around her head like boils.

"Oh, Grandma!" Lindsey threw her sobbing self into my mother's arms. "Ms. Weiss thinks I stole her necklace."

"Nonsense. That woman's off her rocker. Always has been. It's because she puts too many toxins in her body. Can't leave well enough alone, that one."

I locked the door and headed to the kitchen. I needed some colorful stress reliever. I'd gain twenty pounds at this rate. Mom and Lindsey followed with my mother cooing soothing phrases to my distraught daughter.

"Well, Barney, I mean Bruce, was here asking questions." Stretching on my tiptoes, I reached for my candy. Somehow, stashing them on a higher shelf didn't do much to dissuade me from turning to chocolate during a time of crises.

After tossing a handful of colored discs into my mouth, I turned to the other two generations of Calloway women. "We'll just have to prove her innocent, won't we? You know the gossip mill in this town. Another day or two, and they'll have Lindsey robbing the Savings and Loan."

Under the watchful eye of my mother at Crafts from Country Heaven, I stuffed bunnies and embroidered sleepy eyes on them with black thread until life existed in a fog. Did she really think we'd sell this many rabbits in floppy hats and frilly dresses? I gazed with longing at the quilt rack. I'd never finish the Oklahoma Star pattern stretched across it if my whip-slashing-boss of a parent kept me doing mundane chores like this. What was I thinking, moving back home? And staying this long? Oh well, rent was cheap, and I had help in raising Lindsey.

I sighed and grabbed another handful of cotton batting. Robert had made barely enough money to pay bills, much less provide me and his daughter with life insurance. Then, a dark road, a drunk driver, and I became a grown widowed daughter who'd moved back in with momma.

One glance at the counter and I groaned. Six sappy, three-foot rabbits stared at me in various shades of undress. The bell over the door jingled, and I bolted to my feet. Relief at any form of entertainment coursed through me as Lynn strolled inside.

I grinned and managed to take one step before tripping over the plastic bag of stuffing. In nightmarish slow motion, bunnies mobbed me, tumbling down on my head and threatening to suffocate me with their muslin cushiness.

Lynn rushed around the counter, giggling. "I don't understand why your parents didn't change your name to Grace years ago. Have you ever walked across the room without tripping or running into something?"

"When I do, I'll let you know. Make yourself useless and help me pick these up." I cast a glance over my shoulder to make sure Mom was still safely in the backroom.

Lynn lowered her voice and stooped to grasp a bunny. "Sharon is spreading rumors all over town that Lindsey stole her necklace. Now, the woman has got Harvey thinking your daughter took his wallet."

"Lindsey wouldn't steal." She may be a teenager with a smart mouth, but I knew she wasn't a thief.

"I know that, and you know that, but people are going to start wondering." Lynn stood with an armful of stuffed animal. "Where do you want these?"

"The counter." We lined up the muslin rodent soldiers. I straightened my shoulders and folded my arms. "Why didn't you tell me Duane was the new high school coach?"

"And physical education teacher. Don't forget that." Lynn smiled then got serious. "You would've worried all day, and for what? So the guy's back. That shouldn't affect you too much. And I did warn you, kind of. I told you to guard your heart. It's been fifteen years since you married Robert, and ten years since Duane was last in town. You've both moved on." She peered closely at my face. "Right?"

I shrugged. "Of course. Yes. I've moved on. Definitely."

"You haven't! Oh, Marsha." Lynn leaned against the counter, her expression filled with pity.

"Have you seen him?" I fell back into the chair. "He's rocking hot. Looks better than he did before he left. Why do men do that? Age better than women? And, he's coming to dinner tonight. Said he wants to get to know his niece."

"Uh-huh." Lynn's gaze roamed over me. "What in the world are you wearing?"

"Overalls. Why?"

"Not to dinner, you're not."

"Why not? They're comfortable, and I'm definitely not out to impress Duane." Plus overalls hid all my bulges and imperfections.

"Keep trying to convince yourself of that, sweetie." Lynn patted my shoulder. "I've got to go. Don't stress too much over dinner. What are you cooking?"

"Chicken with Hollandaise Sauce."

Lynn laughed. "Yep. Cooking to impress."

The bell over the door jingled. Stephanie Jackson's perfume reached us before she did. Tall, thin, immaculately dressed, every strand of dyed red hair in place, she breezed into the store like she owned it. "Good morning, ladies. I'd like to ask whether I can hang one of these fliers in the window? I'm hosting a yard sale to raise funds for the women's ministry at River Valley Community Church. May I?" She turned before waiting on an answer.

I cringed at her exaggerated, overly-done southern drawl. Only those born and bred in the south could do it right. Imitators only sounded stupid.

"Sure. How's the adoption going?" *Please don't rope me into anything.*

Stephanie halted for the briefest moment before she continued, tape in hand, to the window. "Wonderfully. Should have enough money any day now. Mark and I have been saving every penny."

"As evidenced from the new Tahoe parked outside." I ducked my head before she spotted the smirk I was sure my lips curled into.

"Excuse me?" She turned and raised a finely tweezed eyebrow.

"Nothing. Just wishing you luck."

Sharon pushed through the door, almost knocking into Stephanie. I gnawed the inside of my lip. If River Valley's self-proclaimed elite were going to congregate in my store, I wished they'd buy something.

Sharon stomped to the counter. "What are you planning to do about my missing necklace?"

I twisted a finger in my ponytail and wished for my bag of M&M's. There were a lot of things I could tell her to do with her jewelry, but none of them nice. "Why should I do anything?"

"Your daughter stole it. She came to my house, let herself in, and waltzed off with a precious heirloom. Just as pretty as you please." Sharon's puffy lips tried going into a straight line, instead resembling the result of a bee sting.

"There is no proof that Lindsey took anything. She said you were wearing the necklace when she delivered your dolls." I really needed my stress reliever. Maybe I should take up smoking.

"Goodness." Stephanie clasped her handful of papers to her chest. "I hope little Rosalea isn't such a handful when she gets to be a teenager. Stealing. Imagine." She waved. "Y'all be nice now, ya hear?"

She'd already named the baby she hoped to one day adopt? What if it fell through or was a boy?

Lynn stepped beside me. "Sharon, until Lindsey is proven guilty you shouldn't be making waves."

The woman leaned across the counter and poked me in the chest with her index finger. "Watch your kid. I want my necklace back, and I'll do whatever it takes to get it."

My queen-in-shining-armor emerged from the storeroom brandishing a broom. "You leave right now." Mom's eyes flashed. "Or, Lord help me, I'll do something we'll both regret."

"Or what? You'll rob me of the rest of my possessions? Kill me?"

4

A cheap imitation of Westminster chimes rang through the house. I dropped the spoon, smearing hollandaise sauce down the front of me. Splatters dotted above the V neck of my royal blue blouse, and down the rest of my shirt. A swipe with a dishtowel succeeded in smearing them in a wider swath. One glance at the clock showed that if the person at the door was Duane, he was half an hour early.

Drat the man! His voice rumbled a greeting to Mom. Her higher sing-song voice answered. I tossed the dishtowel into the sink, lowered the temperature on the oven, and snuck up the stairs to my room.

My trusty overalls beckoned from the floor. I whipped off my soiled clothes, tugged on a fuchsia-colored tank top, and stepped into my favorite denims. Who did I want to impress anyway?

"What are you doing?" Mom banged open my door.

I shrieked and whirled. "You scared me."

"You have a guest you haven't greeted yet. Plus, dinner isn't finished, and what are you wearing? Couldn't you put on a dress?"

"I had on something else and spilt food on it. This is more comfortable."

"How are you going to catch a man dressed like a field hand? Do you have eyes in your head? A brain in your skull? Have you taken a look at that walking picture downstairs?" Her eyes bulged from their sockets.

I stared at my mother like she'd just arrived from another planet. Did she not remember the anguish I went through when the so-called hot plate downstairs ditched me? "He invited himself. You agreed to let him come. Not me. *You* wear a dress." I moved to step past her.

"You're thirty-four years old. You've been widowed for ten of those years. Get moving, young lady." Mom popped a dish towel at me. "You're crimping my style living here."

I stopped, caught a glimpse of the very serious look on my mother's face, and giggled. "Are you seeing someone?"

Her chin lifted. "Maybe."

I wiggled a finger at her and winked. "We'll talk later." I headed back to the kitchen. Just because Mom felt the need for a man in her life, didn't mean I did. My life was full with Lindsey and the store. Right. And if I said it enough, I might actually believe it.

"Hey, Mars Bar." Duane handed me a three-layer chocolate cake. "You said to bring chocolate."

The man looked more delicious than the cake, if that was possible. Wearing jeans that appeared made for him, a navy, button up collared shirt, and those scuffed boots that made him walk with a swagger worthy of the old West. I jerked my gaze away and accepted the dessert. "Yes, thank you."

Grateful for something to occupy my hands, I set the cake on the counter and turned back to preparing dinner. "Supper is almost done. Why don't you go on in the other room and visit with Mom and Lindsey?"

Duane stood so close behind me his breath tickled the hair at the nape of my neck. "Marsha."

My heart stuttered. The counter prevented me from moving to a more comfortable distance. If I could I see my face, I probably resembled an animal caught in a spotlight.

"Look at me, Marsha."

"I don't want to." My whispered words filled the silent kitchen.

"Please take a walk with me after dinner." His boots thudded against the worn linoleum on his way out.

I sagged against the counter and struggled to control my breathing. Be still my heart. An evening stroll with Duane Steele. I was doomed. I slid the steaming chicken dish from the oven and carried it into the dining room.

"That pip-squeak Barnett had the gall to accuse Lindsey of stealing the woman's necklace." Mom's scarlet face shone beneath the light. I set dinner in the center of the table and rolled my eyes. From the looks of things, she was just getting started.

"Now look at this face." She pinched Lindsey's chin between her fingers. "Does this look like a thief? Something is rotten in Mayberry, and Marsha and I intend to find out what."

I slapped a chicken breast on her plate. "What did you say?"

"Careful. That's hot." She wiped sauce from her hand. "I heard you tell Lindsey yesterday that you'd get to the bottom of this. So, we'll do it together. Sounds like fun." Mom lifted her fork and stabbed her chicken.

My mother might be unconventional, but her heart was in the right place. A smile tweaked the corner of Duane's lips. My breath caught as I remembered his kisses. Those had been given by a teenager. Would the man do better? Make my knees weak and my head spin? I yanked my gaze away. Don't go there, Marsha. My hands shook. I served his food slowly, careful not to splash or dump anything in his lap.

Duane placed a hand over mine and whispered. "As delicious as dinner looks, I don't think you want to be wearing it." His hand, clutching a napkin, raised to a spot above my overalls. I glanced down. Hollandaise sauce nestled in the small amount of cleavage showing. If my face got any hotter, we'd have to call the fire department. The cad! Mentioning something so embarrassing.

I slapped his hand and turned away to dab myself with a napkin. "A gentleman wouldn't have said anything." Much less attempt to clean such a personal area.

"Now, Marsha—"

"Let's eat." Mom glared at me, before bowing her head, chicken still speared on her fork.

The meal passed with Mom filling Duane in on all the River Valley gossip. His hearty laugh rang across our small dining room, filling the house with warmth. My chicken tasted dry. The sauce bland. I shoved aside my plate. How could I be expected to eat with him sitting across from me? Staring at me with those bedroom eyes?

Lindsey leaped to her feet. "I'm hanging with my friends okay? Be back at ten." She snatched her plate from the table, disappeared into the kitchen, re-emerged empty-handed, then dashed out the door, grabbing her backpack on the way. I sighed and cleared my own plate. What I wouldn't give for an ounce of her energy.

Duane followed my lead, prepared to follow me into the kitchen. "Ready for that walk?"

"A walk?" Mom's eyebrows rose. "That's a great idea. I'll clear the table. You two go on."

Wonderful. I relinquished the dishes and, avoiding Duane's gaze, headed out the front door. "Where do you want to go?"

"Let's just head down Main Street. Is that all right with you? I know you aren't comfortable being alone with me."

That's an understatement. "Duane, it . . ." Ahead of us, Lindsey darted around the corner of a neighbor's house. "That's fishy. I thought she said she was going to a friend's house. Wonder what that girl's up to. Come on." I led Duane into the shadows lining the sidewalk. "Don't let her see you."

"Why are we spying on your daughter?"

We hunkered behind a Rhododendron bush. Duane's cologne drifted on the slight summer evening breeze. A musky, manly scent. I wanted to bury my nose in his neck. "She isn't acting herself. Lindsey doesn't usually skulk around. With this suspicion hanging over her head, she needs to be careful."

"Could she have taken the necklace?"

"No!" I bolted to my feet, getting my hair tangled in the bush. Fighting with the branches increased my irritation. "If you would have stuck around to get to know your niece, you'd know better than to ask that question."

"Let me." Duane reached around me to work my tresses loose. "I had to go, Marsha. I needed to see what was outside this town." He brushed my cheek with the back of his hand. "Do you want to know what I discovered? There's nothing that compares to you."

Help me, Lord, the man stood too close. Goodness! I placed a hand to my chest in an effort to keep my heart from beating free of its cage. Was he trying to kill me?

Lindsey reappeared and moved at a brisk pace about fifty yards ahead of us. I slapped Duane's hands away and yanked my pony-tail free. "Come on. She's getting away."

"Well, okay. But chasing after your daughter wasn't what I had in mind when I mentioned taking a walk."

"Shhh."

"She can't hear us."

Lindsey headed toward the Dairy Queen, but instead of joining the group of young people gathered at the picnic tables outside, she peered around the corner. I stopped Duane with a hand on his arm. Ten minutes later, Lindsey followed a young man who separated from the group.

Duane reached up to smooth my hair. I shoved him away. "Stop touching me."

"Your hair is sticking up."

"Good grief." I stepped away from him and quickened my pace in order not to lose sight of Lindsey.

Duane's boots clomped as he caught up with me. "We're going to have to talk sooner or later, Marsha. You can't keep pushing me away."

"It'll have to be later. I'm busy." I'd make sure it was way later. How would I tell this man I still harbored feelings for him? That being anywhere near him set my blood to boiling? What if I bared my soul, and he dosey-doed on my heart with his cowboy boots?

The drone of a lawnmower reached our ears as we turned down a residential street, still following Lindsey, who chased after the boy. If my daughter ducked behind a bush, we copied. If she paused in her stalking, we imitated her movements. I glared at Duane when a snort of laughter escaped him.

"Sorry. But if anyone sees us. . .On second thought, everyone in town will just say, there goes Marsha Calloway Steele again."

"Ha, ha. You're a regular riot."

Lindsey turned. I ducked, and lunged, barreling into Duane, who once again stood too close. The movement took both of us to the ground. My breath left in a whoosh. Whether from being knocked out of me from the fall or from the close proximity of Duane's lips, was a mystery.

His mouth curved into a slow smile, and he twisted his hand in my ponytail and pulled me closer. His lips seared mine. The stars erupted into a blaze of fireworks, the moon brightened, the…

"Mom?"

5

Where was I? Who was that girl calling me mom? I stared, uncomprehending into a strange man's eyes. His arms tightened around me, melding my body with every inch of his. Goodness!

"Mom!"

"Huh?" Oh, yeah. That's my daughter, and the man beneath me was Duane Steele; the man I refused to give the time of day to. I shoved off him and punched his chest.

"Hey!" He laughed. The sound rang through the approaching dusk.

Lindsey put fists on her hips. "What are the two of you doing making out on the sidewalk? How embarrassing! If Grandma saw you. . ."

"Uh?" I got to my feet and brushed off the seat of my overalls.

"Were you following me?" Lindsey threw her hands in the air. "I cannot believe this! You *were* following me. Why?"

"Um." When did I grow speechless? I couldn't form a cohesive sentence.

Duane placed a hand on my daughter's shoulder. "Your mother is worried about you. She wants to make sure people don't have more reason to speculate about your whereabouts."

Ooh, good save, Duane.

"People are talking about me?" Lindsey's shoulders slumped. Her chin quivered. "I've got to go. I'll see you in a couple of hours." She turned and shuffled away.

"Lindsey, wait." My heart ached for my baby. "Come home with me. We'll watch a chick flick and eat popcorn."

"Let her go. She'll be all right." Duane peered into my face. "Want to go for an ice cream?"

An ice cream with him would be safe, right? "Okay."

Duane grabbed my hand, sending bolts of electricity up my arm and into my numb brain, waking me. I tried to pull away, only to have him tighten his grip. Resigned, I sighed. "Let's head that way for a minute." I motioned my head to the right. "I want to walk past Sharon Weiss's house."

"Why?"

"That's the way Lindsey headed. And the boy she was following."

"You aren't a very exciting date."

"We aren't on a date." Did he think we were on a date? Lord, help me.

Sharon's house came into view, curtains pulled tight on all the windows except a panel in the front door. A small square of amber light spilled onto the front porch. Her neighbor, Harvey Miller, who said his wallet had been taken around the same time as Sharon's necklace, peeked through the sheers of his front window. He let the drapes fall as we strolled by.

"Stop!" A young woman streaked past us, dragged by three Labrador retrievers in various colors. Duane dropped my hand and lunged forward to grab the dogs' leashes and bring them to a halt.

"Thank you." The woman doubled-over, balancing her hands on her knees. "These three always give me a run. I think I need to charge more for their care." She straightened and took back the reins. "I'm Marilyn Olsen, the dog walker of River Valley. At least I think I'm the only one with those particular services for hire." White teeth flashed in a tanish orange face. "I'm saving to get to Hollywood. Do you have any dogs that need walking?"

"Sorry, I don't. I'm Duane, and this is Marsha." He looped the leashes over her wrist.

"You could walk him." I motioned my chin at Duane.

"I don't walk people." The girl obviously didn't know sarcasm. Her gaze traveled from Duane's boots to his head. She cocked a hip and batted her eyelashes. "Of course I might make an exception for you." The dogs lurched ahead. "Nice to meet you." Marilyn tossed a wave over her shoulder and before we knew it the wanna-be starlet with a fake tan disappeared around a corner.

"She even looks like a Marilyn," I said. "The bleached hair, red lipstick, and how many coats of mascara do you think she was wearing?"

"I have no idea. Did she have on mascara?" Duane reclaimed my hand. "Now, can we have that ice cream?"

"In a minute." I slid free and shot him a look that could kill. What had he been looking at if not her face? Her silicon chest? Would've been hard to miss. Even for a blind man. "Look at this street. What do you see?"

Duane sighed. "It looks like any residential street in an Arkansas country town. Or any small town for that matter. Trees line both sides. Homes with character; not cookie cutter houses. Children playing by the light of the porch. Old people sitting in rockers. It's the same scene I've seen a million times."

"Exactly." I let my gaze roam up and down the street. "The same thing every day. Morning, noon, and evening. Now, if someone were to break into someone's house during the day, there would be at least two or more witnesses to the event."

"Okay." Duane nodded.

"If Lindsey went into Sharon's house. . .there." I pointed. "Then next door to Harvey's," my finger showed the path. "Someone would have seen her. A pizza doesn't get delivered in this town without the neighbors knowing what the toppings are."

"Why don't you let the police handle this?" Duane grabbed my elbow and turned me in the direction he'd been working toward all evening. "They'll prove Lindsey innocent and life will go on. The thief, if there is one, is most likely someone passing through."

"You know how our police are. Don't you remember Halloween nights in high school? The officers took the eggs from the boys and gave them to us girls. They aren't exactly on top of things. And what do you mean *if* there is one? You don't think we have a thief?" I planted fists on my hips. "If not, then what are people accusing Lindsey of doing?"

"Maybe they just misplaced those things." Duane dragged me along with him until we stood in front of the town's local hangout: The River Valley Dairy Queen. He held the door open and ushered me inside.

After ordering both of us a chocolate peanut covered piece of heaven, Duane ushered me to a far corner booth. He slid in next to me instead of across. My breath hitched, and I pressed against the wall.

"Now that I've got you cornered, you have no choice but to listen to what I have to say." Duane turned to face me.

Uh oh.

"I know you can't stand the sight of me. . ."

That wasn't exactly true. With his square jaw, sleepy eyes, dark hair, and eye color no man could invent, Duane was some of the best eye candy around. And that hint of a five o'clock shadow made a woman want to.

. . Well, I couldn't go there. Not and maintain my reputation as ice queen, anyway.

"Aren't you going to say anything?"

What did I miss? "Um, sorry?" I reached for the ice cream the teenager who'd taken our order brought.

Duane ran his hands through his hair and slumped against the back of the vinyl booth. "I'm baring my soul, and you aren't listening?"

Great. Now, I had guilt. "Duane, this is very difficult—." I put a hand on his arm, and froze as a commotion outside the window distracted me.

The young man my daughter seemed so fixated on darted past the building. A few moments later, Lindsey slid past, keeping her back against the wall. She reached the corner, paused, then dashed across the parking lot. Behind her, dressed in black, sneaked Sharon Weiss.

"This evening gets more bizarre by the minute." Duane straightened. "I change my mind. No one can say being on a date with you is boring."

"We aren't on a date." I shoved against him. "Let's go. They're getting away."

"You know, Marsha, they have medication for what ails you." He slid from the booth and grasped my hand.

We shoved past a couple entering the burger shop and murmured apologies. The parking lot stood empty. I cast glances to my left and right, then tugged to pull Duane in the direction the sneaky threesome had run.

"There." Ahead, I made out the shadowy form of Sharon.

Duane and I sprinted in her direction. The woman yelled and leaped behind a shrub. Someone screamed. We increased our speed and burst upon Sharon holding my daughter's arm in a death grip. With her free hand, she yanked at Lindsey's backpack.

"I don't have it!" Lindsey pulled free, almost knocking Sharon off her feet.

"It's an heirloom." Sharon grabbed again, her sculptured nails raking my daughter's face.

Lindsey cupped her cheek.

"Hey!" I bolted forward.

"That's enough." Duane stepped between us. "Ms. Weiss, would you please explain what is going on?"

Sharon took a deep breath and squared her shoulders. "Seeing as how things in peaceful River Valley have taken to disappearing, and *this* girl is wandering around after dark, I thought I would do the responsible thing and follow her. Someone needs to protect the citizens of this town."

"That is the police's responsibility." I jerked my arm free of Duane's grip. "Besides, look around you. It's summer time, Sharon. Lots of young people are outside after dark."

"The police are doing a bang-up job so far." Sharon crossed her arms.

Lindsey pulled her hand away and glanced at her palm. I craned my neck, relieved not to see blood. "I didn't take your necklace, Ms. Weiss. You were wearing it when I delivered the dolls. I never saw Mr.

Miller, so I didn't take his wallet." Lindsey's eyes glittered beneath the street lamp. "I'm heading to a friend's house. There's no harm in that, is there?"

What friend was she going to see? She'd roamed the two main streets of town and most of the neighboring residential area. I opened my mouth, then clamped it shut. Better to let things play out without my interference.

"Go home, Sharon." Duane took my arm with one hand and Lindsey's with the other.

"Yeah," I jutted my chin forward. "Before I press assault charges against you."

"Real mature, Marsha." Sharon tossed her head. "Y'all haven't seen the last of me."

6

The sounds in my head whirred to the buzz of the sewing machine. Voices spun, overlapping, tumbling, and weaving like tangle thread. Duane's low rumble begged to be heard over Sharon's shrieking. Lindsey's teenage voice rose in confusion. I couldn't make sense of any of the voices filtering through my mind.

As I sewed, the needle flashed in and out of the flowered fabric before snapping in two. I sighed and pushed back from my chair. "Mom, I'll finish these seat cushions later. I've got to go and clear my head."

"How can you clear something that's already empty?" Her giggle reached me from the storeroom.

"Everyone's a comedian." Outside, I turned right and headed toward Sharon Weiss's street. The way she accosted my child the night before still irked me. Maybe the two of us could sit down like civilized women and discuss things. I glanced at my watch. Nine

A.M. Even a woman of leisure such as Sharon should be up by now.

The drone of a lawnmower drew my attention. Melvin Brown, a familiar sight behind any landscaping tool on most of the town's properties, mowed the lawn next door to Sharon's. He tipped his grungy baseball hat in my direction. Trying to be neighborly, I stooped to pick up Sharon's unclaimed newspaper before heading up the steps to her front door.

Westminster chimes rang when I pressed the doorbell. After a few seconds, I cupped my hands around my eyes and peered through the etched beveled glass. The house appeared dark. No human form approached. The shadow of a cat streaked past on highly polished wooden floors.

I tried the door handle. It swung open at my touch. I glanced over my shoulder.

Melvin shut off the mower and tipped his hat again. "I ain't seen her all morning. Normally, she's outside wearing that slinky housecoat and getting her paper. All dolled up like some movie star," he called.

"New lawnmower?"

He grinned. "Second-hand. Get a new one soon. I'm getting closer to having a real business. Coming into some extra money, ya know?"

I waved and stepped inside. A cool, air-conditioned foyer greeted me. From a room down the hall came the muted sounds of a television. "Sharon? The door's open, can I come in?"

My footsteps thudded against the floor. "It's me—Marsha. I need to talk to you." My voice echoed from the Spartan walls. A shiver ran up my spine, and I had the urge to turn around and forget speaking with her.

"Get out!" Like a phantom, Sharon seemed to float into the hall, some kind of green paste spread across her face, her hair in skinny foam rollers. "Like mother, like daughter. Both sneaky. Both deceitful. Get out." She advanced, her face contorted like something out of an alien nightmare.

Sharon brandished a heavy silver candlestick like a weapon-wielding Medusa. I spun. My legs moved like a cartoon character, sliding on the polished floor surface, yet I couldn't gain traction. I ran—going nowhere. Darn these new boots. My heart banged in my throat. My feet slipped, bringing me hard to my knees. In desperation, I crawled toward the safety of the front door. Glancing over my shoulder, I whimpered as she advanced.

Could she attack me? I *was* in her house. Uninvited. Would it matter to the authorities that the door was unlocked?

After what seemed an eternity of breath-holding, heart-stopping seconds, I made my way onto the front porch. I leapt to my feet, jumped the three stairs to the ground, and dashed down the street. Out of sight of Sharon's house, I leaned against a tree. A fit of nervous giggles overtook me.

I glanced around the corner to where Melvin trimmed bushes. No sign of his having seen anything. I thanked God no one had witnessed what guaranteed to be my most embarrassing moment of many embarrassing moments. Then to start laughing, even as tears sprang to my eyes, had to be the cherry on top of embarassment. Why did giggling when nervous or scared have to be in my DNA blue-print? I sighed and wiped my eyes.

I'd never seen Sharon without makeup and had never been privy to what was obviously an elaborate routine to look her best before starting her day. She wouldn't really have hit me with the candlestick, would she? Of course, the fact that I had seen her not fully made up might give her motive. I couldn't remember having ever panicked before. It must have been the eeriness of the silent house. I shrugged. I'd better go tell Barney, I mean, Bruce, because Sharon was bound to call him.

Being a small town of nosey neighbors, Oak Dale had few yards enclosed by fences. I cut behind several houses until I reached Main Street. I turned left fifty yards then stood in front of the small red brick building that housed River Valley's finest in law enforcement: All three of them.

I straightened my shoulders to bolster my courage, and shoved inside. "Sorry." An officer I knew only by face, leapt to safety to avoid being hit by the swinging door. He scowled at me and slipped outside.

I made my way to Bruce's office. "Hey, Bruce."

He sat in the back of the room, feet propped on his desk. "Marsha." Bruce let his feet fall with a bang to the floor. "I just got an interesting phone call."

"I can explain." I plopped into a plastic chair opposite him. Folding my arms, I leaned back on two of the chair legs, and filled Bruce in on last night's happenings. "Then, I went to her house to speak with her this morning. You know, to smooth things over. The door was unlocked and open, basically, so I went in. She chased me out waving a candlestick. She could've killed me. If anyone was in danger, it was me."

"She's threatening to press trespassing charges."

"What?" I jerked. "Whoa." My arms wind-milled as I fell back. I fell over with a thud. My legs flew over my head before hitting the floor. Ow. One more reason I rarely wore a dress. Flashing unmentionables during clumsy moments would've been hard to live down. "Can she do that?" I lay as still as possible to catch my breath.

Bruce rushed to my aid. "Are you all right?" He held out a hand offering to help me up. "I talked her out of it, but she's putting a restraining order against you and Lindsey. I'll bring it by once the paperwork is complete."

I waved his hand away, and closed my eyes. Movement only promised to bring more pain. "After last night, I ought to put one against her."

He bent over me. "Do I need to call an ambulance?"

"No. Just give me a minute. Once I die, I'll feel better." My mortification was complete. Within hours, possibly minutes, everyone in town would know Sharon considered me a threat. I'd better get up and face the music. I groaned and struggled to my feet. "Oh, well. We weren't really friends anyway."

Mom met me at the door of the store, hands on chubby hips. "You've been busy. The phone's been ringing off the hook. Seems I'm living with a dangerous criminal. What were you doing at Sharon's? I'll never be able to lift my head in this town again. Good thing is— the focus is off Lindsey and on you."

"Please. Something else will happen and everyone will forget about this." I shuffled inside and lowered my aching body behind the sewing machine. I could really use some M&M's about now. A tray that used to contain cookies, beckoned. One last cherry-chocolate chunk called my name. I shoved it into my mouth and sat down to begin work.

"Marsha!"

I jumped. "What? Did you want the last cookie?" I glanced around. The empty platter sat on the counter.

"I don't know what you're talking about." Mom glared at me from the other side of the sewing machine. "What, exactly are you doing with those cushions?"

"Sewing them?" I glanced at my work. They resembled nothing but a lump of striped cloth. My gaze flew to the clock.

Forty minutes, and I hadn't sewn anything? I scratched my head. "Was I asleep?"

"No. Your eyes were open." Mom stepped behind the counter. "I came back from running errands to see you with your foot pressed to the pedal, the machine running about ninety miles an hour, and no cloth being moved through it. Are you daydreaming about breaking and entering into someone else's home?"

"Um." I chewed the inside of my cheek. Didn't we just talk about my visit to Sharon? Ten drummers played a heavy metal beat inside my head. I lowered my face to my hands.

"They aren't going to sew themselves." Mom patted my shoulder on her way to the storeroom.

I glanced at the clock again. Please, God, don't tell me a customer came in and saw me sitting in La-La land. I studied the shelves. Nothing appeared out of place. The counter remained clear of notes. No messages waited on the answering machine. I shrugged and decided to do what I should have done in the first place.

It didn't take long for the thread to break. Probably had something to do with forcing the fabric through too quickly. My hand shook, making it impossible for me to rethread. What was wrong with me? My temper rose. My right eye twitched, and my head spun.

"Mom?" I called over my shoulder. "I'm walking home. I don't feel well."

7

I stumbled over a crack in the sidewalk,
almost falling to my knees. My hands grasped
a fence post to keep me upright. My head
ached and my legs seemed to be the
consistency of jelly. A truck stopped on the
street beside me, and I lifted my head.

"Marsha?" Duane slid from behind the
wheel. "What's wrong?"

"I don't know. I feel weak." My knees
buckled.

He lifted me and carried me to the
passenger side of his truck. "Do you need to
see a doctor?"

"No. Just take me home." I rested my
head against the back of the seat. Having
skipped lunch in my quest to resolve things
with Sharon left my stomach angry with me.
Could the lack of food cause me to feel this
way? I'd have a handful of M&M's first thing
when I got home.

Duane cast several glances my way as
he sped toward my house. If he asked me one

more time if I was all right, I'd slug him. Did I look all right? The comfort of the sofa beckoned.

He pulled the truck into the driveway, cut the engine, then rushed to help me inside. "Upstairs?"

"Heavens, no. Mom will kill me if you take me to my room. That's off-limits to males. Always has been, always will." I could hear her voice as if she stood next to me. "The sofa's fine."

"Can I get you anything?" If he didn't wipe the concerned look off his face, I might start to show him how I really felt about him. Keeping Duane at arm's length became more difficult with each passing day. How would he react if I threw myself at him and planted a big kiss on those delicious looking lips? I'd have to try it sometime when craziness completely took over.

"A glass of water and my bag of candy. It's in the cupboard beside the sink." I sank onto the sofa with a sigh, and pulled a crocheted afghan over me. My eyes closed.

Mom shook me awake. "What are you doing in the house alone with Duane Steele?"

I sat up. "He's still here? How long have I been sleeping?"

"About an hour." Duane leaned against the door frame. A grin spread across his face. "Did you know you snore?"

"I do not." The events of the day were fuzzy. I remembered being chased by a green-faced Sharon, and visiting Bruce, but after that, the day's events vanished. Until now. Did

I have some kind of a virus? "Where's Lindsey?"

"Hasn't come home yet." Mom folded the afghan and placed it along the back of the sofa. "Are you sick? You left the store acting funny."

"I don't know. I feel fine now."

Mom placed a hand against my forehead. "You don't have a fever."

"I saw her wobbling down the sidewalk." Duane moved to sit in the recliner like he'd been invited to stay. "If I didn't know better, I'd swear she'd been drinking."

"Hmmph. I'll fix her some tea. And some for myself. What a day." Mom bustled to the kitchen to brew what she considered her miracle drug.

"I don't drink." I hugged a sofa pillow to my stomach. "I remember sewing cushions, then eating a cookie, but that's it until mom woke me. Did you carry me into the house?" *Please say no*. The poor man could've broken his back.

"Yep." He winked. "You felt good in my arms."

Right. All one hundred and twenty-five pounds of me. "Sharon put a restraining order against me and Lindsey. Well, she's going to."

"Why?"

I explained my wanting to speak with her, then added, "Doesn't that seem a bit harsh?"

"You were in her house." Duane leaned forward. "Why does this bother you? The two of you aren't exactly friends.

Something is obviously going on in Sharon's life. Give her space. She'll work it out."

A glass shattered in the kitchen. Duane and I dashed from the living room and into the kitchen. Mom leaned against the counter, staring into the sink.

"Mom?"

She sighed. "I'm fine. Wet hands and a glass don't mix. Especially when you're distracted." She turned to face us and crossed her arms. "Did you take money from the cash register today?"

"No, why?"

"We're short almost two hundred dollars. Did you wait on any customers this afternoon?"

I chewed my lip. Had I? A chunk of the day seemed non-existent. "I don't think so."

"Did Lindsey come in?" Mom's face reddened.

I fell into a chair. "What are you saying?"

"Nothing. It's just that, well, I heard the bell over the door a couple of times today when you were working up front, then when I came back from running errands, you're in a daze behind the sewing machine. And, well, I'm not saying anything really." Mom pulled up a chair opposite me. The sadness in her eyes almost made me forget she basically accused her granddaughter of stealing. "The cash register receipt says we should have a hundred and ninety-five dollars more than we do. According to the records, we sold a wooden rocking chair, and we *are* minus one."

"I remember now. I sold one this morning." To a young couple just starting a family. I knew I'd put the money in the register. I leaned my chin on my hand, mentally picturing the four fifty-dollar bills and handing the customer back a five. I'd even checked to make sure the money was legit. "Something fishy is going on here."

"Y'all want me to call Bruce?"

I glanced at Mom. I'd forgotten for a moment that Duane stood behind me.

Mom nodded. "I'll finish making that tea while you do." She turned back to the counter, and Duane's footsteps rasped against the linoleum floor as he moved to the phone on the wall.

Duane's low murmur failed to penetrate the fog in my mind. Not being able to account for a chunk of my time today, bothered and baffled me. I might be hyper and ditzy, but my memory had never failed before. Not to this degree.

"He's on his way." Duane pulled out a chair and straddled it, folding his arms across the back. His midnight eyes caressed my face. "Are you sure you don't need to go to the doctor?"

"Positive." I reached up and removed the hair tie from my hair, letting my tresses fall to my shoulders.

Duane's eyes glowed. "You still have the most beautiful hair. Like someone's shining a light from within and the rays shoot from the ends of each strand."

"Uh, thanks." The man might be gorgeous, but he definitely was no poet. Why was he working so hard to get back into my good graces? Despite my determined attempts to stand my ground, Duane's flattery slowly but surely nicked away at my defenses. I didn't want to be vulnerable to him again. My heart wouldn't stand it.

The doorbell rang, yanking me from my thoughts. Duane stood. "I'll get it."

Mom turned back to me, a smirk on her face. "That boy has it hard for you. When are you going to let bygones be bygones and let him have a chance? You've been mad at everyone since Robert died."

"Mom, don't. . ." My cheeks burned. I wasn't mad at everyone, was I? Just the world in general. I sighed.

Bruce marched into the kitchen, followed closely by Duane who resumed his seat. Bruce straightened his shoulders and whipped out a notepad. Pencil poised over the paper, he turned to Mom. "Why don't you tell me what happened?"

I choked back a snort. The man cracked me up when he tried to look official. The skinny mustache, bowed legs, and tiny frame belied the impression he tried to give of a tough cop.

"There isn't a whole lot to tell you." Mom set out four porcelain mugs and poured tea. "We were robbed of some money. Marsha doesn't remember who might have come into the store and taken it. I was gone. It's missing. That's about it."

Bruce looked disappointed. "That doesn't give me much to go on."

Mom shrugged. "Maybe not, but now the police report will be filed. Why don't you take off your cop hat and have some tea. I made cookies yesterday. Chocolate chip."

Bruce reached to doff his hat before realizing Mom spoke figuratively. "Don't mind if I do. I'm off duty in fifteen minutes. Do you think I should wait until then?"

A smile tweaked the corners of Mom's mouth. "I think you'll be all right." She set a plate of cookies in the center of the table.

After grabbing a cookie, Bruce bit into it. "Marsha wouldn't be covering up for anyone, would she? I wouldn't want these cookies to be construed as a bribe." Crumbs dropped down the front of his shirt.

"Come on." I slouched in my seat. "You know me better than that."

"Well, you've been in a lot of trouble lately. You and your daughter." He brushed his shirt with his hand. "How can you not remember what went on in your store today? Have you started drinking?"

"Apparently, I was sleeping." The nerve of the man. We've known each other since grade school. How dare he question my integrity?

Duane sat back with a grin on his face. The big oaf.

"Is everything okay?" Lindsey barged into the room, backpack slinging, and shoes squeaking. "I saw a police car out front."

My gaze fell to her feet.

She wore a brand new pair of expensive gym shoes.

8

"Okay, time for bed." I bolted to my feet and ushered Lindsey out of the room. "Everyone's fine. See you in the morning."

"But, Mom, it's only eight o'clock. On a summer night!"

"Don't argue," I hissed. "Just go." I turned back around with a smile. "Guess I'm really not feeling well. See y'all tomorrow." Taking the stairs two at a time, I followed my daughter.

When I burst into her room, she glared at me from her bed. I closed the door behind me. "Where did you get those shoes?"

"What?"

"Those." I pointed. "Where did you get them?"

"I bought them with the money I've earned this summer. Making deliveries, babysitting. You know." She chewed on a cuticle.

"Stop eating yourself." I moved to perch on the edge of her bed. My daughter was right. She'd been doing whatever odd jobs she could come up with to earn money. Now, instead of being proud of her for her initiative, I was like everyone else and suspected the worst.

"How did you get to the shoe store?" I really needed to cut back on my hours at the store. Lindsey had way too much freedom.

"My friend Patty's mom. I told you this afternoon when I called the store. Don't you remember? You sounded kind of funny, though."

Hmmm. I didn't remember. "Don't wear them for a while." I glanced around the room searching for a place to hide them out of my mother's sight. "With everything going on, someone might think you stole them."

"Like you did?" Lindsey folded her arms. "Besides, wouldn't hiding them be an admission of guilt? If I stick them away somewhere, it's the same as shouting I took them."

When did my daughter get so wise? Or smart-mouthed? "Fine. But you'd better be prepared to answer a lot of questions." My mother's footsteps pounded up the stairs. "Starting now."

She burst through the door. "I didn't raise you to be rude, Marsha." Although she apparently didn't believe my story of being ill, she felt my forehead. Mom's hands were always cool and soothing. "We had guests downstairs. Duane and Bruce don't deserve for you two to run out on them." She glanced at Lindsey and her voice rose to a screech. "And where, young lady, did you get those?"

Lindsey sighed before going into her spiel. Then, her eyes filled with tears. "Why do y'all automatically suspect the worst?"

"Oh, honey." Mom plopped on the other side of the mattress. "Things are disappearing in this town and people are getting upset." She patted Lindsey's hand. "I know you aren't a thief. But somebody thinks you are."

Didn't my own mother question Lindsey's whereabouts earlier? I did. I needed my M&M's.

"Well, we'll just start sticking closer to home at night." Mom stood. "We won't give anyone anything to talk about. There's a thief wandering around town. Marsha, let's snoop around at church tomorrow. Since it will be daylight, we won't seem suspicious then. See what we can dig up."

"I was going to get caught up on work." Didn't she realize all the robberies had taken place during the day?

"You use that excuse every week, and you haven't missed a service yet."

"I can keep trying." It wasn't that I disliked church, it was that Stephanie Jackson never failed to try and talk me into joining the women's ministry. Or I stayed wrapped up in my own thoughts. Now with Sharon's beef, all eyes would be on me. Unless I could discover the real culprit before then. I glanced at my watch. Eight thirty. Plenty of time to wander the town's streets without looking suspicious.

"Good night. Going to bed." I kissed my daughter, hugged my mother, and forced myself not to dash to my room. Mom would know for sure I had something up my sleeve if I ran.

I closed my bedroom door with as much care as possible, grabbed a small shoulder bag from the closet, stuffed a hidden bag of candy into it, then headed for the window. Not having snuck out this way in many years, the ground looked a lot farther away than it had when I was a teenager. I slipped my arm through the bag and eased open the window.

Lifting my leg over the ledge, I reached for the wooden trellis covered with climbing roses. I should've worn gloves. Inch by prickly inch, I worked my way to the ground. When I reached the half-way mark, I glanced over to see my daughter going hand over hand down a drain pipe, looking all the world like a monkey. Or a cat burglar. "Hey!"

She shrieked and lost her grip, to dangle from one hand. A swing back and forth and she retained her grip. "What are you doing?"

"I'm asking you the same question." We hung there like a couple of apes. My thigh muscles quivered, threatening to deposit me not very gently on the ground below.

"You first." Lindsey jutted her chin.

"I'm the mother, you first."

"And I'm the grandmother. Seniority rules." Mom stood below us, fists planted on her hips. "The two of you make enough noise to wake someone on Mars. Get down here."

Good grief. My hands slipped, and I bounced my way down the trellis, landing in a heap at my mother's feet. Lindsey bounded the last foot and skipped to where I lay. She offered me a hand up. I got to my feet and prepared myself to face my mother's wrath.

"I'm waiting." She tapped a foot.

"I decided to go to town and snoop around."

"Me too," Lindsey added.

"I thought if I stayed hidden but with my wits about me, I could discover who the thief is." She couldn't fault me for good intentions, could she?

"Me too!" Lindsey held up a hand for a high-five which I returned with enthusiasm.

"Neither one of you have any wits at all. The best place to find a thief is out in the open. Everyone knows that." Mom dug her car keys from her pocket. "We'll all go. Duane and Bruce left, with a warning for us to let things be, by the way. We should probably listen. But, being Calloway, we won't."

My mouth fell open. I snapped it closed as she marched toward the driveway. "You didn't hear us, did you? You saw us when you came out, right?" No lights flicked on in neighboring houses. No one shouted out their doors to hold down the noise.

She shrugged. "Y'all were still noisy."

"It would be sneakier if we walked." I put a hand on the car door.

"But my corns won't take it." Mom slid behind the wheel of her mile-long, white Cadillac.

"This car glows in the dark. We'll be spotted a mile away. Why don't you put on those special shoes you bought so you can walk?"

"They make me feel like I'm walking on the moon." Mom slid back out. "But, I see your point. Be right back."

As soon as she disappeared into the house, I glanced at Lindsey, she smiled, then we dashed across the street, behind the houses, and emerged on Main Street. My heart gave a momentary twinge of guilt at ditching my mother, but I forgot it as soon as I spotted Melvin and Kyle Anderson standing in front of Wanda's Cafe. Wanda tried to name it something fancy, but most people called it a diner.

The two men laughed at something Melvin said. Kyle didn't seem too broken up over his sister's disappearance. Did the fact she turned up missing have anything to do with the items that were unaccounted for?

I grabbed Lindsey's arm. "Come on. We'll hide behind the cow and eavesdrop."

Wanda's Cafe proudly displayed a massive plaster cow, complete with horns, in a position of honor next to the street. The legs were big enough around for me to hide behind one and Lindsey the other. I glanced at Lindsey. "Can you hear anything?"

She shook her head. "We need to get closer. Grandma said to hide in plain sight, after all." She hitched up her backpack, and stepped out, whistling a tune from a Saturday morning cartoon. When she reached the men, she stopped. "Hello. Oh, look, I've got gum on my shoe." Lindsey kneeled. I rolled my eyes at her attempt at subtlety.

The men spared her a glance and went back to talking. I gnawed the inside of my cheek. I couldn't hear a thing they were saying. I started to move out, and Lindsey waved at me to stop.

After what seemed like hours, the men moved on, just as Mom's giant of a car pulled into the parking lot. She stopped close enough to where I stood that she almost pinned me to the giant bovine. "That was mean."

Lindsey dashed up to us. "Wait until you hear. Hi, Grandma."

"Don't hi, grandma me. I have an urge to leave the two of you here and do my own investigating. Get in the car."

One thing I've learned in my thirty-four years of life was not to argue with my mother when she had her dander up. We followed her orders. Mom turned around and speared Lindsey with a glance. "What did you find out?"

"Well." Lindsey leaned her arms across the back of the front seat. "Seems when Mr. Anderson's sister disappeared, or left, no one seems to know for sure, she took money from his safe." She grinned, clearly pleased with herself. "He's angry because he planned on using the money to put an addition on his house. Now he has to come up with the money all over again and the contractors have already been hired."

"Good job!" We high-fived. Could Karen Anderson be our thief? She moved to the top of my not yet written list of suspects. Her brother became number two.

"Okay. Put your seatbelt on." Mom placed both hands on the steering wheel. "Where to now?"

"Well." I stared out the window. Sharon is missing a necklace. Melvin a wallet. Kyle a sister and cash. Us, cash. Three out of the four crimes took place on Mountain View Road. Seemed as good a place as any. "Go to Mountain View."

"Okey dokey." Mom turned the wheel and stepped on the gas hard enough to throw me against the door. "I said put on your seatbelts."

"A little discretion might be in order here, Mom." I clicked the belt across me. "We *are* on a spying trip."

9

When we passed Sharon's house, I ducked, leaving only my eyes and the top of my head visible. Mom snorted. Lindsey giggled. Despite feeling foolish, and with Sharon having a restraining order against me, hiding seemed safer.

No lights shone from Sharon's house. Her neighbor, Harvey watered a profusion of flowers in terra cotta pots. Melvin marched up Sharon's driveway, dragging his lawnmower behind him, and a German Shepherd practically dragged Marilyn down the sidewalk. An elderly couple strolled, hand-in-hand, creating a sense of nostalgia to the scene.

"I don't see anything out of the ordinary," Mom said as we reached the end of the street and she swung the boat of an automobile around.

"If we drive back the same way, people are going to be suspicious," Lindsey spoke up from the backseat. "This car isn't exactly invisible."

"Stop." I popped up in the seat. "Look."

A delivery man peered in Sharon's windows as he made his way around the house. Before too much time passed, he was back in front, ringing the doorbell.

"It's kind of late for a delivery, isn't it?" Mom stopped the car on the opposite side of the street.

"Doesn't the woman ever lock her door? He's going in." I bet she wouldn't put a restraining order against him.

"Should I call the cops?" Mom leaned for a better look.

"I don't know."

The man burst back outside and lost his dinner in the rose bushes. He sagged against the porch railing and wiped his mouth on his sleeve.

I shoved open my door. "I think you'd better." I rushed to the man's side, narrowly being hit by an ice cream truck in my effort to be helpful. Didn't those things have one speed? Slow?

Before I'd opened my mouth to inquire to the man's welfare, he gagged again and pointed to the open front door. The voices in my head warned me not to go inside. Since when did I listen? I straightened and took that first step, then another and reached for the knob. The hair on my arms rose, the voices screamed to get away while I still could, and the man behind me stumbled off the porch.

I glanced over my shoulder to where Mom and Lindsey rushed to join me. "Stay here, you two. Don't follow me." Bravery wasn't a normal part of my DNA, but I was determined to prevail. Fear swirled in my stomach. Whatever awaited me inside Sharon's house, I didn't want my mother and daughter to witness.

Surprised that they actually followed my order, I stepped into the dark foyer. A small ray of light came from a room to my right, casting more shadows rather than illuminating the space. "Sharon?" I waited to see whether she'd come brandishing another candlestick. "Kitty kitty?"

The house seemed to breathe. The silence grew in intensity. Air rushed through the foyer, ruffling my hair and assaulting my nostrils. I sniffed. A strong metallic odor overpowered the previous scent of rose scented room freshener. I knew I shouldn't go any further, but I went. Three more steps into the shadows and my foot bumped into something. I glanced down, gasped, shuffled backwards, fell, and landed on my rump. I choked down the acid rising in my throat.

Sharon Weiss lay at my feet, gowned in a negligee and robe of black silk. Blood pooled beneath her from a deep gash in her forehead. Even being a non-expert at judging death, I could tell she'd been here a while. The crimson stickiness close to my feet testified to that fact. It had congealed to the appearance of syrup. Ebony syrup in the almost absence of light.

"Mom, have you called the police yet?" I crab-walked backwards. Not until I reached the porch did I remember the restraining order and the fact I wasn't allowed in Sharon's house.

I sat on the front porch, head in my hands, until the police arrived with sirens wailing. The poor delivery man chose to stay as far away from the house as he could without leaving the scene. His forehead rested on the steering wheel of his truck. Mom paced the front stoop. Lindsey twirled her hair, obviously confused about what was going on because I hadn't spoken a word since coming outside

I raised my head when the police cruiser wailed to a stop in front of the house. Bruce climbed from behind the wheel of his squad car. Another officer slid from the passenger side. They both barely spared me a glance before marching into the house. Bruce returned almost instantly.

"You went inside?"

"No." I shook my head with enough force to send my hair flying from its already loose holder.

He pointed at my pants. "Then why do you have blood on your jeans?"

"Eew!" I jumped off, slapping at my leg. "Get it off!"

"It isn't a bug you can knock off." Bruce placed a hand on my shoulder. "I'll ask you again. Did you go in the house?"

"Yes." I took a deep shuddering breath. "But it won't happen again. I promise. Lesson learned. What if she would've needed my help? It was the most horrifying experience of my life."

Mom stepped up. "Clearly, Marsha does not have full control of her faculties. I'll explain what happened." She narrowed her eyes at him. "Aren't you going to write this down?"

Bruce whipped a pen and notebook from his pocket. "Go on."

"We were cruising the street when we saw the delivery guy…why would someone be delivering at this time of the night? Anyway, he stepped inside because the door swung open, then he rushed back out and tossed his cookies in the bushes, if you know what I mean." Mom crossed her arms. "Marsha went to offer aid to the man. He pointed for her to go in. I saw everything. So, being Marsha, she did. Go in, I mean. Then she rushed out. I haven't been inside, and my daughter isn't talking, so I have no idea what's in there. I'd like to, though. Can you tell me?"

"Sharon Weiss is dead."

"Oh, my." Mom unfolded her arms and raised a hand to her throat. "Are you sure?"

"Yep." Bruce snapped his notebook closed. "If you'll excuse me, I'm going to question the driver. Don't go anywhere."

"Are we suspects?" Mom plopped on the step next to me.

Bruce waved a hand over his head and continued toward the street.

"Wow. Now it's murder." Mom's voice dropped to a whisper.

I turned to face her. "What makes you think the thief killed her? You don't even know how she died."

"Tell me."

"She has a head wound. There's a lot of blood." I gnawed my lip and forced the gruesome picture from my mind. Instead, I dug around in the faulty computer inside my head and searched for other images. Things I may not have recalled after catching sight of the scantily clad Sharon.

There'd been no sight of the cat I'd seen the last time. The lamp on the foyer table had been knocked over. . . "I think she hit her head on a table."

"Any sign of a struggle?"

"Not that I could tell."

Lindsey peered inside the door until the other officer ordered her out. "They've got the lights on now. Gross. There's blood on the corner of the table."

Mom nodded. "Accidental death. I guarantee it." She exhaled loudly. "Not murder, then. That's good."

I rested my forehead on my knees. "I'm in so much trouble. I'm not allowed anywhere near her, and I went inside."

"She's not going to be able to press charges." Mom rose. "I'm going to find out what that driver has to say." She marched over and stopped beside the growing crowd of onlookers until Bruce finished his questioning. Then she rushed forward like a dog after peanut butter.

Bruce glanced back. "Get away from there, Gertie."

She grinned and dashed as quick as her plump body and stiff joints would allow, back to where I sat. "He's delivering a registered letter that he forgot to earlier today. Since

Sharon lived on his way home, he thought he would take care of it now rather than in the morning. Lucky man. Wrong place at the wrong time. He still looks green."

"I can't say I blame him." My stomach churned too.

We sat there until they asked us to move in order to wheel Sharon's body away on a gurney, complete with zippered black bag. In spite of our differences, tears welled in my eyes. What were the chances? You're enjoying a quiet evening at home, someone rings the doorbell, you rush to answer it, and bam! You fall, hit your head, and die.

I straightened. "Mom, why do you think Sharon was in the foyer?"

"Someone either came to her door, or she heard something." Mom's eyes widened. "Our search intensifies. We need to find out who Sharon's visitor was. Whoever they were had to have witnessed her death. I know it looks accidental, but what if it wasn't. Something's rotten in Timbuktu, and I'd like to know what."

"Doesn't mean a thing." Bruce stood behind us. "Y'all stay out of it."

We three Calloway women exchanged glances. Intuition, or voices, take your pick, told me someone witnessed Sharon's death. I intended to find out who that person was.

10

"Do you know what could've happened had you gone inside Sharon's house and been caught by her?" Bruce's face reddened. "I would've had to arrest you. I ought to anyway just to get you off the streets. You're a menace."

I pretended to study my fingernails. "Technically, I haven't been served yet so I didn't violate anything."

"You, Marsha Steele, have a smart mouth!"

I choked down words better left unsaid. "Do you think I wouldn't have chosen being arrested over finding her body?"

"You have no respect for the law."

Maybe it's the person enforcing the law I didn't care for. "You have no compassion for a dead person!" By this time, Bruce and I faced each other over his desk, both on our feet, faces inches away from the other, and my hand was curled around a glass paperweight.

"I dare you to hit me." Bruce smirked. "Assault a police officer. See what I do."

With a shuddering breath, I whirled, tossed the paperweight on the floor, and marched out of his office.

A while later, I lay staring at the ceiling, a bundle of nerves. The cuckoo clock downstairs sang out two o'clock. I groaned. Experience told me that no matter how much sleep we missed, Mom would still expect us to arrive on time to church. I didn't think the need to search for a possible witness, or murderer, would trump Sunday morning service. I closed my eyes and prayed for sleep.

The alarm blared country music at seven. I reached for the snooze button then remembered I'd moved the clock out of reach. Sometimes, my desire for efficiency drove me nuts.

Mom belted out Amazing Grace while passing my room, banged on the door, and stomped down the stairs. Her own form of an alarm clock. I tossed the blankets aside, groaned, and crawled from bed.

A shower helped marginally, leaving me with wet hair and still gritty eyes. I stuffed my hair into a ponytail and slapped on some mascara. On my way to the kitchen, I passed my daughter who grunted in response to my "morning." If we were going to continue our night time spying, we'd have to squeeze in a nap somewhere.

Mom had three plates of pancakes on the table and poured a thick layer of syrup on her stack. "About time, you two. You got thirty minutes to eat and get presentable."

She squinted at me. "You in particular need more time, but I can't give you any. Eat up."

I put a hand to my hair, which stuck up in all directions. I hadn't done a very good job of pulling it back. No one at church would care. I'd sit in the back and slip out as quickly as possible.

I scarfed down breakfast like a starving dog then dashed upstairs to throw on a sundress. The only time anyone would catch me, alive at least, in anything remotely feminine was church. When I die, they can bury me in my overalls. The more faded and tattered the better.

Flip-flops in hand, I sprinted down the stairs, grabbed my Bible from the table by the front door, then raced my daughter to ride shotgun. She beat me. Way too early in the morning to play games.

"It's a glorious day, don't you think?" Mom asked. The only conversation during the twenty minute drive to the nearest non-denominational church, River Valley Community. The one we'd called our church home for as long as I could remember. I popped open one eye and gazed out the car window.

"Lovely." I closed my eye. Then straightened in my seat and tried smoothing the wrinkles from my dress.

Duane swaggered toward us, dimples winking, teeth flashing, and looking way too good for this small town. He helped Mom from the car then turned to me.

"When did you start going to church?" I declined his offer, choosing to stick with my hands off attitude.

"About five years ago." He placed a hand against the small of my back. His warmth could've melted the sun. "Want to hear about it?"

"No." I stepped forward so he couldn't touch me. "Don't you have somewhere to be?"

"Yeah, here." He opened the door so I could proceed first.

My eyes hadn't adjusted to the change of indoor light before Stephanie rushed me. "Thank the Lord! Marsha, we're in a dilemma. The Sunday school teacher for the two-year-olds didn't show. Would you be a peach and cover for her?" Stephanie gazed at me. "What's wrong with your hair?"

Could the teacher have been Sharon by any chance? "I, uh. . ." Don't do toddlers.

"We both will," Duane offered.

Great. The man was crazy. "You probably aren't even fingerprinted." I whipped around to face him.

"This morning." He held up his right hand, still sporting black ink on his fingers. "The results won't be back for a while, but I'm clean. Plus, the coordinator is desperate. It doesn't hurt that I'm a teacher."

Before I knew it, I found myself swarmed by at least ten screeching knee biters. A headache threatened, prickling behind my eyes.

Duane rubbed his hands together. "This will be fun." He crooked his arms and immediately two boys latched on and he carried them across the room. The girls screamed to be next.

Yeah, fun. I plopped into the nearest rocking chair. On a nearby table sat a colorful book about Adam and Eve. I sighed, picked it up, and called the children to form a semi-circle around me. After fifteen minutes and several requests to be quiet, I was able to start reading. To my amazement, twenty pairs of eyes in cherubic faces stared at me, quiet, and unmoving, for the most part.

This wouldn't be too bad. I could do this. Maybe I related better to older kids, but this might be fun.

As soon as I closed the book, screaming resumed, with Duane in the middle. He crumpled to a multi-colored carpet that looked like Walt Disney threw up on it and disappeared beneath a swarm of chubby arms and legs. Well, fine. If they were mauling him, I'd be safe, right?

"I gotta go potty." A grubby hand tugged on my skirt.

"Can't you go by yourself?"

"I'm little." A rosy lip pouted. Tears welled. I grabbed the girl's hand before wailing started and led her to the room that held a child-size toilet and sink. Business completed, I headed back, relieved to see Duane had the other children seated with cookies and Kool Aid. I glanced at my watch. Fifteen minutes, and I'd be free.

We lined the children in front of the sink and busied ourselves wiping sticky fingers and smudged faces. Several of them started the potty dance and another line formed. When we finished, I collapsed into a rocking chair.

"That was a blast," Duane said, handing the last child to his parents. "I think I'm going to volunteer for this class once my fingerprints are cleared."

"You go right ahead." I grabbed my purse and scooted through the door.

"You didn't enjoy yourself?"

"I like the older kids. Ones that can talk and go potty by themselves."

He followed me to the courtyard. "Don't you want more kids someday?"

"I'm thirty-four. Time is slipping away." I stood on tiptoes, trying to find my mother and daughter.

"I've got a remedy for that." He laughed.

"Don't be crude." I swung my purse at him, catching him in the stomach, cutting his laugh off into a wheeze. The man's a complete oaf.

He pursed his lips at me, smacked them a couple of times in an imitation kiss and despite myself, I giggled. This was the Duane I fell in love. . .Good grief. I needed to change the subject immediately.

"Marsha!" Mom waved gaily from her group of "red hat" ladies. "Going to lunch. See you at home."

"Mom." Lindsey appeared at my elbow and cast a sputtering Duane a curious glance. "I'm hanging out with Kelly. I'll be home in time for dinner, okay?"

"Okay." I bit my lip, watching her skip away. Trying to hide behind a pillar was the boy she'd followed from the Dairy Queen. A shock of dark hair fell in his eyes. He needed a haircut. Lindsey gave him a nod and continued toward the parking lot.

Duane straightened. "Kelly, huh? Odd name for a boy. Especially since that isn't his name."

"You noticed him too."

He nodded. "Name's Billy Butler. He's on my football team. I haven't met him yet, just his parents. He's supposed to be quite the quarterback. He wants to go to some football skills camp this summer, but his parents don't have the money."

"Seems everyone I meet needs money for something. Melvin the gardener is trying to start his own landscape business. Stephanie Jackson is saving to adopt a girl from South America. Kyle Anderson wants an addition on his house, Marilyn the dog walker wants to go to Hollywood." Me, I just wanted a life. I turned to Duane. "What do you want?"

He didn't hesitate. Instead, he speared me with those incredible eyes and said, "You."

11

Lord, catch me. I never should have left the question open like that. It's completely my fault. This feeling of drowning. Duane didn't even ask if I wanted to go to lunch with him. He took me by the arm and led me to the parking lot.

"Where's your truck? I can't ride a motorcycle in a dress."

"It's not just a motorcycle." Duane crossed his arms. "It's a Harley. A V-Rod VRSCAW. Custom metallic silver paint. I bought her yesterday. Isn't she sweet?"

I still didn't know how I was supposed to ride in a dress. I knew I should've worn my overalls. Or jeans. The bike *was* pretty. But exactly how excited did he want me to act? What would people think when I rode up to Wanda's Cafe on the back of his bike with my arms around his waist? My face heated. They'll think we're an item. That's what. "I can't ride with you."

"Why not? Sit on your dress. The diner isn't that far. Fifteen minutes. It'll be the ride of your life." He grinned. "All you've got to do is hold on to me."

Yeah, that's a great idea. *Wrap my arms around you and lay my head on your back.* Probably wouldn't change people's opinion a bit. I grinned. "Why not?" Since we were headed to the diner, I could eavesdrop on conversations around us and search for a clue to Sharon's murderer.

"Great!" Duane handed me a helmet and swung his leg over the bike. I followed suit and tucked my skirt tightly under me, wrapped my arms around a very firm waistline, turned my head, then closed my eyes.

Being close to the man in front of me without any strings attached, along with the fragrant summer air whizzing past us, made me almost regret my vow not to get emotionally attached to Duane Steele. Not again. Only fools go back to the origin of pain. But he sure did smell nice. A musky, woodsy cologne. I took a deep breath.

Cars honked as they whizzed past us. A couple of local yocals hooted out the window. Mom's Cadillac cruised alongside us. Mom waved and pointed. I waved back, my face hurting from the stretch of my grin.

"Your dress is flapping behind you!" She pointed again. "You're wearing purple panties!"

Oh! My face burned like acid lay across my skin. Duane's back vibrated with his laugh. Struggling to hold on with one hand, I fought to stuff my dress back under me.

Not soon enough, we pulled beside the giant cow advertising the diner and Duane put the kickstand down. I removed the helmet, thankful I'd braided my hair before taking care of the children. At least I wouldn't look like a cave woman. I glanced at my skirt. Gracious! The stupid dress had escaped again and slid to an entirely inappropriate length up my legs. How many town residents had I flashed? My mother's warning of always wearing clean underwear rose to mind. For such a time as this, she would say. I smoothed the fabric before Duane could see and say something embarrassing.

His mouth twitched when he offered his arm, making me suspect the man was up to no good. Before I could ask what he smirked about, he ushered me inside the diner to a corner booth. Too cozy for me, but I pacified myself with the fact that Kyle Anderson and Melvin Brown occupied the booth next to us. I slid into the seat backing theirs so I could snoop undetected.

A bouncy teenage girl handed us our menus. I lifted mine to cover my face and slouched in my seat.

Duane reached across the table and pulled down my shield. "What are you doing? Embarrassed about the exhibition show you gave? My side mirrors reflected a lot, you know. I almost wrecked us a couple of times." He winked.

"Shhh." My face burned. Good grief. Did the man ever quit? "You should have told me, not taken advantage of the situation. Now, hush."

"Are you spying?" He whispered. "Or hiding from me?"

"Yes to both. Now be *quiet*." I hid again behind the laminated list of food items.

"The contractors are really breathing down my neck. Karen did a real number on me by cleaning out my checking account." Anderson's voice lowered. I suspected so he wouldn't be heard by the other patrons, but his words reached my ears easily enough.

"And I've almost got enough for that high-fangled lawnmower," Melvin answered. "If I could get a few more accounts, I'd have enough. I've got a plan, though."

"To come up with more money?"

"Yep. Sure thing. Easy. All I gotta do is—"

The waitress skipped back to the table to take mine and Duane's order. Her hyper, cheery voice drowned out the words from the other table. I scowled. "I'll have a cheese burger, fries, and a cherry diet coke."

Duane ordered the same then leaned back in the booth. "I might as well have come to lunch by myself."

"Sorry." I folded my arms on the table and tried to keep one ear tuned to the men behind me. "But an awful lot of people seem to be searching for money around here. Now Sharon's dead. I think they're related. Somebody wants money bad enough to kill for it." I glanced over my shoulder to make sure my soft words weren't overheard.

"You have quite an imagination, Mars Bar. She fell and hit her head. No sign of foul play."

I cringed. "I'm right about this. You'll see, and stop calling me that."

"Marsha!" Stephanie stopped at our table with a stack of fluorescent pink papers clutched in one fist. "Here's another flier about my yard sale. Don't want you to forget. It would be great if you could donate something."

"I live with my mother. I don't have, or need, a lot." I set the paper on the table. We definitely wouldn't be contributing anything from the store.

"You must have something." Her pasted on smile grew wider. "The women's ministry committee is actually talking about giving some of the proceeds toward the adoption of the little girl I want." She giggled and glanced sideways at Duane. "And here I thought I'd have to go to Mexico and steal one. Saving money is so slow, you know. Bye bye."

"Bye bye," I mocked under my breath. What a fake.

Duane watched the exchange with one brow cocked. "Yikes. It appears you two can't stand each other. Why not?"

I shrugged. Men were so dense. "No particular reason. Personality conflict, I guess." He didn't need to know she'd hated me ever since I'd shoved her into the lake on the night of Senior prom. It'd been an accident, but the murky water stained the white dress she'd worn and destroyed her elaborate hair style. I couldn't remember exactly what we'd fought about, but I had a sneaky suspicion it had been about the tiara I'd worn on my head and the boy whose arm I'd been hanging on. Even then, she'd had her eyes set on Duane. Now, married to the pharmacist of our quaint little town, she didn't seem satisfied. Being unable to bear children because of a sterile husband, she might be looking somewhere else again.

Our food arrived, thankfully halting our conversation, at least for the moment. Duane's lips pulled back and his mouth opened over his burger. Ketchup smeared the corner of his mouth. I decided to focus on my food, instead of watching him. Not that staring at him was bad. Far from it. The man could grace the cover of any country magazine in the world. Put a suit on him, and I'd probably have a heart attack.

"So." Duane set his burger on his plate. "Back to the question you asked me earlier."

"Which one?" My hands shook as I lifted my lunch.

He smirked. His eyes smoldered. "About what I want. What's your response to my answer?"

Sheer terror. I decided to play it cool. "I asked what you wanted out of life."

"Uh-huh. And I answered."

Taking a bite and chewing gave me a minute to compose myself. I should've known better than to come here with Duane. Being alone, even in a crowded diner, was not the wisest thing I'd ever done. The man had always been blunt, even when he dashed out of my life after my senior year. He hadn't pulled any punches then, and he didn't now. Told me he wanted more than this Podunk town. Interpretation—he wanted more than me, Marsha Callaway. Two weeks after that, I'd ran into his younger brother's arms to be consoled, wed a few months later, then got impregnated. Thankfully, in that order.

"Look." I wiped my mouth and folded my hands in my lap. "You can't leave for fifteen years, disappear for the last ten of them, and waltz right back into the heart of the girl you left behind. I am no longer that girl, Duane. I'm a widowed mother who moved back in with *her* mother."

"You still do that eye-lid fluttering thing when you're mad."

"Don't change the subject." Tossing my napkin on the table, I stood and leaned closer, my lips inches from his ear. "I won't deny that I still love you, Duane Steele. You know me too well. But I think it's too late for—us. You killed me that night, and you're still twisting the knife." I straightened. "Either we work at being friends, or you hop back on your bike and ride into the sunset."

Duane's grin outshone the sun, and I willed my heart to slow. "You still love me. Then, Mars Bar, it's only a matter of time. You'll see I'm serious. That I'm changed."

"Puh-leese." Leave it to a man to only pick up on part of the conversation. "You've got an ego the size of that football field you're so fond of." I grabbed my purse. "Come on. I need a ride home."

"So," Melvin's voice drifted back to me. "If you want in, just let me know."

"Oh," Kyle Anderson replied. "I definitely want in."

12

After Duane let me off his two-wheeler, I called it that just to make him mad, I headed straight for my M&M's. With a tall glass of ice-cold diet cola, I plopped into the nearest kitchen chair and listened to the silence. I couldn't get everyone's dire need of money out of my head.

I grabbed a notepad from beside the phone and started my list of people's needs. Melvin, a new lawnmower for the business he wanted to own, Marilyn the dog walker –to go to Hollywood. I scoffed at that one and chewed the eraser on my pencil. Billy—go to football camp. I scratched his name off. He's just a kid. Then I remembered those two brothers on the news a few years back who murdered their parents and put his name back on. Stephanie—money to adopt, Kyle Anderson needs to pay contractors, and his sister, Karen, has conveniently disappeared.

I popped another chocolate piece into my mouth. Plus, someone came into the store and stole from us when I drifted away to La La land. Not to mention Sharon's missing necklace. Or her neighbor's misplaced wallet. It's all connected somehow. I just needed to put the pieces together before someone else accused my street-wandering daughter of being a thief.

And how is Sharon's death connected?

The phone rang, and I pushed to my feet to answer. "Hello?"

"May I speak with Gertie, please?"

"She isn't home. Can I take a message?" I stretched the phone cord to the nearest paper which happened to be my list of names.

"Just tell her Leroy called. I'll try her back in a few minutes. Thank you."

Leroy? The dial tone droned in my ear as I racked my brain trying to bring up a picture of someone I might know by that name. His deep voice sounded pleasant enough. Could this be the mystery man Mom eluded to a few nights before? I grinned and relished having something to pester her about.

"Oh, I didn't think you'd beat me home." She'd obviously hurried. Her cheeks flushed scarlet, and a line of perspiration dotted her upper lip.

I waved the paper in front of her. "Someone named Leroy called. Said he'd call back later."

Mom paused in the removal of her red hat. "Did he say what time?"

"No, but I'm guessing you thought you'd be home instead of me, so most likely any time." I couldn't help but wiggle my eyebrows.

The phone rang, and I snatched the handset from the cradle before Mom could. "Who is he, huh?" I danced around, holding it above my head. If she hadn't refused to get a cordless, I could've made a run for it. "Is he your *boy*friend?"

"Give me that, you idiot. Grow up." She elbowed me, knocking the air from my lungs and effectively halting my taunting. She stole the phone from me and walked around the corner, stretching the cord.

"I was only playing around! No need to get violent." Some people had no sense of humor. "Don't know why you're keeping him a secret anyway. Is he a hunchback or have a bulbous nose?"

Mom stuck her head around the corner and glared at me. When she ended her call and hung up the phone, she folded her arms and turned to me. "What is wrong with you? I taught you better manners than that."

I shrugged. "Just playing. Why are you keeping him a secret anyway?"

She sat in a chair opposite me. "It's embarrassing. A woman my age having a romantic liaison with a gentleman. I haven't dated since your father died. I'm not sure I know how."

"Yep. Fifty-five is really old. There's nothing to dating. It's like riding a bicycle."

"And you're the expert?"

Good point. I held out my hand. "Can I have that paper back? It's got information I need."

Mom scanned the list. "Suspects?"

"I think so."

She handed it to me. "It's silly. Everyone needs money. Doesn't mean they'll steal for it."

"But not everyone goes around town talking about it." I reached for more candy. "Besides, I don't see you coming up with anything better."

"No one's accused Lindsey of anything more. Maybe we should let things be."

I shook my head. "Somehow, I think whoever took Sharon's necklace, took the money from the store. It's all connected. I guarantee it. Now, back to your boyfriend."

"He's just a friend." Mom rose and plodded to the sink.

"Where did you meet him?"

"What is this, the third degree?" She frowned.

"Fair play's what I call it." I grinned, feeling pleased with myself.

"Okay. If that's the way you want it. I ran into Duane on my way home." She wiggled her eyebrows at me in what was most likely a perfect imitation of my earlier move.

Uh-oh. I grabbed a handful of chocolate.

"The man seems to believe you still love him. Says you told him so yourself. Now where would he get that idea?"

My mother is plain mean. "Changing the subject?"

"You bet I am." She smiled an evil grin. I almost expected her to twirl a black moustache. "And, since you're so in love, I invited Duane for a simple Sunday dinner of hot dogs." She giggled and went into the front room. Within seconds, the television blared.

I plopped into a chair. How could she do this to me?

"We don't have any buns," Mom yelled from the front room. "You might want to run to the store."

All right by me. I grabbed my purse. I needed more stress relievers anyway. With a sense of immaturity, I let the door slam behind me and marched down the driveway to my AMC Spirit hatchback—held together with tape and a prayer.

They most likely didn't make the tiny automobile anymore and mine was definitely on its last leg. I stuck the key in the ignition and turned. Nothing. Maybe it was time to buy another car. I popped the clutch and stomped the gas. Finally, it sputtered to life.

The Food Mart was, thankfully, only a spit and a wink from our house. I parked in a black cloud of exhaust from my tiny blue beast and thanked heaven I'd arrived without having to push the thing.

Billy gathered carts outside the store and lo and behold if Lindsey didn't lean against the brick building watching him with love-sick eyes. She gave me a sheepish smile and shrugged. Busted! I waved and told myself I'd be asking Duane more questions about the object of my daughter's infatuation. A cute face did not necessarily mean the insides were as nice.

I pushed through the double glass doors and grabbed a cart before making my way to the bread aisle. Running over the items in our pantry, I remembered other things we were running short of. Next stop, meat. I turned the corner and ran over the foot of a man in a white butcher coat.

"I'm so sorry." My cheeks heated as my gaze drifted to his name tag. Leroy. Could it be? I offered my hand.

"Marsha Steele."

He smiled and returned my shake. "Leroy Bohan. I'm a friend of your mother's. What was all the ruckus earlier?"

I studied him before answering, noting the buzzed grey hair, still muscular build, ocean-blue eyes, and killer smile. Way to go, Mom! "Oh. Uh, just a game. We're having a friend over for hot dogs later. Would you like to come?"

Leroy's smile broadened. "I'd love to. I get off at five. And instead of dogs, why don't I grill steaks? I know a good butcher."

"Perfect. There will be five of us." I grabbed the meat I needed for dinners during the week, then headed to the candy aisle. Yep, revenge tasted sweet.

My smile faded when I approached the register and spotted Bruce with one hand on my daughter's arm and his other clutching a worn brown wallet. Lindsey's eyes shone with unshed tears, and she shook her head. "I didn't. I swear." I couldn't help but notice the new jeans she wore. Faded with jewel stones on the pockets.

"What are you doing? Bruce, release her." My stomach clenched as I put an arm around Lindsey's shoulders. I glanced at the curious onlookers in line. Wonderful. Stephanie Jackson watched with a pitying look on her face, Bill Butler halted in his pushing of the carts, and Kyle Anderson plopped down money at the register faster than an addictive gambler. Well, Stephanie, this is what having kids can get you. One big headache.

"Lindsey dropped this while paying for her soda." Bruce waved the square of leather in front of my face. "Who's name do you suppose is inside? Huh? Harvey Miller, that's who. The same man who reported it missing."

Lindsey turned to me. Tears shimmered. "I don't know how it got in my backpack."

"How am I going to explain to the other officers why I didn't catch this before?" Bruce let go of Lindsey's arm. "They'll say I'm not doing my job because we're friends."

"They won't have to worry about us being friends if you don't stop accusing my daughter." I rose to my not-so-tall height. "If you find Lindsey's fingerprints on Harvey's wallet, I'll bring her to the station myself." *Minus her head!* I leaned forward until our noses almost touched. "It would be very easy for someone to stash it in her pack. She takes it everywhere and leaves it lying around. Let me handle this, Bruce. You find the *real* criminal."

"Oh, no, you don't. You start nosing around and someone else will file a restraining order against you." Bruce rubbed his head with both hands. "How did this happen in my town? You Callahan's are disturbing the peace."

"Sheer luck, I guess." I wheeled my cart through the line and tried to ignore the curious stares from bystanders. Wonderful. Now, I'd have to shop in another town. Everyone here will believe Lindsey is a thief. "Lindsey, wait for me in Little Blue."

Her eyes widened. She hated that car. I ought to give it to her when she turned sixteen, just to be mean, but even I drew the line somewhere. I paid for my groceries and ignored the other shopper's stares.

Five minutes later, I slid behind the wheel of my piece of junk, fought with the car until the engine turned over, killed it a couple of times by popping the clutch, then backed quick enough out of the parking space to burn rubber.

I glanced at Lindsey. "So, did you steal the wallet? Do you want to go to jail? Are you trying to kill me!?"

13

Lindsey stormed upstairs muttering something about an overreacting, drama queen of a mother. I admit the comment about her killing me might have been overboard, but either the girl's escapades lately would give me a heart attack or the M&M's I kept munching on would make me fat enough to have a coronary. Either way—I lose.

I set the groceries on the counter and glanced at the clock. Two hours until dinner. I picked up the phone and dialed Bruce's direct line.

"Officer Bruce Barnett here."

"You're playing right into the thief's hands by focusing your efforts on Lindsey."

"Marsha?"

"Instead of harassing my daughter," I opened the refrigerator and placed the makings of a salad inside. "You might want to consider the possibility someone is framing her."

"Why?"

"It's pretty obvious, really." Maybe by telling Bruce my suspicions, I'd actually believe my daughter's innocence. The new clothes did make me suspicious and where did she keep disappearing to? I slammed the fridge door with my hip and leaned against the counter. "If you're focusing on Lindsey, your mind isn't on the real culprit. Simple."

"Okay, Agatha Christie. Thanks for the tip." I could hear a pen clicking in the background.

Gee, I wasn't aware Bruce read, much less could remember a famous literary character. And he obviously wasn't paying attention or taking me seriously. "Fine. I'll prove it myself." I slammed the phone back in its cradle.

"Trying to break it?" Mom stepped into the room and peered inside the grocery bags.

"I'm trying to break something. Most likely someone's head."

"Uh-huh. You'd never hurt a fly. Too nice. A meek dog who tries to be tough. Someone who runs at the first sign of a fight."

"Okay, Mom, I get it." But this time she's wrong. I intended to fight until Lindsey was either proven guilty or innocent.

Mom took the empty bags and stuffed them into a cylinder made from dishtowels designed to store plastic grocery sacks. "What's got your dander up this time?"

"Bruce accused Lindsey of stealing Harvey Miller's wallet."

"Why would he do that?"

I shrugged. "It fell out of her backpack at the Food Mart. I don't know what to think. Today, she's wearing new jeans with sparkles on the pockets."

"I bought her those. You need to stop jumping to conclusions. Lindsey needs your support while she's being accused, not your condemnation. Especially since you don't have proof." She opened the pantry. "Why'd you buy steak sauce?"

"For dinner." I clapped a hand over my mouth. Oops.

Mom narrowed her eyes at me. "What did you do?"

"Nothing." I really needed to get my own place. Reverting back to my mother treating me like a child grew old.

"Marsha Marie Calloway Steele." She crossed her arms.

"Fine. I ran into Leroy at the store, introduced myself, and now he's bringing steaks to grill for dinner." I gave her a shaky smile. "I wanted to get back at you for inviting Duane."

"Just perfect." Mom threw her arms over her head. "Now he'll think I want to move to the next step in our relationship."

"Why don't you?"

Mom sat in a kitchen chair. "I don't have time. Not with taking care of you and Lindsey." Her eyes widened. "Not that I'm blaming you for my romantic problems. I love having the two of you here, it's just. . .there isn't a lot of privacy."

I joined her at the table. "I'm thinking it's time to fix up the guest house out back. I've enough money stashed away to pay for the repairs. That way, we'll still be close, but you can have company if you want." I winked at her. "And I can still chaperone."

"Pshaw. Like I need that. Let's go take a look at your new home."

My feelings stung at her easy acceptance to my moving out, but it was time. Time for me to get over the pain of betrayal and the loss of a husband who, though I hadn't loved deeply, I had still cared about. Plus, he'd given me a beautiful daughter. Lindsey might be a pain in my backside, but she's mine.

We rose and walked the fifty yards to the small building mom and dad had once called home before they built the two-story farm house we lived in now. Presently, the smaller place was used for storage. The wood paneled door squeaked as I pushed it open. I brushed aside cobwebs and stepped into the murky depths. Mom squeezed past boxes and tool equipment to open the shutters, flooding the room with dust particle filled light.

"Guess we'll have some things to give Stephanie for her yard sale after all." I headed to the small kitchen. "What's in all these boxes?"

"Lawn equipment your father never got around to fixing, files, leftover paint, and I don't know what all. I'm going to check the bathroom."

I turned the faucet on the sink. After a fair amount of sputtering, the water flowed brown then cleared. "Plumbing works." I flipped a switch. Nothing. I moved to another. The bulb overhead illuminated weakly. "Needs new light bulbs." My gaze wandered. It also needed paint, a floor waxing, and a carpet cleaning. I glanced at the ceiling. No water spots. There wasn't anything I couldn't fix within a few days.

Despite the amount of work the house would require, excitement welled within me. The two-bedroom cottage would be perfect.

"Mom!" Lindsey's voice carried through the open front door. "There's some old guy here with Uncle Duane."

I pressed the light button on my watch. The men were right on time. "Coming, Mom?"

She stepped beside me and placed a hand to her hair. "I must look a sight after rummaging around in here."

I plucked a spider web from her head. "You look fine." Neither of us had changed out of our church clothes. *Please, Lord, don't let Duane think I wanted to look nice for him. The man was way too sure of himself already*.

Mom and I strolled around the corner of the house. Leroy's arms were loaded with grocery bags while Duane held a carrot cake. He looked more delicious in jeans and a navy tee shirt than the dessert.

"You didn't buy this, did you?" I took the cake from him. "Or the chocolate one earlier."

He grinned. "Guilty. Baking is my way of relaxing."

I shook my head. "I can't picture you wearing an apron and covered in flour." The man goes to church and bakes. There'd been a lot of changing in the last ten years.

"I look very good in an apron, by the way, and I'm a clean cook. No messy kitchen for me." He gave me a slow smile. "I also cook a mean omelet. I'll show you sometime, if you stick around early enough."

The temperature rose several degrees. I fought the urge to fan myself.

Mom took a bag from Leroy. Her cheeks glowed like a young girl's when he placed a kiss on her cheek. I hadn't noticed before how attractive my mother was. It shouldn't be a surprise a man would notice her. I'd been thrown off track by her "red hat" club. Something her and her friends started as a lark when they turned fifty.

Marilyn walked two German shepherds down the sidewalk. She sashayed past us with tight shorts, a mid-rift shirt, and lips painted their usual fire-engine red. She hollered a greeting and tossed a little wave. I waited to see whether Leroy's gaze would linger. It didn't. Neither did Duane's. Score a point for the men. My spirits lifted.

A half hour later we sat around the table eating and laughing like old friends. I kept my eye on Leroy, relaxing when he acted like nothing but a gentleman. I wished my mother the best of luck. My heart tugged a bit at realizing I might soon have to share her with someone else. Dad died when I was twelve. Other than Lindsey, Mom had been all mine for a long time. Several times I caught Duane watching me, his eyes dark with thoughts I didn't think I wanted to know.

The phone rang. Lindsey jumped to her feet. "I'll get it." She returned seconds later. "Can I hang out with Kelly? I'm just a fifth wheel here anyway."

I began clearing off the table. "Sure, honey. Be home by curfew."

Duane moved to help me and whispered in my ear. His breath tickled, prickling my skin. "Do you want to take a walk with me after we clean this up? Let your mother and Leroy have some quiet time?"

I shrugged. No way would I make this easy for him. He'd shattered my heart fifteen years ago. It would take a while to rebuild, despite the way my blood raced and my heart stuttered. "Mom, why don't you and Leroy go to the front room? We'll take care of this."

"You wash and I'll dry." Duane slung a dishtowel over his shoulder.

"Okay, but you have to bring in the rest of the dishes."

The fragrance of lemon filled the kitchen. My hair curled around my face from the warm moisture rising from the sink. Washing dishes normally relaxed me, but the intimacy of doing them with Duane wasn't lost on me. This was the act of a domestic couple. We weren't even a pair. The man's skillful trickery at getting close impressed me.

He winked and took the first washed plate from my hand. With the second, his arm brushed mine. I could've chalked it up to coincidence until he did it again. I rolled my eyes and took a step to the right. I didn't want his playfulness. Not now. I wasn't willing to accept what he wouldn't offer fifteen years ago.

Why not, I asked myself? It wasn't a crime to enjoy the attention of a handsome man. I'd spurned a few opportunities since Robert died. Men looked past the overalls and ponytail to the pretty woman who stared back at me from the mirror each morning. I squared my shoulders. If Duane wanted to spend time with me, he could help me find the River Valley's thief. That should be safe enough.

Duane filled his hand with bubbles and blew them into my face. I sputtered and grabbed a towel from the counter to wipe my face. Before he could run, I'd rolled the towel and aimed for his leg. The towel snapped. The look on his face warned me I'd better flee. I squealed and darted out the back door and around to the front of the house.

My feet slid as I came to an abrupt halt. With a sinking heart, I shuffled to the driveway.

"Mom?" I called through the open front door. "Where's your car?"

14

Mom burst through the doorway and let the screen slam shut behind her. "I parked it in the driveway like always." She planted hands on her hips then spun and marched into the house. She returned within seconds. "My keys aren't in my purse." Mom patted her pockets.

"Y'all need to see what's on the news," Leroy yelled from the front room. "You ain't going to like it."

The wooden planks of the porch thudded beneath us as we thundered inside and squeezed in front of the television. Mom's great white boat stuck out of the front window of Wanda's Cafe like a stranded whale.

My chin must have dropped to my knees. My darling daughter sat with her head in her hands on the front sidewalk. Across the bottom of the screen, scrolled the words "Local Teen Runs Car Through Diner Window". Well, duh, I could see that for myself. I clenched my jaw.

Lindsey didn't look hurt, but wait until I got finished with her. "How did she get there? I haven't taught her to drive." Billy Butler strolled through the door of the diner, a cup in one hand and a bag of chips in the

101

other. Question answered. Billy drove the car. Bruce's patrol car rolled into the lot, lights flashing, and stopped beside a squad car already parked there. Just great!

Duane chuckled then choked the laugh off when I tossed him a look. Leroy jangled his keys. "Hop in the truck."

"I'd rather walk. I need to calm down before I claim my child." My limbs trembled. I squelched the urge to rant and rave. To scream and wave my arms around. To cry. I definitely did not want to lose it in front of Duane and Leroy. I whirled and marched out the door and down the street. The walk would take fifteen minutes. Plenty of time for my temper to cool.

A glance over my shoulder showed Mom, Duane, and Leroy following. At least two of them knew enough not to bother me when I got into a "state". Leroy had an arm around Mom's shoulders. Duane gave me a crooked smile. I ground my teeth and redirected my attention forward.

What was Lindsey thinking? I'd like to wring her neck. It might be worth going to jail for.

I must be losing my mind! What had become of my little girl? Hardly any trouble until recently. She'd been accused of stealing. Now this. Taking my mother's car. Wrecking it. Running around with a boy I knew nothing about. Instead of calming down, I grew more agitated the closer I got to the diner.

I took deep breaths and counted. One. . .two. . .three. . .It didn't help. Instead, I hyperventilated. The beginning of a headache throbbed behind my eyes. I prayed for peace. My mind refused to focus on anything other than the fact my daughter stole my mother's car. I marched into the diner's parking lot, rounded the giant bovine, and lost all the resolve I'd tried to build.

"Mom!" Lindsey bolted to her feet. Billy's arm slid from her shoulders.

"Are you all right?" I'd try the nice mother touch first. She nodded. "What were you thinking?" My arms flew over my head to accentuate my words. It probably looked like sign language gone mad. "You are definitely trying to kill me or drive me insane!" I paced in front of her. "You ought to just get a knife. It'd be faster. Good Lord, take me now. Take me home."

"Mom, please." Lindsey grabbed my arm. "You're embarrassing me."

I jerked free. "You mean bigger than the embarrassment of you running the car through the window?" The cameraman from the local station swerved the camera in my direction.

"Don't you dare put me on the news!" I jabbed a finger in his direction then resumed my frantic back and forth walk. "Like I don't have enough to deal with. Ugh!"

Duane, Leroy, and Bruce stood side-by-side, arms crossed, and huge grins splitting their faces. The Three Stooges. I wanted to punch them but then I'd probably go to jail for assault. That would be icing on the cake. Mom patted her hair in place and waved to the camera before moving to check on her car.

Remorse the size of a grain of rice kicked in. I knew how much she loved her baby. "Is the car okay?"

"Just a scrape. No dents, thank the Lord. They don't make cars like this anymore." Mom ran her hand down the side. "The store is another thing."

I whirled back to Lindsey. "You could have killed somebody! Who taught you how to drive?"

Lindsey shook her head. "Billy was driving. You have to listen—"

"I don't want to hear another word, unless it's to Wanda about how you're going to pay to repair this window." My head pounded. "Somebody get me a diet coke. No, some M&Ms. Both. I need both."

Duane dug his wallet from his pocket and meandered through the open door. He winked at Lindsey as he passed. I rolled my eyes. Good grief. The man was incorrigible. I suddenly remembered all the trouble he'd gotten into through high school. Sneaking out, borrowing his parents' car, ditching school. The apple didn't fall far from the Steele family tree it seemed.

Mom stepped up to me and put her hands on my shoulders. "Calm down. It will be okay."

"It won't be okay. She. . ." I pointed at Lindsey. "Is. Not. Too. Bright. All the work I've put into raising her. . .well, I don't know what else to say." My shoulders slumped. Duane thrust a coke and candy into my hands then stepped back as if afraid I'd unleash my fury on him.

"Take care of Lindsey." Mom patted my arm. "My car is fine, except for a scrape of green paint. Not sure where that came from. The window can be fixed. Damage you may cause with your words might not be erased."

I glanced at my daughter. Tears ran down her face. Billy tried comforting her by smoothing her hair away from her face. He jerked back when I glared at him. I marched to them, put my fists on my hips, realized I probably looked like my mother, removed them and crossed my arms. "I'm calm now. Talk to me. Why did you take your grandmother's keys? Are you sure you're okay?"

"You aren't calm." She sniffled and wiped her face on her sleeve. "And I'm fine."

"I am calm." Or at least trying to be. I took a deep breath and willed my voice to lower.

"We wanted to go for a ride, and we didn't want to take your car. It would've left us stranded somewhere."

"You shouldn't have taken anyone's car." My eyelids were probably fluttering faster than a hummingbird's wings.

"Okay!" She crossed her arms in a direct imitation of me. "Geez, lighten up. You don't even know what happened."

"I'm trying to find out." How would I survive the teenage years?

"Billy was driving. I did back out of the driveway though. I did pretty good." Her features brightened a bit. "Then we drove around town for a while. Grandma's radio doesn't work very well, by the way. On our way back, we noticed a car following us. Billy thought it might be one of his friends. . ." Lindsey wrapped her arms around her stomach and bent forward.

My heart skipped a beat. I dreaded the rest of her story. Afraid of the direction it headed.

"—so we slowed down." Her eyes widened, and she shook her head. "We weren't speeding though. Billy's a good driver. He even has a license."

I waved Bruce over so he could hear the rest of her story.

Lindsey frowned when he joined us, most likely remembering his earlier treatment of her. "Anyway, the other car sped up. They got right on our bumper. Billy said the lights blinded him." Her eyes shone with tears. "Then he freaked out a little when they bumped us. He said some words I won't repeat. But he was stressed, so don't hold his language against him. The wheel spun in his hands, and we ended up here."

The dinner I'd eaten churned in my stomach. Why would someone run two teenagers off the road? Or had they meant to target my mother? "You could have been killed." My voice shook.

Bruce whipped a notepad from his pocket. "Was the driver a man or a woman?"

Lindsey shrugged. "I don't know. The person wore a President Clinton mask."

15

"Let me make sure I have this right." Bruce tapped his pen against the rim of his hat. His mouth twisted as he chewed the inside of his cheek. "You and your boyfriend stole your grandmother's car then someone with a mask, like a former president's face, ran you off the road, and you crashed into the diner."

Lindsey frowned and nodded.

I whipped toward him. "You don't believe her?" Stealing was a harsh word. Never mind that I'd thought the same thing a few minutes ago. I knew my mother would never press charges against her granddaughter.

Bruce shrugged. "Lindsey's been in a lot of trouble lately. People are accusing her of being responsible for a lot of things." He peered over the dark sunglasses he wore. Sunglasses at night? Geez. "She's been seen wandering the streets after dark. Someone took off with Gloria Simpson's litter of registered Chihuahuas."

"You can't be serious."

"About what? That she's been seen wandering the streets or Gloria's puppies missing?"

I glared at him. "Sounds to me like you're accusing my daughter. What would she do with a litter of puppies?"

"I'm not accusing, yet. I'm just saying, well, people talk. A whole litter of pups are missing. They're worth a couple hundred dollars a piece. Times four that's—"

"I can do the math." I crossed my arms and glared. The man was completely incompetent. Now, more than ever, I'd have to actively pursue this case and clear my daughter's name. "Can we go home now?"

He snorted. "If you can get the car out of the window."

Mom had already climbed behind the wheel. The roar of the engine rose above the chatter of spectators. She honked the horn, stepped on the gas, and hurled backwards like a racehorse headed the wrong way. She spun the wheel and the car slid into a spin. Her grin rivaled the rising moon's. "That was fun."

"Your entire family is a menace." Bruce slapped his notebook closed, shoved it into his pocket, and spun on his heel. "Don't leave town."

Duane stood next to the kids. Once Bruce marched away from me, Duane clapped Billy on the shoulder then made his way to my side. "Everything okay?"

"He doesn't believe Lindsey is telling the truth about being run off the road."

"Hmmph."

"What does that mean?" I crossed my arms. "I'm going to have to go pro-active and find Sharon's necklace." I proceeded to rattle off the facts and thoughts that circulated through my brain the last few days.

Duane frowned. "I don't think you should get involved. If you're right, things are escalating. I'll talk to Bruce if you want, and ask him to lay off Lindsey."

"Why do men always say that? Things are too dangerous, you're a girl, blah blah blah." I glared at him. "Why don't you help me? Lindsey *is* your niece after all."

"Okay, but football practice starts tomorrow." He slung an arm around my shoulder. "Do you want to walk back to your house or ride with your mother?"

Exhaustion weighted my shoulders beneath Duane's arm. Had it really only been Wednesday since Sharon accused Lindsey of taking her necklace? I sighed. "I'm going to ride. It's late, and I've got to work tomorrow."

Duane gave me a warm arm squeeze. "Call if you need me. Otherwise, I'll stop by after practice and go snooping with you."

I nodded and waved Lindsey over. We climbed into Mom's car. Me in the front, and Lindsey sprawled in back. "You okay?" I glanced over my shoulder.

"I was so scared." Lindsey burst into tears.

"Oh, sweetie." I climbed over the back seat. My foot tangled in the shoulder strap of the seat belt and I fell, clumsily beside my daughter. The air left my lungs with a whoosh, and I lay with my head on the floor and my rear in the air until I caught my breath. With a bit of skillful maneuvering, I recovered and wrapped her in my arms.

Lindsey giggled. "You are such a dork."

"Hey, I work really hard at it. Practice makes perfect." Her hair smelled of strawberry shampoo. "I'll do anything to put a smile on your face."

She sniffed. "Billy tried to act brave, but I could tell he was scared spitless. He really is a good driver, Mom. No one could have stayed on the road unless they wanted to get hit."

"Yeah, about that. Taking the car was wrong."

"We'll discuss this when we get home." Mom threw the car into drive and punched the gas. She yoo-hooed out the window to Leroy and sped from the parking lot.

"Great," Lindsey muttered. She laid her head on my shoulder.

I straightened when the car turned right. "Where are we going?"

"To look for a green car that might be missing some paint." She pulled into the lot of the Super Mart and cruised at the speed of a turtle. All three of us squinted through the evening.

"Don't you think they'll most likely have gone home and hid the car in a garage?" I rolled down my window for a better view. Mom slammed on the brakes and I hit the seat in front of me with enough force to bite my tongue. That's what I got for not wearing my seatbelt.

"Is that the car, Lindsey?" Mom thrust her pride and joy in park and shoved open her door. We stopped behind a forest green Toyota.

"Maybe."

Mom marched around the vehicle, searching for scrapes and dents. "It's clean."

"What are you doing?" Mark Jackson glared at us, arms folded, lab coat almost glowing beneath the street lights. "You're blocking me in."

"Just mistook this car for someone else's." Mom flashed him a grin, never above a little flirtation with a handsome man. And Stephanie Jackson's husband ranked close to the top of the list. At least for the men in our town and neighboring ones. "How's the adoption going?"

"We're getting there. Stephanie's doing a great job of saving. A few more months and we should be parents. We've decided on a girl in Mexico."

"That's good." Mom patted his arm. "We won't take any more of your time." She slid behind the wheel and cruised around him.

"Well, Mark Jackson is innocent. Not a scratch on his car. Probably looks as good as it did when he drove it off the lot." Mom turned right again. "Let's cruise the neighborhood."

An hour later, and enough gas burned to set the economy into a downward spiral, Mom conceded defeat for the night and turned into our own driveway. Lindsey sighed and slid from the backseat. She stood with head bowed, no doubt waiting for the lecture from my mother. I followed, ready to watch the show. My mom was the best at giving verbal lashings. I carried scars to prove it.

She placed a hand beneath Lindsey's chin and tilted her face until she looked at her. "Don't take my car without asking again. I'm glad you're all right." Mom kissed Lindsey's forehead and strolled into the house.

Wow. Who was that and who stole my mother?

Lindsey glanced at me and shrugged then a grin spread across her face. "I guess she likes me better than you."

"Oh, yeah. Go to your room. There needs to be some kind of punishment for your actions. Tomorrow, you can clean out the guest house. We'll be moving in soon." I smirked and stalked past her, leaving her mouth hanging open.

Mom sat at the kitchen table with my suspect list in front of her. She glanced up at me. "I've seen a green car somewhere. Do you know what any of these people drive?"

I shook my head and sat down across from her. "I don't pay attention to what people drive. Speaking of, I'm taking off work early tomorrow to find something for myself. Little Blue deserves to be put out to pasture."

I drummed my fingers on the table top and mulled over the day's events. "Did you know someone stole Gloria Simpson's litter of pups?"

"No." Her brow furrowed.

"Can I borrow your car? I'd like to run by her house."

"It's after nine o'clock. That's rude."

"I'll only stop if her lights are on."

Mom shrugged. "Go ahead. But be careful. My baby's been through enough tonight."

Gloria lived on the other side of town so the drive took all of ten minutes. Thankfully, besides the porch light, the one in the woman's kitchen and front room shone through sheer curtains. I cut the White Beast's lights and pulled into the woman's driveway. Her lights flicked off one by one.

Nice try, Gloria. I slid from the car, marched up the steps, then gave three sharp raps on the door. "Gloria, it's Marsha Steele."

The door opened as far as the safety chain would allow. "What do you want at this time of the night?"

"I heard about your Chihuahuas. I'd like to ask you some questions."

The woman sighed. "Ask. I don't know what I can tell you. I didn't leave my house all day. I woke up, had a doughnut for breakfast, the next thing I knew Lucy whimpered and her babies were gone. I went to bed with a dreadful headache. In the middle of the day. Imagine."

"You didn't go anywhere?"

"Nope. At least I don't think so. I might have gone somewhere to buy the doughnuts, but for the life of me I can't remember. I must have though. They wouldn't have shown up by themselves. The day's been kind of a fog."

16

Back home and more confused than ever, I flopped across my bed and dialed my best friend, Lynn's, phone number. She wouldn't care that it was after ten o'clock. Bosom buddies didn't pay attention to tiny details like that.

"Do you know what time it is?" Lynn's sleepy voice rasped over the air waves.

Oops. Maybe time didn't matter during high school, but it apparently did now. "You said I could call you any time."

"Is this an emergency?"

"Not really. I just need to bounce some ideas across you." I twirled the phone cord around my finger. "Did you see the news?" Rolling to my back, I grabbed the remote. On the television, for all the world to see, was me pointing my finger at the camera, scowling, waving my arms, and looking like a complete lunatic. Wonderful.

Lynn giggled. "I've never laughed so hard in my life. What did your Mom say about her baby?"

"Yeah, well, there's a great picture of me on the news right now. The weird thing is, she didn't yell at Lindsey. Must be a grandmother/granddaughter thing."

I could hear her shifting on her bed. "It's probably a good thing it's a silent picture. I can just imagine what you said."

I joined in her laughter. "I was really angry. But seriously, Bruce is accusing Lindsey of pretty much every crime around here. It doesn't look good since Bruce found someone's missing wallet in her backpack."

"Ouch."

"Yeah, and she says that she and Billy were run off the road. Bruce doesn't believe her."

"You're going to prove her innocence."

"Somebody has to." I moved back to my stomach and winced as the phone cord became tangled in my hair. The more I moved, the worse it got. I'd play things cool. No need to let Lynn know I'd done something stupid again. "I mean, Lindsey's a typical teenager but she isn't a thief." Ow!

Tears sprang to my eyes. Drat these old fashioned phones. I laid flat on my back with the phone between my cheek and the pillow and vowed to buy a cordless as soon as possible. "I made a list of possible suspects, but I never learned how to be inconspicuous. Could you do some spying for me?"

Lynn remained silent for several seconds. "Are you serious?"

"Yes. Everyone likes you. They tend to put restraining orders on me."

"Fine, but it'll have to wait until after a meeting tomorrow. I'm not taking off work to spy for you. Speaking of—good night." Click.

I let the phone fall to the floor and stared at the ceiling wondering how I was going to get my hair free. Mom and Lindsey had already gone to bed. I felt the bed around me. A book. I tossed it against the wall. It thumped, I waited. "Mom!" I located a shoe and hurled it with a satisfying thud next to where I'd aimed the book. "Mom!"

She shuffled from the room next door and leaned against my door jamb. "What in the world?"

"I'm stuck." I didn't think I'd ever been this embarrassed in my entire life. If word of this got around. . .no one would be surprised. The thought depressed me.

"I ought to leave you there. You can't get into trouble if you can't move." She sat on the edge of the bed and reached for my head.

The lights went out, casting us in semi-darkness. "Wanna bet?"

Mom reached over and flicked the switch on the lamp. "We probably just blew a fuse. I'll be right back."

"You aren't going to leave me here unable to move, are you?"

She waved a hand. "Don't be such a baby. I'll be right back."

Normally, the dark didn't frighten me, especially a moon-brightened one. But lying imprisoned on my bed did not leave me feeling reassured. Footsteps scuffed in the hall outside my room.

"Hello?" My heart hammered loud enough for the people in the neighboring county to hear. "You're not funny, Mom. Lindsey?" I tried swallowing against the cotton feeling in my mouth.

A person dressed in a black jumpsuit started to pass my room then paused in the doorway and looked inside. I blinked and shook my head. President Bill Clinton? A mask. I thrashed and pulled against my captive phone. The fake president continued to stare at me for a moment, eyes glittering through slits in the molded plastic, then whirled and disappeared. I swore his or her's shoulders shook with silent laughter. Just wait until I got free. I lifted the receiver and frowned at the silence on the other end. "Mom, Lindsey, call 911!"

Lindsey stumbled into my room, rubbing her eyes. She burst into raucous laughter at the sight of me, highlighted by moon beams, and bouncing up and down on the mattress. "Be right back." She disappeared into my closet and re-emerged with my camera. "This is going on Facebook." The flash lit up the room and blinded me. Then, I heard the snip of scissors. On no, she didn't!

She did. I sat up, freed from the phone and sporting a new lopsided hair cut. I patted my head and shrugged. "You might as well make the other side match." Tears spilled down my cheeks. I'd been growing my hair for months.

"I only cut off one curl, Mom. Geez. You can't even tell."

The lights blinked back on and I stared across the room at my dresser. She was right. Barely noticeable.

"Sorry, Mom." Lindsey plopped on the bed beside me. "There really wasn't any other way." She grinned. "I can't wait to show the picture to my friends."

Mom bustled into the room and clamped a hand over her mouth to prevent a snort from escaping. "Oh my." Obviously, you *could* tell.

I lifted my chin and squared my shoulders. "Close the door." Mom raised her eyebrows and did as I asked. "There was someone in the house. An intruder. They stopped and glared at me from the door, then ran off. We need to call the police."

"Probably the same person who flipped the breakers." Mom nodded. "Who was it?"

I shrugged. "Bill Clinton."

Mom frowned. "Can't say I know anyone by that name around here."

"Not the actual person." I rolled my eyes. If I was going to solve this case, I'd need smarter sidekicks. "He wore a mask of the former president. I couldn't tell whether they were male or female, but I intend to find out." I rose to get a closer look at my hair. Not bad. A little snipping on the other side, and I could live with it. I glanced back at the auburn curl on my bed.

Lindsey grabbed the phone. "It's dead."

Mom leaned against the door. "We can't lock this. Give me something heavy."

"Tomorrow, I'm buying a car, a cell phone, and a Tazer gun." I stood with my mother, holding the door closed. "And maybe a dog. A big one."

"I won't have guns in the house. And cell phones give you brain tumors. The dog might be okay, though."

"I'm willing to take the risk with the phone, and a Tazer doesn't shoot bullets, just electricity. We can't stand here all night. I think the person is gone, but we need to make sure." I bumped Mom with my hip and cracked open the door. Silence greeted me. "Okay, who wants to go downstairs and check on the phone?"

"Not me," Mom and Lindsey said in unison.

"You went all the way to the basement, Mom."

"That was before I knew we had an intruder."

Great. It's up to me, queen of the chicken club. I glanced around the room for something to use as a weapon. I grabbed the yard stick I'd used months ago to measure the windows for curtains, clutched it like a sword, and nodded for Mom to open the door.

The wood floor felt cool beneath my bare feet, and I moved soundlessly forward, jumping at every creak of the old house. Something banged toward the front of the house. I spun and knocked a lamp to the floor, shattering the crystal vase. Wonderful. If the intruder didn't kill me, Mom would.

Keeping my back plastered to the wall, I slid my way through the house, holding my breath and leaping around corners in a stance of the Samurai. I'd located the source of the banging. The open front door swung to and fro.

Tacked to the frame around the window fluttered a white scrap of paper.

17

"It says to stop snooping." I waved the paper in front of Bruce's face. "This alone should tell you that Lindsey isn't involved. Someone is setting her up."

He rubbed his chin and paced my living room. "This does shake things up a bit."

"A bit?" I frowned and plopped onto the sofa. "Former President Clinton was in my house and that's all you have to say? We could have been murdered."

"They haven't killed anyone yet."

"What about Sharon?"

"We're ruling that an accident."

"I don't intend to be the first murder victim, Bruce. I'm buying a dog."

He glanced at me and shook his head. "I never could understand your jumping from one subject to the next."

"I'm buying a dog for security reasons." Made perfect sense to me.

Bruce finished searching the house, found nothing, which wasn't a surprise since I told him the intruder had left. The man doesn't believe anything I say. Then he reminded us to lock up after he left. Did he think we were stupid?

Mom pushed to her feet from where she'd slumped in her flowered easy chair and listened to the conversation between Bruce and me. "Once again, it's after midnight and we're not asleep. I'm getting too old for this." She clapped me on the shoulder. "You take off work and buy that dog. A big one that barks. I'm going to bed. Oh, and no guns."

"You're buying a gun?" Bruce frowned. "I don't think you and an armed weapon would be a good idea. I'd have to confiscate it."

"Good grief. It's not a real gun. Are you leaving soon?"

He stood and slapped his hat on his hat. "Yep. Heed my words, Marsha. I'll lock you up if I have to."

Idiot. Like I'd be that stupid. After he left, I locked the front door, checked the windows and backdoor then shuffled to my room. I lay on the bed, heart pounding and tried to come up with a plan to defend my family and solve the case before somebody else died.

***

The din of barking dogs vibrated against my ear drums, promising a doozy of a headache later. That, combined with lack of sleep, left me with little patience. I fumbled in my purse for pain reliever and popped the pills without water.

Three aisles of prison-like cells greeted me as I entered the building. Lindsey had disappeared looking for puppies. I shouldn't have been surprised to see Miss Hollywood Wannabe, Marilyn, sweeping out a cage, but I was. "You work here?"

The smile she flashed my way didn't meet her eyes. "Yep. Gotta make money anyway I can if I'm going to leave this dump. What I make walking dogs isn't enough. I also do some janitor work."

I jumped back to avoid being splattered with a not-so-pleasant smelling gunk of something that slung off her broom. "I've decided to get a dog, but these all look too small."

She motioned her head farther down. "The larger dogs are in the last two aisles."

"Thanks." I headed away and glanced over my shoulder to see her still watching me. Her ruby red lips thinned to where they resembled a slash in her face. The narrow-eyed look she tossed my way sent chills down my spine. Could she have left me the note on the door last night?

I paused before the cage of a big brute of a dog. Grey wiry hair, drooping eyes. Ugly, but kind of cute at the same time. I kneeled. "Hey, boy."

The dog lunged, snarling at the wire door. I scrambled backward, falling into the puddles of water on the cement floor. At least I hoped it was water. I resisted the urge to smell my hand and got to my feet. "Guess I won't be taking you home. Good luck, buddy. With that attitude you'll need it. Have you ever heard the term, dead dog walking?"

I turned the corner and stopped suddenly in order not to run into Marilyn. "Are you following me?"

The corners of her mouth turned down. "Why would I do that?"

"I don't know, you tell me."

"I'm following your daughter." Marilyn leaned closer and lowered her voice. "My boss said she's been in some trouble lately and, well. . ."

"You think she's going to steal a dog that's locked in a cage?" I spun on my heel and marched away. A whine at the end of the aisle caught my attention.

A majestic German Shepherd stared straight ahead. Her ears perked when I stopped before the cage. The sign above the door identified her as one-year-old Cleopatra. Her tail thumped the floor when I squatted beside the cage. "You are beautiful. I bet you'd make a real good watch dog, wouldn't you?" I stood. "Hey, Marilyn! I want Cleopatra. What's a purebred doing at the pound?"

"The owners said they had to move and couldn't take her with them." Marilyn unhooked a key from around her neck. "She must like you. She barks at everyone else. I think that's the real reason she was brought in. Barkers don't find homes very easily. Do you have a leash?"

"No."

"Dog food? Dishes?" She frowned at me. "Are you at all prepared to take in a pet?"

"I have a fenced yard and can buy the rest." I wasn't completely incompetent.

She rolled her eyes. "We'll lend you a leash, but you'll have to return it."

I grinned. "I'll have Lindsey run it by your house tomorrow."

Marilyn thrust a tattered strip of vinyl into my hands, banged the door open, and turned away. "Take her up front to pay your adoption fee."

Cleo sat docilely while I hooked the leash on her and then trotted beside me toward the front of the building. If I was half as regal as the dog or carried myself as well, life would be much better for me, I felt certain.

As I waited in line, I perused the bulletin board of animals for sale. Funny. Why would the animal shelter post ads for other people wanting to sell their dogs and cats? The word Chihuahua caught my attention. Someone posted an ad for the tiny Mexican puppies. I grabbed a pen from the counter and wrote the number on my hand. If it were the same ones stolen from Gloria, I'd be a step further in the investigation than Bruce.

"Mom, can we get a cat?" Lindsey appeared at my elbow.

"Not unless you want our new fierce protector to eat it."

"She doesn't look so bad to me." Lindsey wrapped her arms around Cleo's neck and buried her face in her fur. Cleo licked her face then turned back to me. I couldn't help but feel superior to the unknown faces Marilyn mentioned the dog not liking. She seemed to like us. Animals were supposed to be great judges of character, right?

After becoming the proud owner of Cleopatra, we stopped by the giant pet supply store and headed home. Cleo took possession of the back seat and hung her head on the arm rest between the two front seats. An instant best friend.

***

I sat at the kitchen table with my suspect list in front of me and Cleo lying at my feet. Lynn called precisely at five o'clock. I'd have been surprised with anything else from my A-type personality friend.

"Hey, Lynn, talk to me."

"There's a lot of stuff going around the teacher's lounge at the high school." Her words sound garbled, like she was eating.

"Like what?" I picked up my pencil.

"Lot's of things disappearing. Nothing like Sharon's necklace, though. Small things. Worth a couple of hundred dollars each or such." She paused for a moment. "Sorry, took a drink. Here's the funny thing. . .no one seems to remember anything. One moment they have something in their possession, the next they don't. Like they were sleeping or something. And it's happening at home. Not here at school. It's almost like there's an epidemic of forgetfulness assaulting the town."

I gnawed the end of my pencil, thinking back to the day when we'd discovered the money missing out of the store cash register. "Gloria Simpson said it felt like she'd been in a fog all day. What do you think it means?"

"I don't know."

"Huh." She usually knew everything.

"Okay, change of subject." Lynn sighed. "Tell me what's bothering you and maybe I can point you in the right direction."

What wasn't bothering me? "Duane, Lindsey, an intruder in my house last night." Lynn gasped at that one. "I've bought a dog as a security measure, and I'm getting a Tazer, but I'm not feeling very secure right now."

"Did the intruder threaten you?"

"No, I think they laughed at me."

"Laughed?"

"Well, I was kind of stuck. I'd caught my hair in the phone cord." I closed my eyes, envisioning Lynn face alight with humor.

"Only you, Marsha."

"Considering I could have been killed last night, that's real funny."

"We are cranky, aren't we?"

"Ha ha." I leaned down and scratched behind Cleo's ears. "I think I have reason to be. Plus, I don't know what to do about Duane. I think I still have feelings for him. But there's a lot to get over." Too much to dwell on right now. Unforgiveness and past hurts. "Plus, I've got to solve this case before Lindsey gets arrested for something she didn't do.

"Or something worse happens. Like the intruder succeeding in killing someone." I needed to devise a plan to see who our Clinton impersonator was.

18

The doorbell rang. Cleo barked once and bounded from my bed. I followed, more silently, and smiled when I saw Duane's silhouette through the window. I forgot he promised to stop by.

"Ready?" He leaned against the doorjamb when I swung the door open and tugged on the brim of his cowboy hat. "Where are we off to?"

I took a deep breath to keep from fainting. The man oozed so much charm and masculinity if I could bottle it, I'd make a fortune. "I really need to look for a new car. We'd better buy a paper so I can scan the ads." I pulled the door closed behind us. "Then, there's a notice for Chihuahuas I want to check out."

"Speaking of, did I hear a dog barking?" Duane took my elbow and steered me toward the passenger seat of a truck.

"That's Cleopatra. I bought her today. I'll introduce you to her later. She's great." I slid onto the seat and closed my eyes, anticipating, yet dreading, the next question. One, two. . .

"Why do you need a dog?"

I opened my eyes and rolled my head so I faced him. "Thank you for not bringing the motorcycle."

"Marsha."

"We kind of had an episode last night."

"An episode?" His brows drew together. "This isn't television, Marsha."

"Someone wearing a Bill Clinton mask came into our home. They were obviously surprised to see us still awake. Hence, the need for a dog. Cleo's perfect. She's a German Shepherd and the most beautiful. . ."

Duane removed his hat and ran his hands through his hair. A muscle twitched in his jaw. "First the threatening letter, now this."

"Bruce told you about the letter?" So much for confidentiality. "It's actually all part of the same."

"How much snooping have you done?"

I crossed my arms. "Not much, but I'm going to increase. First a car, then a tazer, then I'll find out who is robbing the town's citizens."

"Lord, help me." Duane turned the key in the ignition, backed the truck out of the driveway then headed toward town.

"I don't know why you're so upset. It's not like it's any of your business." I stared out the window. "I mean, we're friends and all, but --"

Duane stomped the brakes hard enough to throw me against the shoulder harness of the seatbelt and skidded to a stop on the shoulder of the road. His glare froze me in place. "I don't even know what to say to that so I'll try to cover it all. I'm sorry I hurt you. I'm not the same man I was fifteen years ago. I care about you, Marsha. Very much, but I won't waste my time if there isn't a chance between us. If you want to get back at me for the pain I caused you, then fine. Fine! Do it. Hit me."

"What?" He'd gone crazy. I flattened myself against the door. Hit him?

"Think about it, Marsha." He wiggled a finger between the two of us. "We need to have a serious talk, you and I." He returned to the road. "I know who has a car for sale. Stephanie Jackson is selling a Prius. Dirt cheap, I heard." The muscle in Duane's jaw ticked faster.

I ripped my gaze away and stared at the passing houses. How *did* I feel about Duane? I'd already told him I still loved him. Did I want a relationship with him? Could I put myself in such a vulnerable position again? What if he skipped town again? How much can a person really change? "I'll have to think about that tomorrow," I whispered to myself. "Today has enough worries of its own."

"Okay, Scarlett O'Hara. We're here."

We stopped before a three-story, lavender Victorian. Stephanie carted a box to a nearby shed and glanced over her shoulder as we marched up her flagstone walkway. "Be right there!" She tossed the box inside the building, slammed the door, and inserted a lock. But not before I noticed stuff piled to the ceiling. She wiped her hands on her navy shorts and plastered a smile to her face.

"Marsha, how nice to see you. Did you bring some items for my yard sale?"

"Is that what's in your shed?"

Her eyes narrowed. "Yes."

I shrugged. "Looks like a lot of stuff. I'm going to be moving into my mom's guest house. Once we clean it out, I should have something for you."

She clapped her hands together in a semblance of glee. "I can't wait. Gertie's been hoarding for years. What can I do for you today?"

"Do you still have the Prius for sale?" Duane asked.

"I sure do." She batted her lashes at him. "You're fast. I just posted it yesterday." Stephanie led us toward her garage and punched a code into the electronic keypad. "Five thousand dollars, fully loaded, midnight blue; she's a beauty. Hate to part with it, but we're saving for the adoption."

Duane and I walked around the car, my heart lifting with each step. I ran my fingers over the smooth paint. The Prius might be second-hand, but it was still the newest automobile I'd ever owned. Why was she selling it so cheap? I'm no expert on blue book prices, but even I could guess the price was a steal. I opened the door and slid behind the wheel.

I'd have to dip into the life insurance money I'd stashed away after Robert's death, but one look at the cute little hybrid, and I was sold. Having reliable transportation constituted using emergency funds, right? "I'll take it. I'll write you a check, but don't cash it until after tomorrow. I've got to transfer the money."

"No problem. I didn't expect it to sell so quickly."

I felt giddy with excitement and turned the keys in the ignition. The engine turned over without a glitch. No more Little Blue beast. Lindsey would be sixteen soon and the proud owner of an ancient AMC Spirit. I thought my face would split with the intensity of my grin when I turned to Duane. "Thanks."

He winked. "You're welcome. Do you want me to go with you to buy that Tazer?"

"Sure. We'll check the pawn shop first. I'm driving." I got out from behind the wheel and jogged to Duane's truck then reached through the window for my purse and withdrew my checkbook. "I just want something that will serve as protection, not break the bank."

Stephanie fidgeted from foot to foot, smile wavering, and kept glancing toward the shed. A strange whining cry came from behind the door. "Just an old generator," Stephanie assured me. "Thing's been messing up for months."

"Do you want me to look at it?" Duane took a step in that direction. "I'm good with mechanical things."

"Oh, no. Mark's just about got it." Stephanie bit her lip.

I wrote a check for $5,000 and held out my hand for the title. She gave an obvious sigh of relief as she handed me the envelope. "Here's the title to the car." She whirled and hurried toward the shed. Unlocking the padlock, Stephanie slipped into the shed. I couldn't wait to slide behind the wheel of my new baby.

But not before I heard a yelp from behind the shed door.

"Wait a minute, Duane. I heard something."

Stephanie disappeared into the darkness where she stored her yard sale junk. The door closed with a bang behind her.

"I'll be right back."

Duane reached out a hand to stop me, but I sidestepped him and headed on my way. "I've got to check something out." I ran on tip toes to peer into the murky recesses of the shed.

Boxes piled on boxes. What I could only guess was another vehicle lay covered by a tarp. Stephanie rummaged in the corner, offering me an unflattering view of her behind, and the thong sticking up from her waistband. Yuck. Another yelp sounded and I leaped back, tripping over a metal trash can. It fell to its side with a clatter. I clamored to my feet and dashed back to the truck.

Stephanie emerged from the shed. A calico cat curled in her arms. "Are you spying on me?"

I was an idiot. Why did I always assume the worst? A cat could've easily made the sound I'd heard, right? Maybe? Until I had proof of something, I needed to lay low and not make assumptions. I gave her a smile and a wave, pretending not to hear her shouted question then turned to Duane.

"Duane, do cat's yelp?"

"What?"

"Never mind. Follow me home, then I'll drive us to the pawn shop."

I climbed behind the wheel of my new baby and turned the key. Concrete sang beneath the tires as I backed from the driveway. No more groaning or grinding from shifting gears. This baby purred. Like a cat. Dog's yelped, or whined. I wondered what was in Stephanie's shed and if I'd recognize the voice when I called to check on the puppies.

I glanced over my shoulder. Stephanie carried a large cardboard box across her lawn and into the house.

19

Duane must have still been smarting from my less than warm attitude toward him. Instead of leaving his truck at my house, he decided to drive it home, tossing me a wave out his window as he drove past the house. Fine. I had things to do, anyway. I directed my new car to the nearest cell phone store.

An hour later, armed with a shiny new smart phone, I punched in the numbers for the sale of the Chihuahua puppies.

"Hello?" A man's voice answered. A lawnmower roared in the background.

"I'm calling about the puppies." I tried to balance the phone on my shoulder and start the car at the same time. Obviously, the tiny electronic device wasn't made for that. I dropped the phone between my seat and the door. After fumbling for several seconds, I pressed it back to my ear. "Sorry. Are you still there?"

"The puppies aren't here right now. They've, uh, been taken to the vet, for, uh shots. Yeah. Call back in an hour." Click.

O-kay. I stared at the phone for a minute before dropping it on the front passenger seat. The man didn't seem to be in much of a hurry to sell the puppies, did he? I'd expected a woman to answer. I would've sworn Stephanie Jackson was the dog thief, head of women's ministry or not. Appearing to be on the wrong track with my hunch on the dogs, I headed to the nearest pawnshop.

While I drove, I kept eyeing my sleek new phone. The urge to use it was like an addiction. I grabbed it and punched in the number to Gifts from Country Heaven. "Hey, Mom. Guess what?"

"I don't have time for guessing games."

"I'm talking on my new cell phone. You're the first person I called." A weird stranger selling dogs didn't count. I swerved, and a truck roared past me blaring its horn. My heart threatened to jump out of my ribcage.

"Are you driving?"

"Yep." Made me feel important too.

"No driving and talking on cell phones. It's against the law." Click.

Hmmph. I started to dial Lynn, then remembered she wasn't likely to be home and didn't possess a cell phone. That left Duane. He couldn't possibly still be mad at me, could he? I pressed the numbers and waited.

"Hello?"

He sounded wonderful on the phone. Deep, southern voice. Husky as all get out. "I'm calling on my new cell phone."

"Marsha?"

"Of course it's me."

"Are you calling to apologize?"

"For what?" I wracked my brain. What had I done now?

"Call me back when you're ready." Click.

Well, pooh. No one wanted to talk to me, and the whole world was rude. A lonely fifteen-minute drive stretched in front of me. My mother accused me on many occasions of being attention-deficit, but it wasn't until faced with minutes of having nothing to do that it occurred to me she might be right.

Focus, Marsha. Think about clearing your daughter of all suspicion regarding theft, or I could think about how I really felt about Duane. No, definitely not that.

Okay. Point one, Sharon lost a necklace and is now dead. Point two, Harvey Miller is missing a wallet, and Bruce found it in my daughter's backpack. Not good for Lindsey. Point three, Gloria Simpson's puppies are gone, and point four—money is missing from mom's till.

Suspects? Everyone, and no one. I wasn't very good at this. Maybe I should think about Duane. He looked good. Better than when I saw him ten years ago. His muscles had filled out, his dimples had deepened, and his kiss rivaled the sun's heat. I turned on the air conditioner.

What would be the harm of exploring a new relationship with him? Men played around all the time. It shouldn't be different for women. I sighed. I couldn't. Love was a serious thing for me. It was all or nothing. I may not have felt as strong for my husband as I do for Duane, but I'd been the model wife, and Robert had died a happy and content man. I couldn't be satisfied with less than that. Only time would tell whether Duane wanted something serious and permanent with me.

The pawnshop, Other People's Junk, appeared ahead, sparing me the path my thoughts insisted on taking.

I pulled my Prius into the vacant parking lot, cut the ignition, stuffed my phone into my purse, then slid from the car. I stared at the smudges of something unidentifiable on the shop's front door. Uh-huh. Wasn't touching that. Using my hip, I pushed the door open and stepped into the dim recesses of a cluttered, second-hand paradise.

"Hey, pretty lady."

I grimaced at the greasy man behind the counter. Hopefully, I could get what I needed and skedaddle. "I'm looking for a Tazer."

"Self-defense? I can see how someone with your good looks would need it."

Good grief. I nodded.

The man reached beneath a glass counter and pulled out a card deck-sized— something. Never having seen one before, I felt disappointed. A black square. Didn't look very impressive. Didn't they come in pretty colors? "Does it work?"

"Like a charm. If my dog was here, I'd show you." He set it on the counter and leaned on the glass. "A one-second burst will shock and disorient a person; a two-second one will send them to their knees for thirty seconds. A cop's tazer only lasts five seconds. Tazers for civilians are meant to allow you time to get away. Do you want a pretty blue arc, or something that shoots probes? Who do you want to zap?"

"Nobody right now. The arc type will be fine." I turned the Tazer in my hand. If I had the ability to shoot anything, I'd be dangerous to be around. Hard to believe something so small could actually knock a person down. "How much?"

"Twenty-nine, ninety-nine. Comes with a thirty-day guarantee, too. You want a gun to go with it? You'll have to wait fifteen days to get it, but I can sell it to you now."

Fifteen days might be too late. "It's an emergency." I drummed up a quivering chin. "Someone's stalking me. Isn't there any way you can make an exception?"

He rubbed his chin and stared at me. "You don't look dangerous, but you'll have to make it worth my time. An extra fifty dollars and I've got a pretty little .22 pistol you'll fall in love with."

"Sure. That would be great!" A gun, a Tazer, *and* a German Shepherd. Nobody would mess with me.

Purchases tucked under my arm, I practically skipped to my car. I wanted to call everyone and tell them. An evening loomed ahead with hours to play with my toys. Did I live within the city limits? Would they arrest me if I set aluminum cans on the fence post for target practice? I really should work on cleaning out my new home. Maybe I could devote time to both.

My phone rang. I jerked and the car swerved toward the ditch. I straightened out and fumbled in my purse. "Hello?"

"Are you coming to work today?"

"Hi, Mom. I'm driving. Can't talk now."
Two could play that game.

"Don't give me that. We've had an order for three Time-Out Babies. I need you behind the sewing machine." Click.

Why did everyone keep hanging up on me?

The moment I sashayed in the door, Mom thrust bolts of flowered fabric at me. "What took you so long? Duane came by an hour ago. Does it take that long to buy a cell phone?"

"I had another errand to run." I glanced at the clock on the wall. Three o'clock. The store closed in two hours. "I can get one of these sewed. Tomorrow, Lindsey can help me stuff while I sew the others."

"As long as they're ready to be shipped by Friday." Mom marched to the back of the store.

There went my opportunity to play. The bell over the door jangled, and Stephanie waltzed in.

"Hello, Marsha. Have you had an opportunity to see whether you have any donations yet? My yard sale is this Saturday." She glanced around the shop. "There's a lot of stuff in here. Surely, you can spare something. Maybe a doo-dad we can raffle?"

I paused in threading the machine needle. "We cannot spare anything in the store. It's all for sale. This is our business. I'll get to our shed by this weekend. I promise."

She stared at me for a moment, her smile frozen in place like a clown's mask. "This is important to me, Marsha. I'll do anything to achieve my dream of being a parent."

"Point taken." Good grief. Talk about over the top. She acted like I personally wanted to foil her adoption plans. I turned back to my work. "Good afternoon, Stephanie."

A few minutes later, Melvin Brown and Kyle Anderson barged in, arguing loudly over exactly what kind of gift an elderly woman might want. "I'm telling you, she'd like a nice broach to go on a scarf," Melvin said.

"And I'm telling you she'd want something hand-made." Kyle crossed his arms. "That's why we came here."

I sighed and stood. "Gentlemen, may I help you? Who are you shopping for?"

"Our grandmother." Melvin glared at Kyle.

I'd forgotten the two men were cousins. "We do have jewelry, Kyle, and handmade scarves. Why don't you buy one of each?"

Melvin frowned. "They ain't expensive are they? I'm saving for my business. I'm starting to collect a nice little nest egg. Wouldn't want to dip into it for anything."

"Don't be cheap." Kyle riffled through the box of pins I laid on the counter. "I'm the one that was robbed. Got to start all over now. But I've got an idea that might get me into some fast cash." He handed me a pink-stoned pin. "This one. Melvin can choose the scarf."

Melvin ran his hands through the lengths of silk and chose one that matched the pin.

Purchases complete, the two men left the store, still bickering over whether a ninety-year-old woman even needed more jewelry. I shook my head. Before the door could swing shut behind them, Marilyn the dog walker breezed in.

"Hello!"

I sighed and glanced at the still unthreaded machine. I'd never get home at this rate. Where was my mother? Why wasn't she waiting the counter so I could work? "Hello, Marilyn. Can I help you?"

She waved a fluorescent yellow sheet of paper in my face. "I noticed Stephanie had a flier up about her sale, and wondered if I could put one up advertising my dog walking business."

I waved a hand. "Sure, go ahead." I plopped back in my chair. All but one of my suspects had paid me a visit within the last fifteen minutes. If Billy Butler sailed through the door, I'd think God was trying to tell me something. What, I had no idea, but something, for sure.

"You must be selling tons of stuff." Mom plopped a spool of ribbon on the counter. "That bell hasn't stopped ringing." She eyed my idle sewing machine. "And you haven't been working."

"That's kind of hard when I'm waiting on customers. What are you doing back there?"

Her face flushed. "Talking with Leroy. He's taking me out to dinner tonight."

"That's great, Mom." I glanced at the clock. "What time is he picking you up?"

"Five. So I'm leaving now. See you later."

My gaze followed her out the door. Time stopped, along with my heart, when a stern-faced Duane marched in.

20

I swallowed against the Mount Everest-sized lump in my throat. The granite look on Duane's face told me this wasn't a pleasure visit. Thank you, Lord, that Mom left and wouldn't be a witness to the continuing drama of my non-existent-slash-rollercoaster love life.

Duane stopped in front of the counter and took a deep breath. "I can't leave our conversation in the car unresolved. It's making me insane." His amazing eyes smoldered. I couldn't blink. Could barely breathe. "I realized I loved you the moment I walked into your store a few days ago. I'm sorry I left River Valley. It tears me up inside that you married my brother instead of me. That Lindsey is Robert's daughter and not mine. All my fault I know, but it kills me anyway." His breath shuddered. "I walked out of your life fifteen years ago and broke your heart. I'm sorry, Marsha. With everything in me, I want to make it up to you, if you'll let me. Think about it, please. That's all I ask." He spun on a booted heel and strode from the shop.

Wow. My chest hurt from my heart's fierce pounding. Tears I hadn't known were forming streamed down my cheeks and plopped on the fabric. I was a cad. An awful person who held on to grudges way past their due date. The world's handsomest, most wonderful, man loved me, and I couldn't utter a single word as he poured out his heart. Couldn't give him the smallest bit of encouragement. I didn't have to think about whether I loved him; I knew I did. How long did I want him to suffer?

Bolting from my chair, I sped out the front door and scanned the street. Duane's truck was nowhere to be seen. I hurriedly locked the shop and dashed for my car. I'd go by his house and spill my guts. We'd lost too many years already. I didn't want another minute to pass without his lips on mine, and his arms around me.

I broke the sound barrier racing to his house. No cars sat in the driveway. I let my head fall forward against the steering wheel. I'd wait all night if I had to. With a deep breath, I grabbed my purse and slid from the car. A porch swing offered the perfect place for me to wait.

Duane lived inside the city limits. The street running in front of his house entertained me and helped to pass the time. Curtains parted across the street then fell into place when I glanced that way. I smiled. Some old busy-body's gears were turning trying to figure out what I was doing.

Dog walker Marilyn ran to keep up with two large hounds, her face scarlet with the effort. "I can't wait to be rid of you!" She glanced my way. I returned her wave.

Billy sped by on a shiny dirt bike. He stopped and flung dark hair out of his eyes. He started to dismount, caught me looking, and with his face turning the color of a cantaloupe, disappeared back down the road. Handsome boy. I could see why Lindsey would be smitten with him. If only the kid didn't look like a skittish colt every time he was around me.

I wasn't a danger to anyone but myself. Maybe he thought I was still upset about the car through the diner window. What happened with that anyway? Did Mom's insurance cover the damages? Or Billy's parents? If his parents didn't have insurance and had to cover the cost, did that mean I needed to add them to my suspect list of folks looking for some quick cash?

Pushing off with my foot, I set the swing into motion. I was tired of thinking of the case and boredom reared its ugly head as the occupants of Duane's street disappeared inside their homes and porch lights flicked on. A quick glance at my watch, and a grumbling from my stomach, reminded me it was supper time.

Maybe I should just call Duane and let him know I waited. I dug through my purse. What's this? I grinned and held up my two new toys. The barrel of the gun gleamed in the setting sun, and since I didn't want to frighten anyone who might be passing, I shoved it back in my purse. The Tazer was another matter.

I glanced around the yard for something to practice on. No four-legged creatures dared get close enough to me. What could I zap? I'd seen bugs fry against electrical devices before. Was a Tazer the same as a bug-zapper? I'd touched my finger on the electric fly-swatter my mom had. My finger went numb for a minute but nothing more. I needed to make sure my new Tazer would actually serve as self-defense.

"Here, Kitty, Kitty." I rose from the swing then crouched behind a bush. A one-second zap wouldn't hurt a cat, would it? They had nine lives after all. But what if it did? I wouldn't be able to live with myself if I hurt an animal.

I supposed I wouldn't get to practice after all. I pressed the button and oohed and aahed over the blue arc between the connectors.

For the first time since meeting the girl, I wished for Marilyn to sashay by with a large dog. That'd be the perfect guinea pig. Her, not the dog. The deserted street taunted me. Why did everyone in this town eat dinner so early? And what was wrong with me? Would I really torture a defenseless animal, or human, out of boredom?

I lowered myself to the top step of the porch, resigned to the fact I couldn't zap anything. Stephanie's face came to mind. I knew I shouldn't be that way, but the woman rubbed me wrong. Her perfect hair, her designer clothes, big fancy car –and wanting to do good by adopting a third-world child. All reasons to like the woman, but I didn't. She seemed fake to me.

Maybe I was in over my head trying to solve this case. Bruce hadn't accused Lindsey of stealing anything in the last couple of days. I should leave things alone and concentrate on my feelings for Duane.

I'd grown to love my husband, Robert, but he'd never rocked my boat the way Duane did. I kept pushing the button on my Tazer and watched the spark. My and Duane's relationship had been a bit like my new toy. Shocking, beautiful—and capable of inflicting harm. Had it been worth it? Not at the time. But maybe now it could be.

Full dark set in, and Duane still hadn't showed. The Tazer glowed more beautiful. I played around, seeing how close I could stick my finger without actually touching the electricity.

"Marsha?"

"Duane?"

Zap. Holy Mary Mother of ...!

I twitched like a fish on a line. Fire burned through my body. Drool gathered at the corner of my mouth. Pain worse than childbirth ravaged my body. Who would have thought touching that colorful arc would render me stupid enough I couldn't withdraw my finger from the button?

Duane yanked the Tazer out of my hand and tossed it on the porch. He bent his lovely face over mine, and—goodness—proceeded to give me mouth-to-mouth. I'd died and gone to heaven. Except for the pain. That kept me rooted to good ol' planet Earth.

"Marsha." He patted my cheek.

"Iluveu."

"What?" He frowned and bent for another life-giving breath.

Only problem with that was the touch of his lips on mine stole my breath away. No longer jerking like a live wire, I pushed him away and sat up.

"Marsha Calloway Steele, what were you thinking?" He retrieved my Tazer. "These are not toys."

"You startled me, and I was bored." I tried patting my hair in place. My finger throbbed with each beat of my heart. With the condition I was in, this happened with lightening speed.

Duane sat on the step next to me. "What are you doing with this?"

"I have a gun, too."

He closed his eyes for a second. "Thank God you weren't playing with that." He took a deep breath and looked at me. His eyes shimmered. "Were you waiting for me?"

I nodded. "You rendered me speechless in the store. I'm sorry I didn't say anything." Tears welled in my eyes. "I love you, Duane. Always have. . .always will. I couldn't let you storm out of the shop thinking I didn't. I'd have waited here all night if I had to."

His mouth hitched. "Good thing I didn't let football practice go any longer. Of course, it might be interesting to see how long you could've held your finger on that Tazer trigger."

I planted both hands against his chest and shoved hard enough to cause him to lie flat. "Don't poke fun at a serious moment like this."

"I'm sorry." He grabbed my hands in his and pulled me on top of him. "Did you try telling me you loved me while thrashing around on my porch?"

I nodded.

"Then kiss me. Let's see whether you can quiver again."

I lowered my head. The electricity that sparked between us burned brighter than an Ozark summer sun and left me almost as weak as the Tazer.

21

When I floated into the house, Mom and Leroy sat in front of the television watching a game show. She'd been spending a lot of time with the man. I definitely needed to learn more about him.

Mom raised her eyebrows before turning to Leroy. "Uh-oh. My daughter looks like a woman who's been thoroughly kissed."

Leroy winked. "Want a look to match?"

Mom giggled and punched his shoulder. "Silly. Not in front of my daughter."

I rolled my eyes. Dusk or not, I needed to give them privacy, or go blind. "I'm going to work on the shed. See y'all lovebirds later."

The grin on my face must have matched the Cheshire Cat's. Mom's description of the way I looked mirrored how I felt. Thoroughly kissed. Yep, I liked that analogy.

My finger sported a blister from my stupidity with the Tazer. Maybe I should detour to get a band-aid. "What do you think, Cleo? Should I play injured or get to work." My dog's ears rose, and her tail thumped the floor. "To work it is. Come on. You can keep me company while I clean out our new home."

Cleo padded along behind me, clearly pleased and excited to be in my company. The front door to the guesthouse squeaked when I opened it, reminding me I'd need to oil its hinges one day. One flick of the light switch showed Mom had followed through with her promise to have Leroy install new bulbs.

The pile of boxes and plastic crates did nothing to make me excited about the job ahead. They towered above me like blocks stacked by a toddler, threatening to teeter and crash down on my head with the slightest breeze.

"This could be hazardous to our health." I shoved aside dust-covered curtains. The early evening light barely cut through the grime on the windows. "I'm not sure where to start, Cleo girl." I unstacked the nearest pile of boxes and sat cross-legged on the wooden floor.

The first box revealed tax records older than I was. I'd really have to talk to Mom about the art of shredding. The next held old photo albums of sepia-toned and black-and-white family members of decades gone by. I settled down to take a trip back in time. At this rate, I wouldn't have anything for Stephanie to sell at her yard sale, and I'd never have this place habitable for myself and Lindsey before my daughter graduated high school.

Moon beams caressed my legs before I'd finished. My back ached, and my tail bone felt bruised. I carefully replaced the photo albums and reached for the next box. My maternity clothes. Those could go. I shoved them closer to the door.

Nostalgia greeted me with the next one. My father's old medical journals. He'd loved reading through them every time one of his old cronies had some ache or pain. He'd never had the opportunity or means to attend medical school, so he'd done the next best thing; read everything he could get his hands on in the medical field. I wanted to keep these. They'd have a place of prominence on my bookshelf. I pushed them to the side. A faded photo fell out.

I held it to the light. Mom, as a young woman, laughed, her face tilted to my handsome father's. They'd been so happy. Best friends since high school, they'd been completely into each other, yet never left me feeling like the third wheel. I tucked the picture back into the book. Dad died a long time ago, leaving a canyon-sized hole in my heart. As much pain as I'd been in, how much more had my mother? If Leroy could make her happy, then God bless him. Leroy might not be the love of my mother's life, but she would be good to him.

Two hours later, I popped the kinks from my back and surveyed the new stacks; keep, toss, and give away. I started lugging the toss boxes to the garage. There wasn't anything more I could do until Mom went through them. Then, I shoved the ones for Stephanie onto the miniscule porch of the guesthouse. Tomorrow, I'd start the chore of cleaning my new home.

My body ached, my skin itched from the layer of dust covering it, and my throat felt like someone had attacked it with sandpaper. The promise of a hot shower and a long night's sleep kept me moving forward.

Leroy's car was gone from the driveway, and Mom left the kitchen light burning for me. I glanced at my watch. Midnight! I'd been working forever. On the kitchen table sat a hefty chunk of chocolate cake. Without looking, I knew there'd be a tall glass of milk in the fridge. Mom was so good to me. She'd even left a steak bone in Cleo's dish, from Leroy most likely.

I tossed my purse on the table. The gun in the bottom clunked on the laminate top. I'd almost forgotten. Target shooting would've been way more fun than digging through boxes.

As I dug into my cake and milk, and Cleo succumbed to bone-gnawing heaven, I envisioned soda cans lining the back fence. With deadly aim, I'd shoot them off in rapid succession. I crooked my finger and pointed, "Bang."

"Who are you trying to kill?" Mom shuffled into the room.

"I thought you'd be asleep." I lowered my hand.

"Leroy and I took in a late movie." She dropped into a nearby chair. "That man spoils me."

"You need to be spoiled again, Mom. Leroy seems like a nice guy."

"You're okay with this?"

"It's been over five years." Dad's face rose to my mind. It seemed like he smiled and nodded. "Dad would want you to be happy."

"You too, sweetie. How are you and Duane getting along?"

I started sweating. Fair's fair. I asked about her man, she asked about mine. "Pretty good. We crossed a mile-stone today. I've decided to give him a fresh chance. I'm going to forgive the past and move forward."

"You love him."

This was getting way too personal. Pretty soon I'd be telling her how I zapped myself and fell all over Duane on his front porch. "Do you want to see what I bought today?" I dumped my purse out on the table.

"A Tazer, a gun, and a shiny new phone." Mom shook her head. "I've seen it all now." She reached for the Tazer and pressed the button. The electricity arced. "Cool." Her eyes narrowed. "You haven't been playing with this, have you?"

My face heated. "Why would you ask that?"

"I know you." She set the Tazer back on the table. "What's with all this? A dog— now weapons. Aren't you getting a little paranoid?"

"Protection. Three women alone in a house, well,--." I scooped everything back into the sling bag I used as a purse. "A girl can't be too careful now-a-days. Do you think I should get a can of pepper spray?"

"You'll probably shoot yourself in the foot with that gun, and from the blister on your finger, I'd say you've been playing with the Tazer." She pointed at me. "Pepper spray is most likely all you would've needed in the first place, but more than likely even that would send you to the hospital. We live in small-town, America, don't forget. Not a big metropolis. Now, I'll have to add to my prayer time and have God assign extra angels to watch out for the foolish whims of my daughter." She rose. "I'm going to bed. You should too. Got to open the store in the morning."

"I was hoping to clean the guesthouse." And sleep in. "So I can move in this weekend."

"You can clean in the evenings." Mom squeezed my shoulder then left the room. "I need your help."

But I wanted to spend my evenings with Duane, and find out who framed my daughter as a thief. And who'd been inside Sharon's house before she died. The list went on and on. I sighed. I'd gotten very little sleuthing done. Maybe I went around it the wrong way. I needed help. Did they sell books on crime solving? I couldn't ask Bruce. He'd tell me to mind my own business and stay out of things. Lynn would say the same.

"Well, Cleo, girl. Time for what little sleep we can squeeze in before the sun comes up." I slung my purse over my shoulder and headed up the stairs.

I stopped and peered into Lindsey's room. Her empty bed mocked me. She'd obviously taken advantage of my busyness to sneak out past curfew. Well, I'd show her. I dropped my purse and spread out across her pink and yellow quilt. When she waltzed in to go to sleep, she'd find me here, wide awake, waiting, and demanding answers.

I crossed my arms and glared at the doorway. My eyelids grew heavy. I tried keeping them open with my fingers. No such luck. Then I ran over my suspects, again, but that was kind of like counting sheep. I glanced around the dim room. Teenage heart throbs adorned the walls. Clothes hung out of the closet and open drawers. My daughter wasn't very neat. Maybe I should use the time to clean her room. No, I wasn't that desperate.

I blinked against the growing sand paper in my eyes. Why wouldn't they stay open? Maybe I'd close them for just a minute.

The sun streamed through the open curtains and stabbed at my eyelids. I glanced at my watch. Seven o'clock. I'd have to hurry to open Gifts from Country Heaven at eight. I sat up. Lindsey! She hadn't come home last night. I wracked my brain, trying to remember if she'd said she would spend the night with a friend. No, she hadn't said anything.

My heart rate increased. Had something happened to her?

"Mom!" I raced from the room and into my mother's. "Lindsey didn't come home last night."

Mom bolted upright. "Huh? Are you sure? She didn't get a hold of your gun, did she?"

"What?" My mother's rambling stabbed me with fear. Lindsey didn't know I'd purchased a weapon, so wouldn't be inclined to play with it. She'd know better at her age anyway, right?

"Never mind."

"I'm positive she didn't come home. I slept in her bed so I'd know when she came in."

"I'm sure she's fine." Mom slung aside her blankets. "Go change your clothes, then we'll drive around town and see if we can spot her."

"Good idea." I dashed into the hall and to my room.

Lindsey lay curled into a ball, sleeping peacefully in my bed with Cleo beside her. Her shoes left mud on my Battenburg comforter.

22

"Lindsey Marie Steele!" I glared at my daughter. "What are you doing in my bed?"

Lindsey popped up like a child's toy and blinked against the morning light. "You were in mine." She scowled and scratched her head. "Where else was I supposed to sleep?"

"What time did you come home?" I snapped my fingers for Cleo to join me.

"Uh. . .midnight?"

"Wrong answer. You know good and well it was past curfew. The last thing we need is for you to get picked up because you're breaking the law. Where were you?"

She ducked her head. "I had something I needed to do." Lindsey swung her legs over the bed and rose. "It's no big deal, Mom." She squeezed past me. "The dog's great by the way. And you talk in your sleep." Lindsey smirked. "I heard Uncle Duane's name a few times."

I couldn't breathe. Was she serious? Robert never said anything about me talking in my sleep. Did I say anything embarrassing? I talked about Duane? Not about the kiss, surely! "Oh, no you don't, missy. You aren't changing the subject."

Lindsey shrugged on her way out the door. Deliver me from teenagers.

Cleo looked up at me. "Some watchdog you are. Couldn't you at least have barked when Lindsey got home? Marilyn said you were a barker." I plopped on the edge of my bed. My daughter had never given me a lick of trouble before this summer. Now, suspected of theft and caught in the act of sneaking out, I was at my wit's end. My heart ached hard enough for me to clasp my hands to my bosom. What was I doing wrong?

Obviously my training had been lacking. "Lindsey." I stood and pursued her to the kitchen.

She slumped over a bowl of cereal, the latest teen mystery propped open in front of her. She grunted in acknowledgement.

I straightened my shoulders. "You'll come to work with me today. No arguments. Be ready to leave in twenty minutes." There. Tough love. I reached into the cabinet, grabbed a handful of M&Ms, popped them into my mouth, then spun and exited in as rigid a manner as possible. If I hadn't knocked my shoulder against the doorjamb on my way out, I would've made my point better. Lindsey snorted behind me.

Twenty minutes later, a sullen Lindsey slouched in the Prius's passenger seat. "I can't believe you're making me give up an entire summer day."

"I can't believe you stayed out past midnight without permission. Didn't call to tell me you'd be late, and then lied about it. Don't forget that vital part." I backed the car down the driveway then headed toward Gifts from Country Heaven. "There's nothing worthwhile to do at that time of the night."

"That's what you know." Lindsey stared out the window.

Ouch. Since when did my daughter begin speaking to me that way? I'd get to the bottom of her behavior while sewing the rest of the Time-Out Babies. If I timed my question just right, I'd catch her off guard, and she'd answer truthfully before she could think of a lie.

I parked behind the store and cut off the ignition. Lindsey's sullenness alerted me that bringing her with me might be punishing myself more than her. Oh, well. No help for it. I resolved to do whatever it took to be a good parent. I read somewhere that if she hated me now, it was a guarantee we'd be best friends when she grew up.

After grabbing my purse, I slid from the car and waited for Lindsey to join me. "Cheer up, it'll make the day pass faster. You can stuff while I sew."

"Oh, goody."

As soon as we entered the store, I picked up the phone to call Stephanie and let her know where she could pick up our donations to her yard sale.

"Oh, thank you, Marsha. I'll send over something as appreciation."

"You don't have to do that. I'm glad to be rid of the stuff."

"No problem. Bye."

Okay. I hung up the phone and rubbed my palms together. Maybe she'd send over something to eat. I turned to my daughter. "I've sewed the doll over there. You can stuff it now, and I'll get started on these others."

Lindsey rolled her eyes, plunked her backpack behind the counter, and plopped her bottom on a stool. "Don't you have anything more fun to do than this?"

"If a customer comes in, you can wait on them." I slid floral fabric beneath the foot of my sewing machine. As the needle whirred up-and-down, I tried devising a clever way of asking Lindsey what she'd been up to last night. I couldn't come up with anything other than the old tried and true straight forward question. "So, who'd you go see last night? Did you have fun?"

Lindsey paused in her stuffing of the doll's leg. "I was alone, and no, it wasn't particularly fun." She set the half-saggy baby in her lap. "If you thought someone might be doing something illegal, what would you do?"

I pressed the foot pedal hard enough for the fabric to shoot through the feed and onto the table. Oh, pooh. Now, I'd be busy ripping out stitches. "Thought? As in not sure?"

"Exactly."

"I guess I'd try to find out for sure."

"That's what I did last night. Or tried to anyway." Lindsey ducked her head and resumed her work.

My daughter turned the question back on me. She'd told me nothing about where she'd gone, or given me a good reason for breaking curfew. Who did she know that might be into something illegal? Did she have a friend I hadn't met? Did I need to be worried?

My seam ripper jabbed my finger, drawing blood. The spot throbbed in time with my heart. I dropped what I worked on and stood. "I'm going in the back to wash this. Watch the store, please."

Lindsey didn't look up as I passed. A belligerent teenager was an alien species to me. Lindsey and I had always gotten along more like sisters than mother and daughter. Maybe that's where I went wrong. I turned on the water in the restroom and stuck my finger beneath the flow. The water turned a pretty shade of pink as it swirled down the drain.

My daughter had turned fifteen a few months ago. Wasn't it a little too late for me to turn into Nazi mom? She'd always followed the few guidelines I'd set into place. Didn't get into trouble at school, didn't drink or cuss. I sighed and reached above the sink for a Band-Aid. With this new Lindsey, I found myself in foreign territory without a map.

The bell over the store's door jingled, followed by low murmurings of Lindsey and. . .the voice sounded male. I poked my head around the corner.

Billy Butler set a platter of cookies on the counter and leaned over to whisper something in Lindsey's ear. She giggled. Her face reddened then she shook her head.

"I have something I need to do tonight."

He pouted. "Are you sure? There's a great movie playing at the drive-in."

The drive-in! Absolutely not. I remembered those nights. Wrapping the

Band-Aid around my finger, I joined them. "Good afternoon, Billy."

"Mrs. Steele. Someone left cookies."

"Thank you, Billy." I raised my eyebrows, hoping he'd take the hint and leave.

"Oh. Okay. See you later, Lindsey." He dashed out the door.

I studied my daughter's pink face. "Is he the one you suspect of doing something wrong?"

"Billy?" Her eyes widened. "Never. He's wonderful, sweet, smart, athletic, handsome. . ."

"Okay, I get the picture. He's the perfect boy."

Lindsey and I reached for the cookies at the same time. My elbow clipped the tray as her fingers closed around one of the round treasures. The tray shattered on the wooden floor, mixing shards of glass with baked delight. I wanted to cry.

She shoved her rescued treat into her mouth making her look like a chipmunk. Sighing, I grabbed the broom from behind the counter and swept my disappointment away. My stomach grumbled, reminding me I'd skipped breakfast and lunch loomed on the horizon.

Once I had the mess cleaned up, I replaced the broom in its corner and grabbed my purse. "I'm heading to the diner to grab lunch. Want a burger?"

"Yes, please." Lindsey wiped her mouth with the back of her hand. "That cookie was good. Almost too sweet, though. It had alot of Cherry flavoring. Sorry you missed out."

"Sure you are." I shoved out the door and marched down the sidewalk. With the size of my hips, I shouldn't be so upset over shattered cookies, but I loved anything with chunks of chocolate. Cherries mixed in were an added bonus.

Twenty minutes later, I headed back to the store, richer by two juicy cheeseburgers and the best fries this side of the Mississippi. I stopped in front of Gifts from Heaven to see Lindsey with her head resting on folded arms.

Couldn't I leave her alone for a second? I reached out to push the door open and noticed Stephanie headed my way. I smiled a welcome, wanting to know if she'd left the cookies so I could thank her.

Her eyes widened, and her face paled. She pasted on a smile, and ducked into the dry cleaners. I shrugged. Maybe she'd already heard about the destruction of her platter and was upset with me.

I shoved through the door. "Lindsey?"

She didn't move. Her eyes stared unblinkingly at me.

23

"Lindsey?" I shook her then waved my hand in front of her face. "Are you sick?" From the corner of my eye, I caught a glimpse of the cash register. The drawer had been left open a fraction of an inch but to my eye it glared as wide as the Grand Canyon. Still, it took a moment for the facts to sink in.

Had we been robbed again or did Lindsey leave it open after waiting on a customer? I glanced around the store. Nothing appeared out of place or missing. Something was rotten in River Valley, though. The hairs on my arms stood at attention. Think, Marsha! Lindsey's spaced-out look mirrored my own from a few days ago, too much to be coincidental.

Did someone waltz in while my daughter sat behind the counter with glassy eyes? Using my shirt tail, I opened the register and peeked inside. Empty. "Lindsey!" I shook her again. Her head lobbed on her neck as her eyes tried focusing on mine. My heart leaped into my throat.

With another glance at my daughter, I headed to the phone and dialed my mother. "Mom?"

"Yep."

"Could you come to the store now? Please?" I chewed on my ragged cuticles and wished for M&Ms. She'd be livid and would most likely burn me at the stake for letting this happen again. "It's very important. Something's wrong with Lindsey."

"Should you call nine-one-one?"

"I don't think so. I'm not sure."

She sighed. "Be there in ten minutes."

I hung up and called Bruce then settled back to wait. Lindsey lifted her head from the counter with a tad more alertness shining in her eyes. "Welcome back." I started to frown, then remembered my battle against wrinkles and fought to keep my face impassive.

"Huh?" She blinked her eyelashes like hummingbird wings.

"Here's lunch." I slid the bag in her direction. "Did we get any customers?"

She shook her head and unwrapped a burger. "Not a single one. It's been really slow."

"How do you feel?" I took a bite of my lunch and wiped the delightful flavored grease off my chin with a napkin. Why did everything that tasted good have to be bad for you?

"Fine, except for a headache. A little bit of an upset stomach. I kind of feel out of it, why?"

"Because while you were sleeping someone robbed us." I motioned my head toward the register. Just like the time when I'd been alone. "You aren't dizzy? Sick to your stomach?"

She shook her head as her hand paused half-way to her mouth. "I was here the whole time. Honest. I don't think I even left to go to the bathroom. How could someone come in and me not know about it?"

"I believe you, but I doubt Deputy Dog Bruce will." With all the other accusations against Lindsey, he'd probably want to drag her to the station. An odd sense of de ja vu came over me as I remembered my own feeling of disjointedness after our last robbery. There had to be a connection. I just needed to find it. Soon, before something more drastic than robbery and an accidental death happened.

My daughter tore into her lunch like as starving dog. I'd barely been able to hold my head up. What happened to her stomach? Could the difference in our ages have something to do with it? Despite the differences in our behavior after returning from La-La-Land, I was pretty sure we were being drugged somehow.

The bell over the door jangled, and Mom marched in with a scowl on her face and Bruce at her elbow. I took another bite and set my lunch aside. I might as well get the unpleasantness over with.

Bruce raised his eyebrows. "Robbed again?"

"Hello to you too, Bruce."

He frowned.

"What?" Mom whirled toward him then back to me. "You didn't say we'd been robbed."

I shrugged. "I didn't want you to get into an accident on your way over."

"So it was better to let me think something was wrong with my granddaughter?" She crossed her arms and scowled. Her face softened as she turned to Lindsey. "Are you all right?"

Lindsey nodded and tossed her burger wrapper in the garbage. "Better now that I ate."

Bruce whipped a notepad from his pocket and glared at me from lowered brows. "Start from the beginning."

"I left Lindsey alone while I went to get lunch. When I got back, she looked like she'd been sleeping, and the cash register was empty. That's it."

"Empty?" Mom dashed around the counter. "Last time they only took a couple hundred dollars. We had at least that amount in there today. Maybe more."

Bruce made a noise in his throat. "Mind if I check your daughter's backpack?"

My shoulders slumped. "She didn't leave the store, Bruce."

"Just procedure."

Lindsey dragged her pack from behind the counter and tossed it at him. "I've nothing to hide."

Bruce rummaged through it. "No cash."

My daughter rolled her eyes then tried to resume a straight face when Bruce stared at her. Her eyebrows rose, her lips pursed, and her eyes widened in an attempt to portray innocence. I choked back a giggle and pretended to cough.

"Lindsey didn't take the money." I rose and paced, walking a circle around the other three, forcing their heads to swivel in order to keep up with me. "It's the same as when the money disappeared the last time. I 'woke up' to discover the money gone. Except I didn't feel well. Lindsey was hungry. Minor difference in details. I'm still positive the two thefts are related." But how? There had to be a way to find out. A trap I could set.

"Okay, Sherlock." Bruce shook his head. "I can't keep up with all the things disappearing around here. And I don't need a clumsy amateur getting in my way, making it harder."

Of all the. . . I took a deep breath. "Any ideas at all who's behind it?"

"I'm thinking it's a gang. It's got to be more than one person. They're all over the place. In people's homes, their place of business. . .and they aren't taking just cash. We've got a stolen Prius, Kyle's sister, a litter of puppies. . ."

"A Prius?" If someone was targeting that particular brand of car, I'd have to be sure to get an alarm installed. I loved my new baby.

"Yeah, doesn't make sense, does it? They aren't usually the type of automobile people steal, but somebody seems willing to take anything that isn't nailed down or locked up. Oh, well. I'm keeping my eyes open. If y'all see anyone up to no good, call me. Y'all might as well go home. I'll be sending someone over to fingerprint and can't have you contaminating my crime scene." He gave a curt nod and scuttled out the door.

I couldn't help but glance at Lindsey, considering her words about what she'd been up to the night before. She'd have to tell me who she followed. If she thought, even for the slightest moment, that someone was doing something wrong, she needed to come clean. What if it had something to do with all the other things going on in Oak Dale?

Mom collapsed into one of the rockers we had for sale. She tapped her finger against her forehead. "There's something familiar about all this. Something I read in the paper a few years ago, but I can't get my mind to spit out the details." She slapped her thighs. "It'll come, sooner or later. Let's close up shop and head home. One of us should stay, though."

I really wanted to see Duane. Maybe he could make sense out of all this. I glanced at my watch. Weight training should be over by the time I drove to the high school. "I'm meeting up with Duane. Catch you two at home."

"Great." My mom muttered something about leaving her holding the door open for the investigators as I grabbed my purse and rushed outside.

The summer sunlight blinded me as I dug for my sunglasses. I spotted my cell phone at the bottom of my purse and grabbed it to call Duane. I punched in his speed dial number and listened while the lyrics to "I Love Rock and Roll" played. His voice came on the line asking me to leave a message. I didn't leave a voice mail and hopped in my car. I knew he was there and that he wouldn't mind a surprise visit from me. After all, we loved each other.

I grinned remembering the kiss he'd bestowed on me after I declared I'd always loved him. The feeling still flooded me with heat.

Lost in my daydreams, I arrived at the school with no recollection of having driven there. I laughed. My reason for drifting into space rested solely on the shoulders of a man with hazel eyes.

After shutting off my car's ignition, I slung the strap of my purse over my shoulder and headed to the gym. Silence greeted me through the door of the weight room. I knocked then pushed the door open when I didn't hear a response. I was pretty certain Duane had said his office was at the back. My gym shoes slapped against the tile floor, echoing with all the joy of a horror movie. Surrounding me were tall skeletons of iron monsters waiting to give me sore muscles. All I lacked was a knife wielding maniac in a mask.

Finally. A door ahead with a plaque that read 'Coach'.

A giggle stopped me, and I pressed my ear to the door. There it was again. High-pitched and nervous sounding. I pushed the door open. My world fell apart.

Duane leaned over the desk on which reclined a very pretty, tussled, red-faced, and giggling, Marilyn Olsen. Minus her dogs. I gasped and stumbled backward against the wall.

Duane glanced up. "Marsha?"

I shook my head and whirled to dodge behind the nearest door. A shriek burst forth as I shielded my face with my purse. Footballs players in every stage of undress gawked at me. Some shouted ribald comments. Others laughed. Why did boys have to be so crude?

I began to hyperventilate. My blood boiled like it could burn through my skin. *Be careful little eyes what you see!* I sprinted out the opposite door and down the hall, mumbling the childish Bible song.

Once I leaned against the door of my car, I labored for breath, choking against the sobs ravaging my breath. I fumbled inside my purse. I had no doubt Duane would follow me. And I'd be ready. Me and my Tazer.

24

Footsteps pounded behind me. I whirled and held out my weapon. Duane skidded to a halt. He blinked, smiled, and scratched the side of his mouth. "Do you plan to zap me?"

The laughter in his voice stiffened my spine. How dare he? One look at my face ought to tell him the situation wasn't humorous. I clamped my lips together in an attempt to keep my chin from quivering.

"Tazering is too good for the likes of you. I wouldn't want to waste the battery."

His face fell, and I hardened my heart against the sadness reflected there. "Marsha, I don't know what you think you saw, but--"

"I *saw* you bent over another woman and tenderly cupping her face." Saying the words out loud was like shoving a knife into my gut. The wound throbbed and bled. "I poured out my feelings to you, and this is how you repay me?" The tears escaped and ran down my cheeks.

Just like the summer we graduated. We profess our love, and Duane throws it back, shattering it like slivers of glass, cutting into me, and dousing me with saltwater. An overkill of emotion, maybe, but the most appropriate metaphor I could come up with.

He looked like he was going to laugh again. The corners of his mouth twitched. A person had to give him points for self-control. Either that or my expression warned him not to let the laughter escape. Duane held out his arms to me, drawing back when I jabbed the Tazer toward him. He crossed his arms and leaned against the hood of my car.

"Marilyn is a part-time janitor at the high school. She got something in her eye, and I was helping her get it out."

"Her face was red and she was giggling. Not exactly signs of a damsel in distress." My hand drooped, and I steadied it. He ought to be happy I didn't pack my gun.

"The football players made some off-color comments about me poking around in her eye. Obviously, she was still laughing when you barged into the room."

"Barged? I thought it would be a pleasant surprise for me to show up. I needed to see you and thought you would be glad to see me. My mistake." I opened the door to the Prius. "I need to get home. We were robbed today." Before words could escape his gaping mouth, I climbed in, tossed the Tazer on the passenger seat, slammed the door, then roared out of the parking lot.

Something in her eye my foot. Oldest ploy in the book. I glanced into my rearview mirror before switching lanes. Uh-oh. Duane followed in his truck, a grim look on his face. I pressed the accelerator. The Prius's whine increased faster than its speed.

I rocked back and forth, encouraging it to go faster. Duane pulled alongside me and pointed toward the road's shoulder. I shook my head and stared straight ahead. *Come on, car!*

My cell phone rang. I glanced at it then back to Duane. He held his to his ear. Was he kidding? No way could I dig in my purse for the phone and talk while driving seventy miles an hour on a curvy mountain road. Was he trying to kill me? Ha! That would solve all his problems. Then he'd be free for Marilyn the dog walker slash man stealer.

It was stupid of me to think I could have any future with Duane Steele, Captain of the football team and all around heart throb. Movie star good-looking with a sculpted body that should be illegal. He could give those young boys in the locker room a run for their money. Nothing had changed since we were teenagers. It was the cheerleader all over again. I sped forward.

Duane honked. I honked back. We repeated the silly process until I spotted a dirt road to my right. I whipped the wheel and shouted in triumph as Duane continued past. No way his beast could handle a turn that sharp. Thank goodness he hadn't chosen to ride his motorcycle. After a couple of minutes, I backed out and headed home. My heart sat like a lump in my chest. The weight of the world rested on my shoulders. The Tazer beckoned from the seat. I ought to follow Duane and put us both out of our misery. Zap him until he twitched like a dying fish.

Who was I kidding? Duane was Duane, and I was plain old Marsha Calloway. We both did what came natural. I repelled, he attracted. The thought did nothing to cheer me up.

After pulling into the driveway, I put the car in park and leaned my head back, choosing to think on the stolen money instead of my broken heart. What did money from our store, a vintage necklace, and puppies have in common? They all equaled roughly two hundred dollars a pop. Except for the stolen car. Or the money missing when Kyle Anderson's sister disappeared. How much exactly was he missing? I pounded the steering wheel. I was getting nowhere fast on solving this case. Somebody wanted money now and would take it however, and in any increments, they could get.

I marched in the house, called for Cleo, tossed my purse on the foyer table, then made my way to my soon-to-be new home. The boxes planned for Stephanie's yard sale still sat piled beside the door. Huh. Guess she wasn't in as big of a hurry as she said.

A bucket rested in a closet beside the kitchen. A mop nestled inside. Fresh tears sprang to my eyes. I should be cuddled up with Duane right now, gaining comfort from his strong arms after being robbed again. I kicked the bucket. The mop clattered to the floor. Fitting.

"Marsha."

I shrieked and whirl to face Duane. "What are you doing here? Where's your car?"

"I parked down the street. You wouldn't have stopped if you saw my truck." He leaned against the door jamb.

"Go away." I grabbed a broom and sent furious clouds of dust over his shiny cowboy boots. The delicious sense of pleasure I felt sent ripples down my spine as I swept dirt on his babies.

"Hey!" He jumped back. "Would you stop and listen to reason? You're jumping to conclusions, Marsha and —"

"I am not!" I hurled the broom like a spear. Duane leaped out of sight.

"Hello?"

Cleo growled. The hair on his neck bristled.

"Good protector." Duane poked his head through the window.

"She didn't protect me from you!" I hurled a scrub brush.

Stephanie Jackson stepped through my doorway. "You must be angry with that broom. Or Duane." She gave a shaky smile. "The door was open. I hope you don't mind. I'm here to get the yard sale items."

"They're in the boxes outside the door." I turned and picked up the cleaning supplies, more as a ploy to wipe my wet eyes on my shoulder than as a hint for her to leave.

"Okay, thanks. Are you fixing the place up to rent?"

"No, for me and Lindsey to live in. It's time to give my mother her privacy." I righted the mop and bucket.

"It'll be very quaint when you're finished. It's perfect place for a single woman like you." She smiled again and lifted the first box in her arms.

I glowered at her retreating back. Is that all I could hope to accomplish? Something quaint? A small, two-bedroom cottage that didn't have enough room for a man?

So be it. While Stephanie carted boxes, I attacked the dirt and cobwebs with a vengeance. Obviously Duane had left with his tail between his legs. Cleo sat out of harm's way and watched me with soulful eyes, occasionally glancing toward Stephanie. Her tail thumped erratically, stiffly, whenever the other woman came near, and a low growl rumbled deep in her chest.

When Stephanie opened the back to her Tahoe, Cleo bounded to her feet and dashed outside barking. Stephanie screamed and plastered herself to the truck. "Call off your dog, Marsha!"

"Cleo! Come."

Cleo leaned and put her front paws on the truck's bumper. Whines escaped her throat. I called again, and with a final whimper, she obeyed and trotted to my side. I grabbed her collar. "Sorry. She's okay now."

"You shouldn't have such a vicious animal." Sharon tossed the boxes in her automobile and slammed the hatch. "She's going to bite someone one of these days."

I pulled my new best friend into the house. "What was in there you wanted so bad, huh? Doggy treats? Did someone toss an old ball into the charity boxes?" I patted her head and went back to work.

By dusk, dirt covered my skin, cobwebs rested in my curls, my back ached, and I looked over a spotlessly clean new home. I'd sleep beneath its roof that night, satisfied with a job well done.

I flicked off the light, motioned for Cleo to follow me, took a step toward the door, and screamed. A man's silhouette blocked the way.

"Have you cooled off enough to listen to reason?" Duane's husky southern voice washed over me like a spring rain. For a moment, I forgot he'd ripped my heart out.

"Sic him, Cleo."

The stupid dog wagged her tail and padded over for a pat on the head. Some watch dog she turned out to be. If Duane had been a deranged killer, I'd be dead for all the warning she gave me.

"I'm not talking to you. Please move away from my house."

"You're living here now?" He flicked the light on. "Cozy. More privacy for make-out sessions."

He wished. I tried squeezing past, yelping when he grabbed me to his chest. "Help, Cleo. Attack." I aimed a kick at his shin, and missed when he side-stepped.

"The dog likes me." Duane dragged me to the sofa then yanked the sheet cover from it. "Almost as much as you do."

"Right." I plopped down and crossed my arms. "What do you want?"

He sat next to me, keeping his body turned to face me. "For you to listen." He tilted my chin. Eyes the color of a summer haze locked with mine. I was doomed. "Nothing is going on between me and Marilyn. It's just as I told you. She's mortified

that you saw us in a compromising position."
He chuckled. "Of course, the guys on the team
are cracking jokes about you seeing them in
their birthday suits."

Boys had no modesty. My face flamed.

"I love you, Mars Bar. Always have;
always will." His hand caressed my check
before plucking a dust bunny from my hair.
Against my weak will, he cradled my head
against his chest. I sighed and breathed in the
scent of him.

"Am I forgiven?"

"Only if I get to Tazer you. I've always
wanted to see what it would do to someone.
Other than myself, that is." I lifted my face for
his kiss.

25

I wrapped my hands around a mug of coffee and stared out the window at my cottage. Duane had stayed too late last night for me to move over my clothes or bedding. Instead, we'd snuggled, kissed, and watched an old black and white romance on the ancient television. The perfect evening. One more night beneath my mom's roof hadn't hurt me. It wasn't until Mom ran Duane off around eleven o'clock that he reluctantly left.

Sighing, I blew into my drink. Ripples spread, reminding me of the scattered clues in this disjointed case I felt determined to solve. Why, I didn't know anymore. They hadn't accused Lindsey of anything new.

Beside me sat a notebook ready for notes. All I had so far was a list of suspects. The motive for everyone was the same; money.

"Earth to Mom." Lindsey grabbed a granola bar and flopped into the chair next to me. "What 'cha doing?"

"Nothing." Obviously.

"What's with the names?"

"I'm trying to make sense of all the things that have been happening around here." I tapped the pencil against the pad.

"Maybe I can help. Sometimes all a person needs is a fresh perspective."

I jerked. Hot coffee sloshed over the rim of my mug and onto my hand. Hissing against the sting, I grabbed a nearby napkin and cleaned the spill. Sometimes Lindsey sounded so grown up it frightened me. "What have you been reading?"

She grinned. "It's something I heard."

It couldn't hurt. My daughter might be right. "Here, you jot, while I ramble."

"Okay." Lindsey tore out the old sheet, wadded it into a ball, then sent it across the room and into the trashcan. "Score! Okay, shoot. This might be fun."

"Sharon Weiss has her necklace stolen, then she dies. I'm not sure her death is related; could be an accident, but write it down." I rose and began to pace. "Harvey Miller's wallet goes missing the same day. They're also neighbors. You're accused of both these thefts. Gloria Simpson's puppies are taken right from underneath her nose. Kyle Anderson's sister is gone and so is who knows how much money. Plus, our store was robbed twice."

"Both times while we were sleeping." Lindsey's pencil scratched across the paper. "In broad daylight. It's not like you or I take naps."

"What?" I stopped and stared at her.

"Neither one of us remembers what happened. Plus, Mrs. Weiss only thinks I went into her house because I was the last person she saw, or *remembers* seeing. Mrs. Simpson was home when her puppies were taken. Both of these people have a time lapse they aren't aware of." Lindsey wielded the pencil like a sword. "And don't forget about the president impersonator running me and Billy off the road and coming to your room."

"Who is it you suspect is doing something wrong?" Bam. Right from the barrel. Hopefully my ploy works and I've caught Lindsey off guard. "You said you were following someone."

She froze. "I was mistaken."

"Who, Lindsey?" I gave her 'the mom look'.

"Billy."

Didn't I ask her if it was him before? She'd told me no and gushed about how wonderful he was. I crossed my arms. "Why would you suspect him?"

She shrugged and lowered her head. "Because he wanders around, alone, at night and wants money really bad so he can go to football camp." She took a deep breath and met my gaze. "But I asked him, and he said he wasn't the thief. He walks around to think about the songs he likes to write. I believe him."

Love could be blind. No one knew that better than me. "Okay. Put him at the top of our list of suspects."

"Mom!"

"Just do it." I reached for my M&Ms and popped a few in my mouth. "Melvin Brown, Kyle Anderson, and his missing sister, Marilyn Olsen, and Stephanie Jackson, are all vocal about their need for money." Marilyn's name under Suspects gave me a thrill of pleasure.

I'd like nothing better than to pin the whole rap on her platinum blond head.

"I want money. Should you write me down too?" Lindsey sneered.

"Don't be ridiculous. I'm doing this to clear your name." I resumed my seat at the table. "The fact the robberies occur during the day, and with no one remembering anything, really has me baffled."

"See, that leaves Billy out." Lindsey tossed the pencil on the table. "He only wanders at night. I bet if you figure out who the president is, you'll have the guilty person."

"They wore a mask."

"Throw a masquerade party. If someone shows up as President Clinton, voila, the culprit."

Could it really be that easy? Today was Thursday. Saturday night, after Stephanie's yard sale, would be a good time for a party. "Make some fliers and distribute them around town today. Masquerade party, Saturday night, seven p.m, Calloway place."

"What's the occasion?"

"Huh?"

"People don't just throw parties for no reason. Not in this town." Lindsey looked at me as if she were the parent and I were the child.

Mom waltzed into the room with a grin to rival any beauty queen's. Plus, her hair was already styled, and she wore makeup. When she moved her hand to grab a cup of coffee, I spotted the ring.

"Yes! Masquerade party on Saturday to celebrate . . . are you engaged?" Her and Leroy dated for what, a week? My world was spinning off its axles, and I barely held on with both hands.

She dangled her finger in front of my face. A gold band with a solitaire diamond adorned her ring finger. "Isn't it beautiful?"

"You just met him."

"Don't be silly. At my age, you take things as they come. Who knows how many more years I'll have."

"You're fifty-two. Hardly ancient." I fell back into my chair. At least now we had a reason to throw a party. "Wonderful. We're having a party on Saturday. Find a costume."

She giggled. "I'll come as a blushing bride."

"Don't you dare." My mother—engaged. My mind could hardly wrap around the news. Ridiculous. She acted like a love-struck teenager.

Lindsey's face paled, and her eyes widened. "You're getting married? That's gross."

"Why, because of my age?" Mom stopped dancing.

"Well, yeah."

Mom planted a kiss on Lindsey's head. "You are the best. But don't worry about me. You're never too old for love and there's no age limit on marriage. You'll see when you get older." She straightened and speared me with a glance. "So, why are we *really* throwing a party?"

"To see if anyone shows up in a Clinton mask." Lindsey unwrapped her granola bar. "I guess it's a good thing we're moving into the guest house. You'll want your privacy. Doing … you know … gross things."

Mom laughed. "You're a hoot. I'm looking forward to those *gross* things, you're talking about. But, I don't think anyone is going to show up looking like the ex-president. Especially, if they're guilty of our recent crime spree. Thank the Lord we don't have a murderer running loose. The party ought to be fun. I'll get started on a menu right away. I wish there was time to have it catered. I'll be cooking all day Saturday."

"Go to the warehouse store. Cold cuts will do fine." I gulped the last of my coffee. "I'm going to work. Lindsey?"

"I'm going to help Grandma. I might as well spend time with her before Leroy steals her away."

My daughter the drama queen. Of course my heart drooped a bit, too. It'd been the three Calloway women for the last five years. Although I didn't begrudge my mother her second chance at love and happiness, I would miss not having to share her. Widowed for ten years, I'd gotten use to not having my own man around. After all, my father had been alive for ten of those years. Anything I needed, he took care of. Now, seeing my mother's happiness, I wanted some for myself.

Duane's face loomed in my mind. Could he be my second chance?

I grabbed my purse and headed outside to my car. Bruce's squad car streaked by, sirens wailing. That didn't happen often in River Valley. I tossed my purse through my open window, yanked the door open, then slid inside as fast as possible. This might be something I didn't want to miss. When the ambulance roared by, I was certain.

Within seconds, I sped down the road after the whirling red lights. Tires squealed as we careened around corners, and I gripped the steering wheel tight enough to whiten my knuckles. My cell phone rang. Who'd be calling me at a time like this? I frowned and ignored it.

Our little convoy whipped through town and toward the outskirts. Fortunately, there was very little traffic at 7:30 in the morning so less chance of me crashing into something. A NASCAR driver I wasn't. By the time we pulled up in front of Kyle Anderson's house, sweat poured down my face, and my hands were frozen in position around the steering wheel.

I groaned and peeled my fingers free, then shut off the ignition. Bruce and another policeman, hands on the butt of their weapons, approached the house at a snail's pace. The medics waited outside their vehicle.

Within seconds of entering Kyle's house, Bruce led a handcuffed woman outside and escorted her to his squad car. I chewed the inside of my cheek. How could I find out what was going on here? I slid from my car and approached one of the medics.

"Who is that?"

The man shrugged without looking at me. "Karen Anderson. Kyle's sister."

I glanced toward the dark-haired woman. So, she wasn't dead. Even through the tinted glass of Bruce's car I could tell her shoulders shook with sobs. "Why did they handcuff her?"

"We got a call fifteen minutes ago that said Kyle Anderson was dead. I'm assuming Bruce thinks she's the murderer."

26

Kyle's sister was back in town? How could I find out where she'd been? Her tear-streaked face beckoned me from the backseat of the squad car. She might be the first viable clue in this whole case. "Was she the one who called the police?"

The medic shrugged and moved toward the house. "Maybe you should speak with Bruce. I've already said more than I should have."

Bruce marched to another officer, leaving Karen Anderson alone. The door to the squad car remained open as a special invitation. Before I had time to think of the ramifications if I were caught, I headed her way.

"No comment." She lifted her head long enough to glare at me. Dark circles ringed eyes the color of dark mud. A pasty complexion, covered with an oily sheen, gave me the impression the woman indulged in activities not recommended by health officials. I felt greasy just standing next to her.

"I'm not with the press." I squatted and hoped it would make me harder to see. The last thing I wanted was for Bruce to haul me away before I had the opportunity to ask questions.

"My name is Marsha Steele. I'm co-owner of Gifts from Country Heaven." If the uncomprehending look on Karen's face was any indication, I was going about this wrong. I took a deep breath and decided to dive in with both feet. "A lot of things have been happening in this town. Things missing. Accidents. My daughter has been blamed for a couple of them. Kyle told anyone who'd listen. . ." I peeked over the door frame. Bruce glanced my way. Better hurry. "That he was missing a chunk of money, and you took it."

"I did take it. But only to help get me back on my feet." Karen sagged against the back of the seat. "I didn't kill my brother. Believe it or not, I came back to repay some of what I'd taken. He's lying in his kitchen with a hammer in the back of his head. Next to him is a peanut butter and jelly sandwich. Who would do something like that?"

Who indeed? "I'm going to try and find something out. Do you mind if I visit you in jail?"

Karen shrugged. "Sure. No one else will."

I dashed back to my car before Bruce started yelling. He might be on the scrawny side, but there wasn't anything wrong with his volume, and I didn't need the whole town knowing I was digging into the mystery. Behind the steering wheel, I watched as they wheeled Kyle's body out of the house. What was happening in this town? *Lord, I'm a little frightened, I've got to be honest.* Sharon's death appeared to be an accident, but what if it wasn't? What if the thief had progressed to out-and-out murder? I shivered and turned the key in the ignition.

Maybe a gun, a Tazer, and a big dog wouldn't be enough protection. This "criminal" seemed to float in and out of homes and businesses leaving no trace.

My mind flitted toward thoughts of God, then skittered away. I knew I needed to be more regular in attending church and stop letting myself get roped into any job that kept me out of the sanctuary, but sometimes the sermons made me uncomfortable. And I was totally into comfort. Could I ask for His protection even if I didn't step foot into His house regularly?

My cell phone rang. I jumped and reached for it.

"Marsha." Duane said my name with his husky drawl, and I almost forgot what I'd been thinking about. "Where are you?"

"Actually, I'm sitting outside Kyle Anderson's house watching the paramedics wheel his dead body away."

"Excuse me?"

"Kyle is dead. I was wondering whether the weapons I bought are going to be enough against the murderer. Maybe I should've bought a bigger gun."

"How do you know Kyle was murdered?"

"Because his sister, she found the body and Bruce arrested her, said Kyle had a hammer sticking out of his head. Clearly someone hit him with it, Duane. It's not an accident that frequently happens to people: hitting themselves in the back of the head with a tool."

"And you just happened to be at Kyle's house as all of this went down?" I could almost hear him shaking his head. "Meet me at the gift shop in ten minutes." Click.

I backed the car out of Kyle's yard and headed to work. Duane waited outside the door, arms crossed, and a scowl on his handsome face. With his jeans, cowboy boots, and tee shirt, he ought to grace the cover of Manly Magazine. Providing he wore a smile of course. What did I do now?

Shutting off the engine, I smiled at Duane through the window using all the feminine wiles I wished I had better control over, but didn't. A certain pout on my lips that Marilyn had. Or a sexy swing to my hips. Instead, I possessed a crooked smile and all the grace of a drunken elephant. Duane crooked an eyebrow and motioned his head toward the door. Fine, be all serious.

I grabbed my purse and slid from the Prius. "What's up?"

"Wait until we get inside, please. No need to alert the town to what Marsha Calloway Steele is up to now." Duane pushed the door open after I unlocked it and let me enter first. "I don't want you getting involved, Marsha."

"I'm already involved, remember?" I stashed my purse behind the counter and chose not to act like I didn't know what he talked about. Pretending would only prolong the inevitable. "When they accused Lindsey of stealing, they practically shouted for me to get involved."

"We're talking about something a lot more serious now." Duane's brow furrowed. "I doubt they will accuse Lindsey of murdering Kyle. Hopefully, his death will clear her of the theft charges. I want you to butt out. This is too big for you."

"But I'm not *doing* anything."

"Following a police car to a crime scene *is* doing something."

Good grief. How did he find out about me doing that? I plopped in a chair. Bruce must have called Duane. Big tattle-tale. "I'm trying to clear Lindsey's name. I agree today probably took care of that. But what if the events aren't related? My gut tells me they are, though." I smiled up at him. "Are we having a fight? Because, this would be our second since we got back together."

"Not yet. But if you continue, we might."

"Are you coming over tonight?"

"Changing the subject?" The corner of his mouth twitched.

"Is it working?" I hoped his smile warmed my inside for the rest of my life.

He nodded. "We'll talk later. I'll bring pizza for dinner and an action flick this time. You owe me after that sappy chick flick the other night." Duane leaned and kissed my forehead then patted my curls. "I like your head and don't want to see any foreign objects hanging from your skull."

Him and me both. "I'll see you later."

Once the door closed behind him, I rummaged in my purse for the list of suspects. I now had a name for Kyle's sister, but seriously doubted she was behind the crimes.

Sharon Weiss fell and hit her head while clearly waiting for someone. My cheeks warmed as I remembered the lingerie she'd been wearing. Kyle Anderson. . .well, I needed to get inside his house. Sure, he most likely didn't hit himself in the head, but maybe I'd notice a clue the police missed. How much trouble could I get in if I went back after dark? A lot. I sighed. This was impossible. Duane would never agree to my crazy scheme.

I shoved the notebook back in my purse then situated myself behind the sewing machine and angled to get a clear view out the store window. In a true snooping fashion, I planned on making notes of everyone I saw today and the times they appeared. Just in case something happened. With Kyle's murder, there was sure to be an uproar of excitement in town, guaranteeing a flurry of activity on our one major street. If I got really lucky, people would waltz in to chat.

Within the hour, Lynn sauntered into the store with a plate of cookies. She wasn't someone I expected to see in the middle of the day. When school wasn't in session, she stayed busy tutoring students in preparation for the new academic year.

"Gifts from a friend." She set them on the counter.

I eyed them suspiciously. "Seems like every time I eat a cookie, I fall asleep with my eye open." What was with the people of this town always bringing food when they visited? No wonder I needed to lose weight.

"Maybe you have a sugar problem." Lynn bit into one then brushed crumbs from her lap. "A little birdie told me you're trying to solve the case of River Valley's missing items."

"Duane's a stool pigeon."

Lynn laughed. "He wants me to talk some sense into you. I told him it was a wasted effort. Any sense you might have had at one time has been all used up."

"Ha ha." I tied off the thread on the doll pattern I finished. "I'm missing something, Lynn. Something obvious. Something right in front of my face. Have you noticed how off the wall some of these robberies have been? Like the Chihuahuas, for example. Or Harvey's wallet. Not a lot of money at a time. What does that tell you?"

"That someone wants money, and they don't care about the amount. It all adds up in the end." She helped herself to another of the cookies she'd brought.

I tossed the empty doll body on to the counter and reached for the last one. Marilyn, boyfriend stealer slash dog walker pranced by the window. A bag hung low over her shoulder. Sticking out of it was the miniscule head of a Chihuahua puppy. I jumped out of my chair fast enough to send it careening into the wall behind me. Lynn stared open mouthed as I dashed out the door.

"Marilyn!"

"Hi, Marsha." Red lips parted over startling white teeth.

"New puppy?"

"It's not mine. I'm taking it for a walk, but the poor thing's barely old enough to walk more than a few feet without getting tired. So, I guess that makes me more of a puppy sitter." She swung the bag around and opened it wider. "Want to see him? He's adorable."

"Who does he belong to?" I peeked at the tiny rat of a dog.

"He's Melvin's. The silly man said he wanted a dog that could ride on his lawnmower. It'll be a pity when he runs over the tiny thing."

That didn't make a pretty picture. I chewed my inner cheek. "Are there any more in the litter?"

Marilyn shook her head. "Melvin said he got the last one. At a discount too. There were four in the litter to start with."

Not an uncommon litter amount for a small breed. "Oh, well. I doubt Cleo would take to another dog anyway. Thanks."

She pushed the puppy back into place and sashayed on her way. What were the odds the tiny mutt once belonged to Gloria? The woman couldn't be the only breeder in the near vicinity, could she? I made a mental note to check with Melvin on where he'd gotten his dog. Maybe I could hire him to mow the yard. That'd make him happy enough to talk.

I went back inside. Lynn rocked back and forth in one of the rockers. I'd actually expected her to be sleeping with her eyes open. Everyone else seemed to after eating cookies. "Hope you're free Saturday night. Lindsey and I are throwing Mom and her fiancé a masquerade engagement party."

"That's great! I hoped your mom would find someone else to love."

"Leroy's a great guy."

"That's unusual, though." She stopped rocking.

"What? The engagement or the party?"

"The theme of the party. Usually engagement parties are more upscale than a masquerade, but then we are talking about you, aren't we?" Lynn rose. "I'll be there. Enjoy the cookies. I made them myself. They're your favorite. Cherry chocolate chunk." She grinned and stepped into the summer sunshine.

My friend was evil personified. I reached for the plate.

27

Saturday morning dawned bright and muggy. The ceiling fan in my new cottage bedroom barely stirred the breeze, and I lay in a sodden tangle of blankets. I tossed the sheet off my body and made a mental note to have the air conditioner serviced.

A hot drink did not sound appealing on this sweltering day. Instead of my usual coffee, I reached for a diet cola from the refrigerator and toasted a couple slices of bread into the toaster. The clock on the wall read six a.m. Why did yard sales start at such an ungodly hour?

Mom honked outside. I grabbed my purse, meager breakfast, and sprinted to her boat of a car.

"If we don't hurry, we'll miss all the good stuff." She glared. Apparently the engagement bloom didn't apply to mornings, or maybe just not me.

"What could you possibly need?" I clicked the seatbelt across my lap. "Why buy someone else's junk? I got rid of boxes of stuff you never used anymore. You'd better not buy back our own discards."

"It's for a good cause." She stepped on the gas. The car roared from the driveway and growled down Mountain View Street, daring any other vehicle to get in its way. If the army drove tanks designed like my mom's Cadillac, they wouldn't have to be afraid of land mines or air missiles. Traveling dignitaries could barrel their way through enemy lines.

I laid my head against the seat and wished for my pillow top mattress. Exhaustion hovered, and I yawned wide enough to pop my jaw.

Yesterday had been spent finishing up orders at work, sending Lindsey to post fliers advertising the party, and getting nowhere on solving the crimes. Not a single person, other than Lynn, had strolled through the store's doors. Obviously they were saving their cash for the yard sale.

While a pleasant diversion from my mundane life, I wasn't cut out to be a detective. Procrastination became my greatest enemy. I still hadn't visited the jail or hired Melvin to cut the grass. Plus, I had a strong suspicion Lindsey snuck out again last night. If I could get out of bed and follow her, I might gather a clue. At least to what she was up to.

Mom perked up at the sight of our destination. Stephanie's yard swarmed with eager bargain seekers. She stood behind a folding table with a metal cash box in front of her and dollar signs in her eyes. I sighed and followed Mom from the car. Mom scurried forward and joined a group of women surrounding a table full of cookbooks and knick knacks. I rolled my eyes. Mom already had more dust catchers than ten people needed.

It looked like the entire town came out to support Stephanie in her quest to adopt a child from south of the border. Melvin searched greasy engine parts, Marilyn browsed a rack of evening gowns, Billy dug through a box of odds and ends, Mom moved on to dishes, and I stood staring at the minimum of twenty others caught up in the thrill of discovering a "Good Deal". With such excitement in the air, I should at least make a pretense of looking interested. Maybe by keeping my ears peeled, I'd learn something, or find a deal I couldn't live without.

Someone grabbed me from behind. I whirled and shrieked, fist raised for attack. Duane laughed down at me. I punched him in the arm. "You scared me."

"Couldn't resist. Why are you standing on the outskirts of this craziness?" He grabbed my hand and dragged me behind him. "Let's join the frenzy. I want to look at the tools."

With all the work still waiting on me to prepare for the evening's party, I had a hard time concentrating, even when Duane exclaimed with delight at some blackened, oily, piece of metal. I meandered away. Maybe I'd find something suitable for my new home.

Melvin lifted a hammer from a battered cardboard box and turned the object in his hands. "I can't believe Kyle is dead. It's even harder to imagine a sweet girl like Karen bashing him in the head."

Who told Melvin that Kyle had been killed with a hammer? It hadn't been in the morning's paper. They'd only mentioned blunt force trauma to the head. I'd have to write this piece of news in my notebook. Was Bruce aware of it? "I'm sorry for your loss, Melvin. I know you and Kyle were close."

"Off and on. We were either best friends, or at each other's throats." Melvin cleared his throat. "We'd argued earlier that morning about Grandma's gift. Again. He said a brooch and scarf wasn't enough for someone who'd lived as long as she had. I said it was the thought that counted, and I was trying to save money. I wonder where he put her gift." He dropped the tool back in the box and shuffled further down the line of tables.

Had they fought enough for Melvin to kill Kyle? I shook my head. *Grasping at straws, Marsha. You're good at that.* People didn't kill over someone else's present, did they?

Mom chattered nearby, showing her ring finger to anyone who'd stop and listen. Piled at her elbow was a basket full of assorted colors of yarn and bolts of fabric. She'd scored a boatload for the store, it seemed. Duane leaned against a table talking sports with a man whose name I didn't know. Lindsey finally showed up and followed Billy around like a puppy. Good. Anyone who could've advised me not to interrogate suspects was occupied. I moved to the rack of clothes where Marilyn held a sequined gown up to her.

"Look at this, Marsha." Marilyn twirled, the gown's fuchsia sparkles catching the sunlight. "Only ten dollars! I could use something like this in Hollywood. No one needs to know where it came from. Where do you think Stephanie came up with all these gowns?"

"No idea." I idly fingered a white dress on a hanger. She'd most likely gotten them for company Christmas parties from years gone by. Maybe I could go to the masquerade party as Marilyn Monroe in the Seven Year Itch. I grabbed the gown and tossed it over my shoulder. Sure enough, a blond wig lay in a basket at my feet. I reached for it the same time as Marilyn.

"Oh, no you don't." Her normally pretty face twisted. "I'm going to your party as Marilyn. I share the name and have the body for it." She raked her gaze from my flip-flop clad feet, up my overall shorts and up to the hair tied back in a ponytail.

That did it. No one insulted my curves but me. I shoved the wig under my shirt. "I got it first, and I'll make a perfectly fine Marilyn Monroe." At least I was pretty sure Duane would think so. "You're hair is already the same color. You don't need the wig." And if she didn't stop being mean I'd rescind her invitation!

Marilyn took a deep breath, then forced a smile to her lips. "Fine. I'll go as a different Hollywood starlet. Maybe Jane Mansfield. It makes no difference to me."

"Obviously it does. You were willing to fight me over it."

She stuck her nose in the air. "You've been mean to me ever since you met me."

"I have not." What was she talking about?

"I hear things, Marsha. I have eyes in my head, and if you knew what was good for you, you'd be a bit more careful about how you treat people. It always comes back to get you in the end." She spun and stomped away.

Talk about coming out of left field. I treated everyone like the Golden Rule. Kind of. Had she threatened me or only been mad because I got the wig? I should've asked more questions. Maybe having the party as open invitation wasn't a good idea. Someone could kill me while pretending to be someone else. I shook off the gruesome thought and moved to the next table.

"Hey." Duane picked me up and swung me around. "I thought I was going to have to break up a cat fight. What was that all about?"

I kissed him. "Silly, really. All over a blond wig we both wanted for the party tonight. Did you find anything?"

"Some great tools and old issues of Sports Illustrated." He shook his head. "People get rid of the best stuff."

"Imagine that." I tapped his shoulder. "Put me down before you break your back."

"I volunteered to help Leroy set up for the party. What time do you want me over?" His arm fell around my waist, and we strolled among the tables.

"Noon or one at the earliest? It doesn't start until seven." And I'd done nothing to prepare. No twinkling lights strung, the lawn still needed mowed, and. . . "I'll catch up with you later, Duane. I need to talk to Melvin." I dashed off.

I caught up with him as he climbed into his truck. "Hey. Could you come over and mow before the party tonight? I'll pay you thirty dollars."

"Sure. I'll be over in half-an-hour. Can't afford to turn down money, no matter how cheap." He slammed his door. "See you later."

Asking Melvin about the puppy would have to wait until later. Also, if he was so hard up for cash, why pay Marilyn to watch a puppy that could stay in a crate while Melvin worked?

A glance at my watch sent me rushing toward my mother. We'd been digging through junk for an hour. A stack of books caught my eye, and I skidded to a halt. How had Stephanie gotten a hold of my father's medical journals? I gathered them into my arms and marched toward the buying table.

"Wow, you've found quite a few things." She grinned and opened her box.

"These. Are. Mine." I fought not to clinch my teeth.

"But you gave them to me to sell." Her smile faded.

I shook my head. "These were not included. How did you get them?" I glared. "I made it perfectly clear which boxes were for you. What else did you take?"

Her eyes widened. "Go ahead and take them, Marsha. I can see it was a mistake, but you owe me for the dress and wig."

I clamped my lips together, forked over the astronomical amount of ten dollars and stormed to Mom's car. These books hadn't been anywhere near the yard sale donations. I was positive they'd been sitting *inside* the cottage, ready for a place of prominence on my soon-to-be-put-together bookshelves.

Someone had been in my house. Why?

28

I twirled in front of my full-length mirror. A mighty fine version of Marilyn Monroe reflected back. All I needed was the air vent beneath me. I pretended to hold down the skirt, and giggled.

"Who are you supposed to be?" Dressed as a boy, Lindsey leaned against the door jamb. "And why are you primping like that?"

My bubble burst. Of course, Lindsey wouldn't recognize the famous star. My face heated, and I straightened. Thankfully, most of the party guests were adults. "Never mind."

"Oh, now I recognize her. She's the girlfriend of President Kennedy."

Good grief. What were they teaching her in school? I shoved past my daughter and sauntered outside. The yard looked wonderful. Once the sun set, the lights wrapped around every tree trunk would lend a festive air. I placed ribbons and lace on my mom's and Leroy's table. Candles flickered from borrowed tables of every size and shape. I grinned. Pretty good for a hillbilly festivity thrown together in two days. Leroy had even sprung for a country and western band.

I paused on the back step and searched the crowd for Duane. He wanted his costume to be a secret. A horn blasted in the front of the house. Holding my skirt in place, I rushed around the corner. Laughter burst from me with all the force of a summer storm. Sitting behind the wheel of a vintage convertible was Duane's imitation of a playboy. Slicked back hair, leisure suit, and a breeze carrying a whiff of delicious cologne. I should've guessed he'd figure out my costume. The wig and dress slung over my shoulder must have given me away.

He bounded over the side of the car without opening the door and sprinted to my side to swing me up in his arms. "Before the night is over, I expect you to sing me 'Happy Birthday, Mr. President'." He nuzzled my ear. "You look hot."

"Dream on, big guy. Besides, you don't look anything like a President." Dangerous would be a more apt description. "Even compliments won't get me to sing for you."

"Too bad." Duane put me back on my feet and escorted me to the party.

The band started a rousing two-step, Lindsey and Billy splashed each other with water bottles, and Mom linked arms with Leroy as they walked to the area set aside for dancing. In the shadows, fireflies added their merriment. Not one person wore a President Clinton mask. So much for that aspect of sleuthing. Oh, well. A night of fun and celebration beckoned. Plus, I hung on the arm of the handsomest man in the entire state of Arkansas.

Stephanie, dressed in a trench coat and hat with lips painted redder than mine sat at a table with her husband, Mark. He wore his pharmacist coat. The man obviously had no imagination since he worked as a pharmacist. Marilyn wore the sequined dress and a black wig with tresses hanging half-way down her back. She flirted with a young man I didn't know. Only one of my suspects was unaccounted for. Melvin hadn't returned after doing his job earlier in the day. Bruce stood near the buffet table, getting an early start on loading his plate.

"Stop sleuthing for one minute and dance with me." Duane swung me into a two-step.

"Who said I was sleuthing?"

"It's obvious." His breath tickled my neck. "Now, suppose you tell me why you set up this little shindig?"

"My mother's engagement." I found it difficult to talk and concentrate on my steps at the same time. Luckily, Duane was lighter on his feet then me and kept his toes away from harm's reach.

"Uh-huh."

"Okay. Lindsey and I thought someone might show up in a Clinton mask. A long shot, I know, but I'm ready to try anything."

"Why?"

I stopped and turned to face him, knowing exactly what his one-word question meant. "I don't know, really. It started as a way of clearing Lindsey's name. Now, I just want to know what the connection is. I'm certain there is one and it's driving me crazy."

He led me back into the dance steps. "You've always been impetuous, but this could be dangerous. You need to think everything through carefully."

"Excuse me?" I yanked free of his grasp. "I'm not stupid."

"I never said you were." Hurt feelings radiated across his face.

"You insinuated." I planted fists on my hips.

His brows drew together. "No, I didn't. I'm just giving you a word of caution because I love you."

"Humph." I whirled and stalked to the buffet table then grabbed a glass of pink lemonade. Duane stood where I left him, his jaw set, and a stormy look on his face. What was I thinking? Two hot heads in a relationship? We were doomed to failure before we get started.

"Mom." Lindsey approached with Billy in tow. "This is Billy Butler." My daughter lifted her chin. "I thought it was time for y'all to formally meet."

The young man in front of me shifted from foot to foot, but held my gaze. Long dark hair fell forward over one eye. His strong chin sported a cleft. It wasn't hard to see why he'd caught Lindsey's eye. I stuck out my hand. "Nice to meet you, Billy."

"Ma'am." He nodded. "Lindsey said you suspected me in the thefts. I'm here to clear your mind of that idea."

I opened my mouth then shut it. Lindsey had accused him more than me. What did my daughter have up her sleeve? "I have several people on my list."

"It's true that I need money for camp, but I'm working, doing odd jobs here and there. I'd never steal." He squared his shoulders. "My mother taught me better than that."

"I can see that." And I could. A light shined from Billy I wished I saw in myself when I looked in the mirror. But I couldn't help reminding myself history showed many good men were brought down by the greed of money.

He grinned and grabbed Lindsey's hand. They strolled away, leaning into each other, leaving me alone with Duane across the yard. His face softened and he hurried to my side. "Still mad?"

"No. I wasn't really. Just frustrated, I think." I melted into his arms. "I'm missing something obvious."

"What can I do to help?"

I leaned back and gazed into his face. "You'd help?"

"If it will keep you out of trouble."

"I can't guarantee that." His arms wrapped around me provided my own slice of heaven. "Duane."

"Hmmm?" We swayed in time with the slow song the band played.

I closed my eyes. "I just can't figure out why people aren't remembering what happened when they were robbed. It's like they black out. I know I did. And now, two people are dead."

"I don't know, sweetheart. But I still wish you'd leave things to Bruce."

"You promised to help." And Bruce's ego-swaggering, little-man syndrome, didn't instill a lot of confidence in me.

"And I will." His chin rested on my head.

A shriek of metal against metal rang from the driveway. Duane grabbed my hand and dragged me with him. I fought with my billowing dress, trying, without success, not to flash my assets. Someone gave a wolf whistle and my face could've set the barbecue on fire. I felt a definite summer breeze in places meant to be covered.

Duane stopped at the edge of the yard sudden enough I rammed into him from the back. I lifted a hand to my throbbing nose.

"Uh-oh."

I glanced at Duane. "Uh-oh, what?" Stepping around him, I cringed. Melvin sat on top of his lawnmower which sat flush against my Prius. What had he done? I dashed across the gravel driveway, trying not to fall on ankles that wobbled in high heels. "Melvin Brown. Look what you've done!"

The odor of liquor slapped me in the face, and I staggered back. "You've been drinking."

He shook his head. "Only a drop." His chin fell forward and sobs wracked his body.

Uh. I glanced to Duane for help. He nodded and moved forward.

By this time, most of the guests gathered around us, lemonade or soda in one hand, plates piled with food in the other. Our town sure could draw a crowd anytime there was food, music, or disaster. If a person could sell tickets, they would make a fortune.

Duane clapped a hand on Melvin's shoulder. "What's wrong, buddy?"

Melvin shook his head, still unable to speak. I'd never seen the man so distraught. Disgruntled, yes. Grouchy, definitely. But like his world had ended? Never.

"Can we call someone for you?" Duane peered into the man's red face.

"I need to speak with Bruce. Someone said he was here."

"Are you hurt?"

Melvin wiped his eyes on the sleeve of his stained tee shirt. "When I was over here mowing, someone broke into my house and took all the money I've been saving to start my own business."

29

Melvin had been mowing at my house when he was robbed, which meant he'd been awake, figuratively speaking. That seemed to throw my theory of the thief drugging people out the window. If I *had* a clear theory, that is. This case was murkier than a stirred up river bottom.

"Break it up." Bruce strolled up, his chest puffed out like a rooster. "Let the police do their job. I'll handle this." He whipped out a notepad and pencil from his pocket. "Start from the beginning and tell me what happened."

Melvin sniffled.

"After you stop crying." Bruce rolled his eyes and shook his head. Obviously the little monkey thought it unmanly for Melvin to shed tears over the theft of months of hard work.

Repentance shot through me. Mom would be scandalized to know I harbored uncharitable thoughts about someone. But Bruce could be a regular thorn in someone's side. "Be nice." I scowled. "He's lost his life savings."

"So he says. That's what I'm here to find out." Bruce's look clearly told me to stay out of it; which made me more determined to stick around.

Duane put an arm around my shoulder and pulled me close. Most likely to hold me in check, rather than a sign of affection.

Melvin took a deep shuddering breath. "Like. . .I said. I. . .mowed the Calloway's yard. The grass was real long so it took about an hour."

Mom gave me a look. Mowing was usually my job, but between work and clearing Lindsey's name, I hadn't found the time.

"When I got home, I noticed my back door was open. You got to yank on it to get it to latch, and I'm real careful about locking up when I leave. So, I pushed it open real slow like." He speared Bruce with a glance. "Could've been killed on my doorstep by a deranged murderer for all the protection we get in this town. Anyway, I didn't see anything out of the ordinary ... at first."

Melvin wiped his eye with the back of his hand. "But when I went to hang up my coat, I saw the shoe box I'd been keeping my money in was moved about an inch. I opened it and. . .it was empty." Sobs retook control of his body. "Gone. All of it. I had close to a thousand dollars."

How did someone know where Melvin hid his money? A shoebox in the coat closet wasn't a common stashing place, was it? "Melvin, how many people knew that shoebox was in your closet?"

Bruce glared at me. "I'm handling this, Marsha."

"I think I told Kyle, but he can't pass the information on. He's dead."

Thanks for the reminder. I shuddered. Someone told somebody. Kyle could've before he died. If he did, it wasn't his sister. She still languished in the town's one jail cell.

I studied the faces of the curious onlookers. Most stuffed their faces with the contents of their plates like popcorn at a movie. Others whispered with curious glances toward Melvin and Bruce. No one showed a smidgeon of a guilty conscience. It would make solving this case easier if someone had shifty eyes, or kept looking everywhere but at us. I'd take scuffing of a foot in the dirt at this point.

"Think harder. You must have told someone."

Melvin raised red-rimmed eyes to me. "I don't know."

"I told you to butt out, Marsha. Do you have cotton in your ears?" A muscle ticked in Bruce's jaw. "If you don't stop, I'll haul you to the station for obstruction of justice."

He wouldn't dare arrest me! Fine. I'd question Melvin myself later.

Duane must have recognized the look on my face, because he bent low and whispered, "Heed Bruce's advice, Marsha."

I plastered on the sweetest smile I could. "Of course."

"Do you have other money stashed around your place?" Bruce's pencil scratched the surface of the paper.

Melvin's eyes widened. "I ain't telling you that with all these looky-Lu's here!"

Bruce continued to scratch notes on his pad. "You come down to the station in the morning to sign a statement. I ought to haul you in now for public drunkenness, but what the heck."

Duane nuzzled my ear. "I know what you're thinking, so at least let me go with you on snoop patrol." My man knew me so well. Duane kissed me then led me to the side of the crowd as Bruce slapped his notebook closed and marched past us to his patrol car. Melvin roared his lawnmower to life and cut a short swatch through my lawn on his way off the property. I'd give him fifteen minutes to get home, then Duane and I could sneak away.

The crowd parted like the red sea to let me pass to the back yard. Duane headed to the drink table to grab two water bottles. Mom caught up with me, a bit unsteady on her high heels. She wore an outdated, one-size-too-small wedding dress. I bit my lip to keep from grinning.

"What is going on in this town?" Penciled eyebrows rose.

"Wish I knew. But someone is raking in the dough." And it wasn't us.

"I haven't heard of any big deposits down at the bank. You know Ira would've told me. Woman can't keep her lips from flapping to save her life. No one's throwing money around. Not with today's economy, anyway." Mom tapped her lip with a press-on French-manicured nail. "Whoever's doing the stealing, is keeping a low profile."

"Keep an ear out, okay?" I gave her a quick hug. "Duane and I are headed over to question Melvin some more."

"Perfect. I'll eavesdrop during the rest of the party." Mom yoo-hooed to Leroy and sashayed in his direction, her hips swinging like a bell.

Good grief. Sometimes she acted like a teenage girl on the prowl. Crooking a finger in Duane's direction, I marched to his truck, hiked up my dress, and climbed in. The itchy wig I wore, soon sat next to me on the seat. Fifteen minutes later, we pulled in front of Melvin's ranch-style house.

Even in the dusk of evening, I could see his landscaping could win an award. During the day, the lawn must burst with a rainbow of color. It was as lush and plush as expensive carpet. A porch light illuminated a rock walkway. As soon as I came into enough money of my own, I'd hire Melvin for more than mowing. He could design a backyard paradise.

"Wow. Nice yard." Duane slid from behind the wheel and stared almost reverently at the grounds. "This guy has talent. No wonder he wants to open his own landscaping business."

"Yep. Let's go see if he has answers." A rising breeze whipped my dress up around my waist. Duane laughed. Good thing I'd had the foresight to wear those shorts teenage practiced cheer in.

Melvin greeted us on the porch. "Figured you'd show up, nosey woman. Howdy, Duane."

"Melvin." The two shook hands, leaving me to stew about Melvin's comment.

Nosey! I'd find out what was going on around here, then everyone would be thankful I had an inquisitive nature. Swallowing my pride, I motioned toward the door. "Can we step inside?"

"Sure." Melvin led the way. So much for modern-day chivalry. At least Duane held the door for me. "Ask your questions."

"Can I look at the closet?"

He raised his eyebrows. "It's just a place to hang my coats and stash my cash, but sure."

The closet in question sat right beside the front door. No way could they both be opened at the same time without hitting against each other. So, logically, someone could've been in and out within a couple of minutes. But there was still the fact they had to know the money was kept there.

On the top shelf rested a single box. The solitary object practically shouted, "Open me." No hats or gloves shared the space. Easy to guess someone would've lifted the lid and taken a peek. I glanced around the room. No throw pillows on the sofa. No magazines on the glass top coffee table. Not even an empty soda can marred the clean surfaces. I never would've figured Melvin for a neat freak.

"Why don't you use the bank, Melvin?"

"Are you nuts? I ain't giving the government none of my hard-earned money. Other than what I have to pay in taxes, they ain't getting a dime."

I rolled my eyes. "Think. Who knew you had money?"

He sagged into an easy chair. "Anybody. I talked about saving money for the last few months. The only thing they didn't know was how much I had or where I kept it. Most of the folks around here know I don't trust banks."

This would be a hard case to crack. Someone knew the occupants of this town, and knew them well.

30

After church, and another hour of reading to and wiping noses of toddlers in their Sunday school class, I stood on the front steps of the church and took a cleansing breath of an Ozark summer day. The humidity filled my lungs with liquid air, but at least it didn't smell of peanut butter crackers or "accidents". I tried to dredge up at least a little excitement due to ministering to God's little ones, but instead wanted to pinch Duane for volunteering us again.

My shoulders sagged. Not really. The little tykes were growing on me, and they were like little sponges soaking up whatever we taught them.

After a quick glance at my watch, I scurried for my car, deliberately avoiding the spot where Melvin's lawnmower had hit it. I didn't want to know the extent of damage to my paint job. Not yet. I only had thirty minutes before visiting hours at the jail, and needed to compose myself. Karen Anderson was at the top of my very long to-do list.

Duane was nowhere in sight for me to tell him where I was headed. I checked my cell phone to be sure it was on, then turned my car toward the other side of town. Duane could call if he needed me.

River Valley's jail-house, a modest red brick building shaded by massive oak trees, sat about three hundred yards back from the highway. I cut the engine to the Prius and stared at the unimposing building. Except for the sign and the black and white's parked out front, a passerby wouldn't have a clue what the building housed. Formerly, administrative offices to an elementary school long burned down, the building had one holding cell, and rarely any occupants.

I'd spotted Bruce at church so knew he didn't work today. Grabbing my purse, I slid from the car and marched to the front door. An electronic signal bonged when I pushed open the door and a small-framed, heavily made-up woman peered at me over tortoise shell rimmed glasses. "Yes?"

"I'd like to see Karen Anderson, please."

The receptionist cocked her head to one side. "Oh, a guest here." She smirked and slid a form for me to sign across the desk. "You'll have to leave your purse, jewelry, belt, etc. Lockers are over there."

"Can I take a notebook and pen?" I wanted to take notes. Karen had to know something about her brother's death. I scratched my signature on the line.

"Let me see them." She wiggled her fingers in my direction.

I withdrew the small spiral notebook and ink pen from my purse. The woman studied the items then handed them back.

"I suppose you can. You'll be under the watchful eye of an officer anyway. We're pretty small time here."

Did she think I would try to bust Karen out? I stifled a giggle and smiled. She waved me through a heavy wooden door where an officer waited. The door banged shut behind us, my skin prickled. What if I needed to leave in a hurry? There wasn't an emergency button in sight. Perspiration dotted my upper lip, and I hugged the tiny notebook to my chest.

"Sit here." The officer motioned to a chair on one side of a pocked laminate-topped table. Another chair sat opposite.

I sat motionless and stared straight ahead for the eternal ten minutes it took for the man to lead a handcuffed Karen Anderson to the table.

"Hello?" Her brow creased.

"Hi, Karen. I'm Marsha Steele. Remember I spoke with you at your...uh...arrest?"

"Yes, I remember." She plopped into the seat. Her handcuffs clanked the table. "What can I do for you?"

"Like I told you a few days ago, I'm trying to clear my daughter of suspicious charges." It wasn't a complete lie. They hadn't suspected her of anything lately, but they had at first.

Karen arched an eyebrow.

"You also said you had taken your brother's money, but returned it."

"Some of it." She nodded. "I returned it the day before his death. I was there the next day to have lunch." Karen leaned forward. "I paid back exactly three hundred dollars. Kyle seemed more relieved to see me than about the money."

"Can you tell me how much you took?"

"Five hundred dollars. Not much by some people's standards, but it was enough to tide me over until I found a job in St. Louis. Not that I have one anymore." Her shoulders slumped. "I have to be back on Wednesday. Somehow, I don't see me getting out of here by then."

The firing of my questions, and the scratching of my pen, made me feel like a big-shot reporter. Maybe I'd missed my calling. Marsha Stele, Investigative Reporter. "Tell me about finding your brother."

Karen shuddered, and her she paled to the color of Cream of Wheat. "I was an hour late. After knocking on the front door, I moved to the back. It was open. I stepped inside and saw Kyle lying there with a sandwich in his hand and a hammer in his head. I called the cops right away."

"Were there signs anyone was there before you?"

She chewed her lip, catching a piece of dried skin between her teeth. "This is the weird part. I'd called Kyle and told him I was running late. He said no problem. So why the sandwich? Why didn't he wait on me? Plus, I could've sworn I smelled a flowery perfume when I entered the house. Kyle never mentioned having a girlfriend."

"Was anyone outside? Did anyone seem overly curious about Kyle's house?"

"Yes." Karen nodded. "There was someone. A woman. Blond, curvy, walking a dog. A red head in a dark car drove by. I notice things like that." A sad smile crossed her lips. "Comes from keeping an eye out for cops, I guess. I also saw Melvin on his lawnmower. He was driving it down the street like it was a car or something. I know he was a friend of my brother's, but that is the strangest man."

Keep her on track, Marsha. "Did anyone check for the missing money?"

"I don't know. Kyle kept it in the cookie jar shaped like a monkey." Karen laughed then choked on a sob. "I told him not to do that, but he said no one would ever find it there. I bet someone did, right after they killed him."

I needed to get inside Kyle's house. "Thank you, Karen. I'm going to try and find out what happened. Hopefully, I can get you back to work on time and put a murderer behind bars." Standing, I allowed the officer to lead me out of the room. I wrote a note telling Bruce to check Kyle's house for a monkey cookie jar and dropped it on his desk.

"Don't believe everything she says," the officer told me. "The woman had recreational drugs in her system when we booked her." He pushed a button to allow the steel doors to open. "Have a good day."

Marching past the stern receptionist, I stepped outside and blinked against the sunlight assaulting my eyes. My conversation with Karen swirled through my mind. So, many questions. It wasn't surprising that I believed her. Drugs or not, the woman already sat behind bars. Why lie? Of course, I tended to take people at face value. Often I found myself proved wrong, but sometimes people were truthful.

Two officers shoved past me, sprinting toward their cars and pulled me from my musing. Ever curious, I dashed to my own vehicle, prepared to follow.

My Prius had a tough time keeping up with their speedier squad cars, and I fell behind. No matter. Only one place resided at the end of the road we traveled. Mountain View Community Church.

By the time I arrived, the squad cars had parked and the officers surrounded Stephanie Jackson. Her sobs carried across the parking lot. I jammed my car into park, shut off the ignition, and bolted from my seat. What could have happened to send the woman into hysterics?

Duane met me half-way. "What happened?" I gripped his arms and glanced toward Stephanie.

He led me to a wooden bench beneath a magnolia tree. "Seems there's been another robbery."

"What? Who?" My blood froze.

"The women's ministry money is gone."

"How is that possible? Stephanie keeps it locked in the safe." I rose to go to her but Duane pulled me back down. "Only a handful of people have access."

He cupped my face, forcing me to look at him. "The money wasn't in the safe, Marsha. Stephanie had it out on the desk. Counting it and getting it ready for deposit tomorrow."

I didn't want to know, but I had to ask. "How much?"

"Two thousand dollars."

"Did she leave it lying there?" The look on his face pulled the rug from beneath me. "Duane?"

He took a deep breath. "According to her, two people came in. One male and one female. Stephanie said they kept their hands in their pockets and acted like they had a gun."

"Where was everyone else?" It didn't make sense. People congregated after church. Somebody would have seen something. The way Duane continued to stare at me told me he wasn't finished.

"Sweetheart." His hands lowered to grip mine. "Stephanie said one of them wore a green backpack with white polka dots."

31

If I hadn't been sitting, I would have fallen. Instead, I shook my head and clamped my trembling knees together. "Stephanie's making that up. Besides, Lindsey isn't the only teen in these parts with that color backpack." No way would I believe it. My daughter a thief? A murderer? Uh-uh. I yanked my hands free of Duane's. How dare he entertain the thought?

"The evidence doesn't look good. Bruce is more convinced then ever that Lindsey is involved somehow."

I set my jaw and tilted my chin. "Ridiculous."

"I'm just saying that—"

"And if you believe her capable of this, I don't want anything more to do with you."

"Marsha." The pain in his voice ripped through me as effectively as a razor.

"No." Without another glance, I tore away and fled to my car. Tears blurred my vision as I roared from the parking lot. My Prius didn't make the sound I would have liked. More like an electronic purr, but I hoped the sight of my rear bumper got my point across. Through the rearview mirror, I caught a glimpse of Duane standing in front of the church looking like a boy who'd lost his best friend. The sight tugged at my heart. I couldn't focus on him right now. Not when finding Lindsey was so imperative.

Maybe someone stole her backpack. Yeah, that had to be the case.

Ten minutes later, I crunched gravel pulling into our driveway. Since every light in the house was on, despite it being early afternoon, I made an educated guess that Lindsey was home. *Play it cool, Marsha. Casual conversation. Don't blurt out the questions.*

I cut the ignition and squared my shoulders. What was I afraid of? She didn't steal anything. The innocent always won, right? I slid from the seat and closed the car door as quiet as possible. With heavy steps, I made my way to the porch.

Two voices reached my straining ears. I clinched my jaw. Lindsey knew she wasn't supposed to have a boy over when no one was home. Their words slipped through the open window.

"That was way easier than I thought." Billy laughed.

Cold chills ran down my back.

"Did you see the look on her face?" Lindsey's giggle joined his merriment. "My backpack weighed a ton. I never thought I'd make it home."

"I told you to let me carry it."

"No way. You're too careless. Besides, it was worth it." Ice clinked in a glass. How could they drink at a time like this? I put my head in my hands.

"What we did today should provide years of entertainment." Billy laughed again.

My heart sank like a stone, and I collapsed on the porch swing. Things didn't look good for my baby.

The front door creaked as my mom pushed it open. At least Lindsey hadn't broken one of my rules. Mom made a more than sufficient chaperone.

"Why are you sitting out here?" She dried her hands on a dish towel. "Are you all right? Can I get you some lemonade? An aspirin?"

I shook my head and pushed off with my foot, setting the swing in motion. "Someone stole the women's ministry money after church today."

Mom folded into a wicker rocking chair. "Do they have any idea who?"

With a deep sigh, I motioned my head toward the front window. "Lindsey."

"Not that again! Why won't people open their eyes?"

"The suspect carried a green backpack with white polka dots." Tears stung my eyelids. "And I heard her and Billy through the window. They were talking about how heavy her backpack was and. . . "

"The only thing those two brought home today was the biggest cat I've ever seen. The thing's a monster! Its purr sounds like a Mack truck." Mom shuddered. "They were so excited about 'saving' it, I didn't have the heart to make them get rid of the thing.

Carted it home in her backpack. Howled like the dickens when they walked through the door. Then Cleo started barking. It was total mayhem."

A twinge of guilt pricked my conscience. Call me the queen of jumping to conclusions, and I'd practically persecuted Duane just for being the bearer of bad news. "She tried getting a cat when we went to the shelter to get Cleo. How's Cleo taking to the animal now?"

Mom gave a dismissive wave of her hand. "They act like old friends." A car rolled in front of the house. "Bruce didn't waste any time."

"He wouldn't. Fancies himself too important." I steeled myself to do battle. He wouldn't be taking my little girl anywhere based on circumstantial evidence. Not while I had breath left in my body. I rose to meet him.

"Marsha." He at least had the common courtesy to remove his hat.

"Bruce."

"Guess you know why I'm here."

"Not really." I crossed my arms. *Lord, give me strength and guard my tongue.* "Grasping at straws?"

"You don't know about the money missing from church?" He frowned.

"I heard about it."

"Then you also heard the thief carried a backpack matching your daughter's."

"And any number of other teenage girls. Doesn't mean a thing."

"It means Lindsey's our number one suspect." He sighed. "I need to speak with her, please."

"I'll get her." Mom rose and marched into the house. But not before giving Bruce her famous 'Mom' look.

I continued to glare until Mom, Lindsey, and Billy joined us on the porch. From the surprised look on his face, Bruce obviously thought we'd invite him inside. That would also be over my dead body. Never in my thirty-four years had I felt this type of animosity toward another human being. The fact it radiated toward an officer of the law bothered me. They were sworn to serve and protect. Instead, I felt Bruce was here to issue a warrant upon an innocent child.

"Good. You're both here." He pinched the bill of his hat. "I need to know where y'all were after church today."

Lindsay glanced at Billy. "We went to get Grandma a wedding gift."

"That cat's my wedding present?" Mom shook her head and placed a hand at her throat.

"Don't you like it? We walked all the way out of town. The ad in the paper said loving cat free to a good home. Mom got a dog; we thought you'd enjoy a kitten."

"That thing is not a kitten." Lindsey's face fell, and Mom wrapped her arms around her. "He's just unexpected is all. I'm sure I'll grow to love the beast."

"His name is Goliath."

"Of course it is." Mom raised her eyebrows then turned to Bruce. "There you have it. They were getting me a cat."

"Any witnesses?"

"Look, Bruce." I took a step toward him. "Get to the point. Are you going to arrest Lindsey or not? Because if you aren't, then leave."

He moved back. "Are you threatening an officer of the law?"

"No. I'm telling a guy I've known since grade school to skedaddle."

"You're stepping over the line, Marsha."

"Then arrest me."

"Don't tempt me!" Bruce slammed his hat on his head and marched back to his squad car. He stopped, one hand on the handle. "Don't try and skip town. I'll have more questions when you women settle down. And I want to know where you got that cat and who else was there."

Three generations of Calloway women, and one lonely boy, stared as he backed from our driveway. Remorse flickered through me at my actions, but not enough for me to want to apologize. What was going on in this town, and why did someone have it out for my kid? It became more important that I got to the bottom of the thefts.

Duane arrived as Bruce left. My breath left me in a shuddering rush. What could I say to him after the gut punch I'd delivered? I glanced at Mom. "Can you take the kids inside, please?"

She nodded and ushered them through the door. "Come on, you two. I'll make popcorn."

Lindsey sent a worried look over her shoulder. "I'm sorry, Mom. We really didn't mean anything by getting the cat."

"I know you didn't. It isn't about Goliath." I forced a smile to my trembling lips before turning back to Duane. Why did this man keep coming back for more torment? I wasn't the easiest person to be around, especially when one of my family members was threatened.

He stopped before climbing the steps, putting us at eye level. "I didn't suspect Lindsey. I only wanted you to prepare yourself for what others are saying." He gripped my hands. "If you want me to go, just say so. But I won't be back again, Marsha. I can't go through another fifteen years thinking about you, and not being able to see you or hold you. A knife in the gut would hurt less than your words. I know I hurt you terribly, but that was a long time ago. Please, stop punishing me for a stupid young man's mistake."

Tears ran down my cheeks, and I threw myself in his arms. "I'm sorry. Really. I don't want to break up. Sometimes the words fly from my mouth without a filter." I buried my face in the crook of his shoulder. He smelled like heaven. "Forgive me?"

Duane scooped me in his arms. "Always." He carried me back to the swing and sat, keeping me on his lap. Nothing could hurt me while his arms were wrapped so tight around me. "Are all the Calloway women as prickly as you?"

"Yep."

His chuckle vibrated against my cheek. "You should come with a warning label."

"I don't deserve you." I sniffed. "But I am eternally grateful to God for putting you back in my life. Now, if you can help me. . . "

"Tell me what you want me to do."

32

"Good morning!" Mom's loud, cheery welcome resonated inside my head.

I lifted my blurry eyes from my mug of coffee. Sleep the night before had been a distant friend. At a loss as to how to clear my daughter's name, I'd tossed and turned before falling into a fitful sleep where I dreamed of visiting Lindsey in jail. Most likely brought on, in part, by my visit to Karen Anderson earlier yesterday. Duane's offer of help had gone untaken. How could I ask him to do something, when I didn't know what needed to be done? "Morning."

Goliath jumped on the table and rubbed his big orange body against my head. Trying to push him away was like shoving against the rock of Gibraltar.

"Isn't he the cutest thing? Slept by my side all night. Sounded like a freight train, but it was a happy sound."

So, now my mother liked him? She bustled around the kitchen, humming and chattering until I wanted to plug my ears. I've never been a morning person. Why start now?

"Someone needs to warn Duane about your morning attitude." Mom slipped two slices of bread into the toaster.

"Why?" I sipped my warm drink.

"He might change his mind about marrying you."

That woke me up. "Who said we were getting married?" Did she know something I didn't?

"Anyone can see it's only a matter of time. All anyone has to do is see how the boy looks at you." She poured a cup of java.

"We just got back together less than two weeks ago." Sheesh. I rose long enough to grab my bag of M&M's. Was I ready to get married again? Lindsey was fifteen. Mom would tie the knot soon. Yeah, I was ready. Years of being alone loomed ahead of me. Much better to spend them with eye-candy like Duane.

"We could have a double wedding." Mom sat across from me.

"Enough talk about me getting married." I tossed a handful of candy-covered chocolate therapy in my mouth. I was sure to do something to run Duane off before long anyway.

"Hey." Lindsey shuffled in the room and grabbed a slice of toast from my mother's plate. Mom frowned and got up to make more. "I've been thinking."

"Dangerous." I downed the rest of my caffeine. "About what?"

"I think I'm being framed." Lindsey grabbed the other slice from Mom's plate. "I know, and you know, that I didn't steal anything. Besides, if I had taken all the cash that's disappearing, wouldn't I have something new? Like a car or something? We're talking a lot of dough by now."

"You're making sense. Go on." Mom brought over several slices of toast and set the plate in the middle of the table. "What do we do?"

I shrugged. "I don't know. All my suspects are being stolen from. I'm at square one."

Mom took a bite of breakfast and stared at the ceiling. "To my way of thinking, someone stole from themselves to take the attention off. Like an episode on Murder She Wrote."

"Is that show still on?" I shoved my bag of candy out of arm's reach before I made myself sick.

"Reruns. Not important." Mom waved her hand. "We need to do some stakeouts, and spy on everyone on your list."

Kyle was dead, and I no longer suspected Billy, so that left Melvin, Marilyn, and Stephanie. But who would take who? What if I was wrong and it wasn't any of them? We'd be wasting our time and end up looking foolish. "What about work?"

"I'll put a sign on the window. It won't hurt to close for one day." Mom's eyes lit up like a Christmas tree. "Who do I get?"

"You and Leroy take Melvin, Lindsey and Billy can follow Marilyn, and I'll tail Stephanie."

Mom clapped her hands. "Let's go! We'll meet at the diner at eleven."

I made a quick call to Duane.   "I'm tailing Stephanie today." I balanced the cell phone between my ear and shoulder and slid behind the wheel of my car.

His sigh vibrated over the air waves. "I wish you'd wait until I got off work."

"I'll be careful. She won't even know I'm there. Mom is spying on Melvin and Lindsey is following Marilyn. We've got it covered." Besides, I had my gun and my Tazer. Of course, I hadn't learned how to shoot the cute little pistol yet, but I had plenty of time.

Mom roared out of the driveway behind me on her way to pick up Leroy, and Lindsey sped-walked down the road. I grinned. The Calloway women; out to save the world.

Stephanie pulled out of her driveway as I drew near. I continued on a few feet then did a U-turn in the middle of the road behind a pickup truck. A thrill of excitement coursed through me. If I could keep another automobile between me and my prey, I'd continue undetected. Detective work and I were made for each other. I waved as Mom and Leroy passed in the opposite direction. Mom gave me a thumbs-up and waved toward Stephanie's Tahoe.

First we stopped at the dry-cleaners, then I waited with all the patience of a toddler at Christmas while Stephanie ran into the grocery store, then we stopped in front of her husband's pharmacy. All above board it seemed. I was right earlier. What a waste of time. Couldn't she do something other than everyday mundane?

Two Labradors dragged Marilyn down the sidewalk. Why did the woman wear heels to walk dogs? I shook my head then smiled as

Lindsey and Billy followed her, hand-in-hand. Casual enough. Marilyn wouldn't suspect a thing.

Good grief. The woman's been in there for five minutes. I cranked the radio station I listened to up another notch and proceeded to sing along.

A sharp rap on the window pulled me from people watching and off-key harmonizing. I shrieked and turned to stare wide-eyed into the stern face of Stephanie Jackson.

"Why are you following me?" She arched a brow.

I rolled down the window. "Excuse me?"

"You are following me. Why?" One tear managed to trickle down her cheek. How did she manage that? "Haven't I had enough heartache in the last twenty-four hours?"

"I, uh, wanted to talk to you." My face heated.

"You could've called." She crossed her arms. "Ask."

"It's about the women's ministry money."

Stephanie sighed. "I really don't want to relive that, Marsha. It was horrifying. Two terrifying people threatened me with a weapon. They could've killed me. Besides, with your daughter as the main suspect, I don't think I should be discussing it with you. Have a good evening." She spun on her stiletto heels and tapped her way back to her vehicle.

Wonderful. I'd accomplished absolutely nothing but waste a morning that could have been spent unpacking the last of my boxes or making money at the store.

Wanda's Cafe loomed ahead. It wouldn't hurt to show up early. Maybe I could enjoy a soda in peace and process the lack of information I'd covered. I parked the Prius in the shade of the massive cow and cut the ignition. Grabbing my purse, I headed inside, noting the new window installed after Lindsey drove through the old one. Thank God for insurance.

Mom, Leroy, Lindsey, and Billy already sat in a booth. So far, nothing had gone as planned. Why did I bother? I plopped my purse on the table and pulled up a chair.

"I got nothing." I slouched. "Stephanie caught me, played the martyr act, and refused to say a word."

"Don't feel bad, dear." Mom patted my hand. "Melvin didn't leave his house all morning."

"And all Marilyn did was walk a dog, then try to walk two big hyper ones, then headed to the shelter." Lindsey slurped a milk shake. "If Billy hadn't been with me, I would've died of boredom. This being accused of a crime is ruining my summer vacation."

"Look on the bright side." Leroy took Mom's hand in his. "I spent a couple of hours with the most beautiful woman this side of the Rio Grande."

"Oh, stop." Mom's cheeks darkened.

I rolled my eyes. If Duane wouldn't have had to work, I could've boasted almost the same thing, except he probably wouldn't have let me go sleuthing. "What a waste of time."

"I see your attitude hasn't improved." Mom wiggled her eyebrows at me. "Leroy took the liberty of ordering all of us cheeseburgers. You'll feel better once your blood sugar is up."

Bruce strolled into the diner, gave us a stern look, then took a seat at the bar. I gave an impish wave and grinned when he turned away. He couldn't say anything against us having lunch, could he? His constant stares toward our table made me perspire. My hand shook as I reached for my drink.

A young waitress brought us our burgers and knocked my purse to the floor. My gun skid across the floor.

Lindsey's eyes widened. "Mom, why are you carrying a gun?"

"Shhh." I dove to the floor, almost kissing the shiny tips of Bruce's boots, and scooped up my scattered items as fast as I could.

"Hand it over, Marsha."

Drat. My pretty toy. "Hand over what?"

"The gun."

I handed it to him and got to my feet.

"Do you have a permit to carry a concealed weapon?" Bruce tucked it into his waistband.

"Do I need one?" I glanced over my shoulder at my family. "Everyone around here carries a gun. They usually keep them in their truck gun racks, but . . . oh! Not concealed."

"Yes, oh." Bruce sighed. "Look. I'm off duty and don't want anything more to do with the Calloways for a lifetime of Sundays. I'm confiscating this until you obtain a permit. Got it?"

"Got it." Off by the hair of my chinny chin chin.

Leroy laughed. "Life with you three won't be boring. I'll look forward each day to a new adventure."

I rested my head in my hands and wanted to cry.

33

With the smidgeon of dignity left to me, I clutched my purse and stumbled from the diner. Good grief. I'd never shot the gun, so why the remorse over it being gone? And crawling around on the floor, ugh. I clamped my lips together. Mortification. That was it. I needed M&Ms, and I needed them now. The nearest convenience store beckoned.

One elderly man in a John Deere hat filled a rust-pocked truck at the gas pump, two teenagers slurped sodas in front of the store, and a red Mustang convertible sat in front of the large store window. Good, in and out, and I'd soon be relaxing at home with a forty-two ounce soda and a bag of therapy. I had a moment of car envy at the sight of the convertible, then patted the wheel of my Prius.

"Sorry, old girl. I'm perfectly happy with you." My phone rang before I'd gotten out of the car so I settled back into the seat. Caller ID showed Duane. "Hey."

"Hey, yourself. How'd sleuthing go?"

"She caught me. Mom and Lindsey didn't do any better."

"I have to admit I'm glad. I worried about you all morning."

Wasn't he sweet? "And Bruce took my gun away."

"What? Who were you aiming on shooting?"

I sighed. "My purse fell off the table, and he confiscated it because I was carrying a concealed weapon without a permit."

"Oh. I should've known about that. You could've gone to jail. Where are you now?"

"The Corner Store. Why don't you come over for dinner around five?"

"That's the best thing I've heard all day."

"Really?" I smiled. "How about I love you?"

He chuckled. "Even better."

My heart warmed, and the stress of the day melted away. I wanted to listen to his soft drawl for the rest of my life. Regardless of my actions toward my mother's hinting of marriage. I wouldn't even have to change my name. "See you later."

I hung up, tossed my phone on the seat, and exited the car. Birds sang from a nearby oak tree, and the sun blasted my shoulders with its Southern intensity. The only thing making the day bearable was a soft breeze that kissed my skin on its way past. I dug in my purse for a hair tie and lifted the mess of curls off my neck. Previous experience proved I looked like a curly-haired Pebbles, but having the weight lifted definitely felt better. With a sigh of relief, I pushed open the double glass doors and stepped into air-conditioned heaven smelling of sweets and roasting hot dogs.

An auburn headed girl in black athletic gear chatted with the young man behind the counter. It wasn't hard for me to guess she most likely drove the Mustang. Her shrill giggle echoed in the almost empty building.

An entire candy aisle screamed my name. I almost shouted in glee when I realized the store had started carrying one pound bags of dark chocolate M&Ms. I clutched my prize to my chest and moved to the soda fountain. Thrusting the largest cup the place carried under the carbonated stream, I waited for cup to fill.

A rush of hot air hit my back as another patron entered. The red head screamed.

My hand froze. Chilly soda ran over my hand and onto the floor. I whirled to face the cashier. My feet slipped on the wet floor, and I grabbed a magazine rack to steady myself.

A person dressed in black from head-to-toe, and wearing a Clinton mask, approached the counter. One gloved hand held a pistol. I couldn't help but think how hot the person had to be in the heat of the day. Those masks weren't made for comfort.

I sat the overflowing cup on the counter and squatted behind a display of chips. What should I do? The obvious answer would be to call the police, but I'd left my phone in the car. I slid my hand in my purse and wrapped my fingers around the Tazer. Could I get close enough to use it?

My heart pounded with the strength of a heavy metal band. Sweat broke out on my forehead and upper lip. *God, please don't let the person shoot anyone.*

I peeked around the corner of the rack. Baggy clothes, thick jacket, and the fact they had yet to utter a word, didn't give me a clue as to the burglar's gender. Auburn hair girl continued to shriek until the person in black pointed the gun in her direction then held a finger to their vinyl lips. The girl shuddered and dropped to the floor. Better for all of us in my opinion.

The burglar made a movement for the cashier to open the register then turned to face the rest of the store. I shrank back against the wall and swallowed the acid taste of fear. I scooted. The metal shelf grabbed my uplifted hair in its cold fingers. Footsteps scuffed closer. Held prisoner, I shoved my purse behind a bag of pork rinds and closed my eyes only to open them when the president impersonator tapped me on the head with the weapon. The genderless specter motioned for me to move to the front of the store. Most robbers are men, right? I chose to believe so.

"I can't. I'm stuck." Adrenaline rushed through me, speeding my breathing.

The bad guy shook his head and pulled a knife from his pocket. *Oh, God, I don't want to die in a convenience store! Please make it quick.* I tugged harder to release my hair and wilted when the thief cut me loose. I lifted a hand. Did he have to cut the entire pony tail off? It took me years to grow it this long. Tears welled in my eyes. *Stop it, Marsha. Now is not the time to cry about your crowning glory.* I sniffed. Duane loved my hair, but considering my recent habit of getting it tangled, maybe this was for the best. Clinton motioned again toward the counter.

Sure thing. No argument here. I scrambled on my hands and knees until I sat with my back against the counter. I laid my chin on my overall clad knees.

Where were all the customers? By now there ought to be at least five dozen people traipsing through the door. Okay, maybe one or two, but I'd take anyone. I glanced out the window and pressed my candy closer. Everyone had disappeared like an old episode of a Twilight Zone movie. "Is that gun even loaded? Why won't you say something?"

The gun whipped in my direction and pointed at my foot. No words needed.

"Okay, don't try it out on me." Good Lord, save me from my mouth. "You must be pretty desperate to rob The Corner Store. It isn't like it's a booming business. Have you tried the bank? They actually keep money there." Maybe if I kept talking, I could distract the person. "Are you the one whose been stealing from the residents of this town? Because they're blaming my daughter, and if it's you, you should say something and clear her name." My chest started to hurt from all the pounding.

"Here's all the cash." The cashier's voice squeaked as he tossed a bag on the counter. "It isn't much. We've had a slow day, and I don't have the combination to the safe."

The robber grabbed the money, rifled through the passed-out debutante's purse, grabbed her wallet, then dashed out the door.

"Call the police!" I dashed to my feet and sprinted after the black dressed he/she. The robber disappeared around the corner as a van full of kids roared into the parking lot. Perfect timing. Now we get company.

I turned and went to refill my soda. By the time Bruce arrived with an officer I didn't know, I sat on the curb slurping an ice cold drink and had eaten a fourth of the way through my bag of candy.

The store clerk stood in the doorway. "Lady, you talk a lot. Blabbering like that could've gotten one of us killed."

I shrugged. Thank you very much young man with the puberty sounding voice. When scared, I tended to ramble through no fault of my own.

"I should've known you'd be involved." Bruce glanced my way as he pushed into the store.

I held up my soda. Couldn't a person buy a coke in this town without being accused of a crime? To top things off, the adrenaline disappeared, leaving me with shaking limbs and an overwhelming urge to start bawling at the top of my lungs.

By the time the media showed up, my blood pressure had returned to normal. I held a hand over my face and dashed to my car when they wanted a statement. The hounds turned their attentions to the two police officers. Could I be arrested if I went home before Bruce talked to me? He held up a finger for me to wait. Wonderful.

I called Duane. "You'll never guess what happened to me."

"You won the lottery."

"No. The Corner Store was held up while I was inside. If I would've had my gun, I could've held up the person holding up the store. I'd have been a hero."

"Tell me you're joking."

"Nope, I'm completely serious." I tossed another handful of candy into my mouth. "They pointed a gun at me and everything. Plus, they cut off my hair. Better that then my head, right?"

"Are you all right? Because you're running off at the mouth like a tsunami."

"I'm fine. Peachy. Right as rain." Tears slid down my cheeks. My hands trembled. It took me two tries to get my straw in my mouth. "No, I was terrified. I thought I was going to die and would miss out on more of your kisses." A sob escaped me. "That would be horrible, wouldn't it? I mean, you enjoy kissing me, right? Because I do love kissing you. It's the best thing ever."

"Are you still at the store?"

"Y . . .yes."

"I'll be right there." Click.

Within five minutes, Duane's motorcycle pulled up alongside my car. He leaped off and yanked on the door handle. "Unlock the door."

I pushed the button. "Let go of the handle."

"I'm not holding the handle."

"Well, I'm unlocking the door."

He stood back and held up his hands. "I'm not holding the handle."

"Oh." I pushed again, and Duane slid inside. He turned to face me.

"Woman, you're going to be the death of me."

"You? I'm the one who faced a gun. All you have to worry about was getting tackled by a high school student. Or Gatorade dumped on your head."

Duane yanked me against his chest. "Your phone call scared me to death. I can't let you out of my sight."

"Can I have a kiss?" My gaze focused on his chiseled lips.

"For the rest of your life. Lord, may it be a long one." He tilted my face and planted a kiss hot enough to melt my gym shoes.

34

"What happened to your hair?" Mom glanced up from where she sat watching a movie. "When did you have time to get it cut? And whoever you hired needs to be fired."

"I didn't go to have it cut." I plunked my purse on the coffee table. "The Corner Store was held up. I got my hair stuck in a rack of chips, and when I couldn't move when the burglar wanted me to, he cut me free."

Leroy laughed so hard, tears sprang to his eyes. "A robber with a conscience. I would've loved to have seen that."

The big doofus! Maybe I wouldn't let him marry my mom after all. "I don't see anything funny about losing my hair. I probably look like a poodle!"

Duane wrapped his arms around me from behind. "I like it. Makes her look sassy. Now her hair matches her personality."

Cleo bounded down the hall and planted her front feet on my chest. She stared into my eyes as if checking to see whether I was really me. She gave a huff, and apparently satisfied, padded to lie down by the window.

"I'm going to the bathroom." I wiggled free from Duane's hold and shuffled down the hall. Once inside the guest restroom, I stared into the mirror. The new do, shorter in some places than others, made me look younger as the tighter curls framed my face and highlighted my eyes. A visit to the beauty parlor would fix the unevenness. I did like it, and since Duane agreed, almost everything was right with my world again.

Cleo barked from the front room. The click of her nails against the wood floor as she dashed to the backdoor compelled me to follow. She scratched and whined until I let her out. I followed with Duane close on my heels.

"Cleo, what is it, girl?" I sprinted after her as she made a beeline toward my new home. She growled and disappeared into the trees. I skidded to a halt. Running into the woods at night without a flashlight wasn't wise; especially with my habit of getting into trouble. "Cleo, come!" She responded with a bark and stayed out of sight. As I turned to leave, a flash of white caught my eye.

Tacked to the front door of the former guest house was a sheet of copy paper. I climbed the stairs and pulled it free from its tack.

Stop trying to figure out what's going on in River Valley. Cutting your hair was minor compared to what can happen. Look at Kyle Anderson.

Ice water ran through my veins. I'd faced a murderer today; someone who was prepared to kill again. And they had their eye on me.

Duane caught me as my knees buckled, and he lowered me to the top step before taking the warning from me. "We need to call Bruce. He's going to be mad that we took the note off the door."

Was calling Bruce the answer to everything? Handling this on our own had merit. Seeing that man more than once a day was my equivalent of torture, but then, again, I'd been threatened. Something I most likely couldn't handle alone.

I nodded. At least the note might remove some of the suspicion off Lindsey. "Cleo went into the woods after whoever left this. I need to find her."

"Oh, no, you don't. They have a gun and already admitted to one murder."

"I must be getting close to figuring this out if the person responsible has resorted to leaving notes." If I only I knew what the thief thought I did.

"And now you're finished." Duane grabbed my hand and pulled me to my feet. "No more sleuthing for you."

"You promised to help me."

"That was before your life was threatened."

I couldn't stop now. Not when I was so close. The thief thought I knew something and wouldn't stop now unless my investigating halted permanently. Caution was the key here. I needed time to sit and process the last two weeks. Something lurked in the murky recesses of my mind. I just needed to dig it up.

One look at Duane's stern face told me I'd have to do so without his knowledge. The thought sent a stab of pain through my gut. Going against his wishes left a sour taste in my mouth. But, I needed to find this threat of a person before they confronted me. Or worse, I found myself with a hammer in the back of my head.

Before we entered the house, Duane turned me to face him. His gaze bore into mine. "I know what you're thinking, and I realize you're going to do what you want to. But do my wishes count in this at all?"

"Of course they do, but I've started something I have to finish." I beseeched him with my eyes, pleading for him to understand. "That person could've killed me today, and chose not to. I don't think they feel *that* threatened by me." I hoped. Halting me under the pretense of armed robbery would've made murdering me easy. Deep down, I didn't feel the person really wanted me dead. Just out of their business.

Duane sighed and ran his hands through his hair. The strands stood up like the blond tail feathers of a chicken. He'd never looked cuter. "Okay. Please promise me you won't go anywhere without someone knowing where you are at all times. Keep your phone and your Tazer with you. Always."

"That I can promise." I wrapped my arms around his waist and laid my cheek on his chest. His heart beat a steady rhythm. A reassuring thump thump that helped keep me cemented to Planet Earth.

He returned my hug and squeezed. "As much as I'd like to stay this way, it's time to make that phone call."

I frowned. "You're right."

We walked to the main house. While Duane placed the call, I strolled to the living room and handed the note to my mother. She fished her reading glasses from the end table and perched them on her nose. Her eyes widened as she read. "Where did you get this?"

"Tacked to the door of my house." I plopped on the sofa next to her. "Duane is calling Bruce."

"That little man might as well move in here." She tossed the note toward the coffee table. It missed and fluttered to the floral area rug like a wounded moth. "This has got to end. We should put a notice in the paper or something. Flush this character out."

"Setting a trap might not be a bad idea." I crossed my ankles on the table. "They're very interested in me. All I'd have to do was stand in the middle of the road with a 'come and get me' sign around my neck."

"It's a horrible idea." Duane squeezed in between Mom and me. "You aren't the police. Leave it alone."

"Party pooper."

"Nope. Just trying to keep the woman I love alive."

"I'm thinking the women might be onto something, Duane." Leroy's feet clunked the floor. "Except, I'll be the bait. I'll spread it around town that I've made a withdrawal for repairs around the house. I'm an old man.

Folks won't think anything odd about it. Look at Melvin. He kept his money in a shoebox."

"I don't want you in harm's way." Mom leaned forward and patted his arm. "And fifty-five isn't old."

"But it's okay for a couple of women?"

"Don't get your dander up, Leroy. Watch your blood pressure."

"It's a bad idea all around." Duane laid his arm around my shoulder. "Let the police handle it."

"Are you afraid, son?" Leroy peered at Duane over the rim of his glasses.

"Not for me." Duane returned the stare. "If y'all want to set a trap, I'll set it." You could almost smell the testosterone.

"Good grief. You two roosters stop prancing around the living room before someone gets clawed. We won't set up a sting." No matter how much fun it sounded. I rose. "We'll keep going along with our little lives and let Lindsey keep getting blamed for anything that goes wrong in this town." With a tilt of my chin, I stormed into the kitchen.

Life had dealt me bad hands before. This was mild, comparatively. So, what had my bloomers in a wad? I planted my hands flat on the kitchen counter and stared into the deepening dusk toward my cozy little house. Where was Cleo? Please, Lord, don't let her be hurt.

"Marsha? Bruce is here." Mom's voice rang from the front room, disrupting my thoughts. "Make some coffee."

I shook my head and reached to fill the pot. One of my friends, or close acquaintances, was a thief and murderer. The realization churned the acid in my stomach. Someone in a peaceful, country town had committed the unthinkable.

Sure, we've had our share of deaths. Hunting accidents or drownings, mostly. And that one husband who killed his wife in a jealous rage. But that was years ago. Evil didn't have a handhold here. A few trains had run over cars until they installed the new guard over the tracks. We had the occasional drunken driver. All in all, life drifted along in peaceful tranquility. What could make someone kill in order to steal? What could they want so badly? I couldn't imagine resorting to murder for money or for anything, actually.

There were other ways of getting what you want. If you need cash, get a job. If you insist on taking something that isn't yours, you don't have to take a life in order to get it.

I measured out the coffee grounds and started the java brewing. As soon as the aroma wafted from the pot, the others drifted into the kitchen. To my relief, Cleo scratched at the door. I let her in, taking a moment to scratch under her chin. "Did you catch that nasty person? No? Well, better luck next time, you ferocious beast. Don't take off like that again. You had me worried."

Bruce was the first to drop his skinny body into a chair. He shook his head at me. "A record in this town, Marsha. Twice in one day.

Remarkable. You would probably qualify for the Guinness Book of World Records. I'll send a photographer over tomorrow to take your picture."

"Ha ha." I handed everyone a mug.

"Duane gave me the note." Bruce leaned back on the chair's hind legs and folded his arms. "Leave it where you find it next time. Now your finger prints are all over it. I don't think anyone is playing games here."

"Really? I thought after Kyle's death and all the robberies, that we were having a party." How did the man ever get a badge? "You really think it'll happen again?"

"Your store was robbed twice." Bruce held up two fingers. "Then we have Sharon's necklace, Melvin's money, Harvey's wallet, those Chihuahua pups, and the women ministry's money." He put down his fingers to accept the cup of coffee then banged all four chair legs back to the floor. "Now, the convenience store. I have to admit, I don't think your daughter is guilty of these crimes. Not anymore."

"Well, thank you very much."

Duane gave me a 'cut-it-out' look.

I pulled up the only vacant chair. "Half of the crimes took place with the victim not recalling what happened during the time the stealing took place. How is that possible?"

"Drugs." Mom slapped the table. "It's always drugs. Just watch any crime drama."

"Don't jump to any conclusions, Marsha," Bruce said. "There's a reasonable explanation for all this. We haven't figured it out yet."

"You're running out of time. Somebody else will die, I just know it." And I didn't want it to be me.

35

I tossed and turned. Grit coated the back of my eyelids. Instead of sleep, visions of my day flicked across my mind like the words of a stuck phonograph. Over and over I saw the burglar, the words of the note, and piles of money. How much was the stolen total anyway? A few hundred here and there, but it all added up, and in today's economy, who didn't need cash? But desperate enough to steal? It was hard to imagine anyone I knew stooping to such lengths.

Lindsey's voice drifted through the wall as she talked on the phone. I glanced at the clock. Midnight. Ugh! I wrapped the pillow around my head to block her conversation and Cleo's snores out of my head. How many times had I told her no phone calls after nine o'clock on week nights?

"Lindsey, enough!"

I removed the pillow to blessed silence. Thank you, Lord. Mom always told me a sure fire way to get to sleep was to pray for other people. Where did I start? With thanking God no one had been harmed in the day's robbery. Then I prayed for Melvin and his heartbreak. For Marilyn and Stephanie's dreams, for Mom and Leroy's future happiness, for Karen Anderson. Surely the day's events would help clear her name. For. . .

"Mom?"

My eyes popped open from my short slumber to peer through the dark at Lindsey's wide eyes. "What?"

"Shhh." Her gaze darted to the window. "Someone's outside."

I sat up and took another look at the clock. Two a.m. Cleo growled deep in her throat, her paws on the windowsill. Had the thief returned? Flinging off the sheet, I stood, the wood floor cool on my bare feet.

"Get behind me." I searched the dark for a weapon. Idiot! I'd left my purse on the kitchen table, along with my Tazer. A quick check of the bedroom phone revealed silence on the other end.

"Does the phone in your room work?"

"No. It cut off while I was talking to Billy."

"What could you possibly have to talk about this late?" I rolled my eyes. Teenagers.

"Mom, I'm scared." Lindsey clutched my arm.

So was I. But a mother must be brave for her child. I straightened my shoulders. "Stay beside me. We'll make a run for the big house."

"Are you crazy? They might have a gun." Lindsey's nails dug into my flesh.

"Do you have a better idea?"

"We could hide in the closet. If they don't find anything, they'll leave."

Cleo let out a sharp bark. Lindsey and I screamed. If our visitor didn't know we were awake before, they did now.

"Let the dog out. She'll scare them away."

"Or get shot." I didn't want that to happen. My furry friend was important to me.

"Why'd you buy her then?"

I shrugged. "Protection. I feel safer with her by us."

Cleo's barks increased in intensity, and she clawed at the window. I turned. Eyes shone by the moon's glow as someone peered in at us. My heart leaped into my throat, and I choked back a shriek. The intruder tapped the window with the barrel of a pistol. Last time, I'd been tangled in the phone cord. Not this time.

Lindsey's sobs spurred me to action. I shoved her through the bathroom door. "Lock it!"

"Mom."

"Now." I grabbed Cleo's collar in one hand and the base of my crystal lamp with the other. Not much of a shield against a bullet, but the action raised my confidence. "Come, Cleo." I pulled her from the room and into the kitchen where I traded my ridiculous weapon for the Tazer.

"Okay, girl. I'm going to open the door, and you rush out. Be ferocious, put the fear of God into that intruder, and don't get shot, please." I shoved the door open and flattened myself against the wall to peer through the window. Cleo burst outside, her barks strident in the night.

Lights flicked on in Mom's house. Her silhouette showed dark against the glow from her kitchen. "Cleo! Stop that racket."

"Mom, call the police!" Please let her hear me. "There's an intruder."

Cleo yelped, then her barks turned to a high pitched yip. She needed me. I bolted through the open door, finger on the trigger of my Tazer. Dew coated my feet as I raced around the corner of the house, my nightgown flapping around my legs. The light from the bathroom where Lindsey hid highlighted a narrow swatch in the yard. Cleo stared into the trees bordering the property; the hair on her neck bristled. Mom joined me. The moon's rays glinted off the butcher knife in her hand. "What do you plan on doing with that?"

"Defend myself. Who is it?"

"I don't know. They stared through my bedroom window."

"Pervert." Mom raised her knife and clutched the neckline of her robe closer around her throat. "Isn't the first Peeping Tom we've had in this town."

"It's not a Peeping Tom." I glanced at her out of the corner of my eye. "I was sleeping, not getting dressed. I'm pretty sure it was the burglar from The Corner Store. He, or she, wore the same type black nylon jacket. Come on. They're gone and we shouldn't be standing out here if they come back." Snapping my fingers for Cleo to follow, I led Mom back to my humble abode.

"Whoever that was is playing with me." I dropped the Tazer back in my purse and grabbed my cell phone.

"What do you mean?" Mom slumped in a chair.

"That's twice they could've shot me. Instead, they're playing some sort of silly game." I shuddered and punched in Bruce's private number. It became obvious the thief knew me and knew me well.

"This better be good." Bruce grumbled in a sleepy voice.

"Hello to you too. Someone was here. They cut my phone lines and waved a pistol at me through the window." I slammed cabinet doors looking for my M&Ms. Surely I didn't leave them at Mom's. "I'm pretty sure it's the same person from earlier today. They didn't wear the mask. Their face was covered by a one of those ski beanie things."

Bruce's growl rivaled a bear's. "This can *not* be happening. I'll be there in fifteen minutes." Click.

"Mom?"

Lindsey! "You can come out now, sweetheart."

Her bare feet slapped the floor boards as she sprinted to my side. "I've never been more frightened. We could've been killed." She wrapped her arms around me. "I'll never take life for granted again."

Teenage dramatics. At least they were good for a smile. I patted her back. "Sit down, and I'll make some hot chocolate while we wait for Bruce."

"That man is going to have a coronary." Mom giggled. "Bet he wished he worked in a different precinct. Are you going to call Duane?"

"Later. I don't want to disturb his sleep." He'd want to camp on my doorstep after tonight's adventure. Not that I would mind too much, but Mom would have a fit and the ladies at church would have gossip fodder for years.

Right on time, Bruce barged into the house without bothering to knock. "Which window were they looking in?"

"My bedroom. West side of the house."

"Y'all stay here." With a hand on the butt of his weapon, Bruce headed back outside.

Mom, Lindsey, and I sipped hot chocolate and waited for Bruce to return. Ten minutes later, he strutted back in. "Shoe prints outside the window. Looks like a man's shoe, but the soil is wet and the print not deep. Could be a woman wearing a man's sneaker."

"So, we're no closer to finding the suspect then we were before."

"Not really, but I suggest you and your daughter move back into your mom's house until this perp is caught."

"Do we have to?" I so dearly wanted my own place. Would I ever be allowed to grow up and be independent? Maybe I shouldn't wait for Duane to propose. I could do it myself. After all, it's the twenty-first century. It wasn't unheard of.

"I can't make you, but I strongly advise you not to stay out here." He gave us a nod and left the way he'd come.

"I don't think this town has had this much excitement since the tornado five years ago." Mom rose and placed her cup in the sink. "Might as well try to get some sleep. There's clean sheets on your old beds. Come on. Work comes mighty early."

She wasn't kidding. By the time I finally closed my eyes against visions of the black-robed demon, Mom knocked on the door to let me know it was time to wake up. Could a person call in sick when they were one of the owners?

36

Bleary eyed, I sat behind the counter of Gifts from Country Heaven, chin propped in my hand, and watched the world pass outside the window. A group of women, mom included, wearing red hats and purple tee shirts pranced by to their weekly lunch at the diner. Billy yelled out a car window at Lindsey who swept the sidewalk. Normal every day activity that did nothing for my mood. Sleep would help. I sighed. Nothing to do about it. We couldn't close the store two days in a row.

Mom left me a mile long list of things to do, most of it sewing. Said it would keep my mind off my troubles. With a deep breath, I grabbed a bolt of cloth and cut off the two yards I would need for throw pillows. Then I grabbed another bolt and cut two more.

"Hey, Marsha!" Marilyn breezed through the door, thankfully minus dogs. "Just dropped in to say goodbye. In case we don't run into each other again."

"Are you going somewhere?" I paused in cutting.

"Hollywood! I've saved enough money to enable me to live for three months. If I can't break into showbiz by then, I'll start over and head to Broadway." Ruby lips spread across white teeth.

"I wish you all the luck, Marilyn. I really do." Despite our having fought over who would be Marilyn Monroe at mom's party, I wished her nothing but the best. "You could always try being a vintage pinup model. With your figure, that platinum hair, and your lips, you'd be a cinch."

"Really?" She put a matching sculptured nail to her mouth. "I hadn't thought of that. Might be a way to make money if I don't break into show biz right away." She winked. "Of course, a sugar daddy wouldn't help."

I grimaced. "There's always that option, I guess."

"Well, bye!" She bounced back out the door.

The newspaper boy banged the news against the window, startling me from my thoughts. Lindsey snatched the paper from the sidewalk and brought it in. "Guess what's on the front page!" She slapped it on the counter.

Wonderful. There I sat with soda in hand on the curb of The Corner Store. The cameraman must have snapped the shot before I stuck my hand over my face.

"We're making the paper a lot." Lindsey grinned. "With me running the car through the diner and you getting held up, we're like celebrities!"

"I'd like to be in the paper because we found out who the thief is, not because we did something stupid or almost got killed."

"Something is better than nothing. It's probably good for business." Lindsey plopped in a rocker. "Melvin drove by with a brand new riding lawnmower. Where do you think he got the money? His was stolen, right?"

Good question. "Maybe he lowered his principles and took out a loan." Or maybe he stole it before peeking in my window last night. And what compromises did Marilyn make? Bruce did say it could've been a woman wearing men's shoes. I should've looked at her feet. She stood several inches taller than me. It might work. I wondered whether Bruce would be interested in my deductions.

"I'm heading to the diner to get something to drink." Lindsey pushed to her feet. "Do you want something?"

"A diet soda would be great."

Stephanie pushed past as Lindsey headed out the door. The woman smiled, without revealing her teeth, and stared at me.

"Can I help you?"

"I want to buy that rose-colored quilt."

My eyes widened. "It's three hundred dollars."

She smirked. "I know how much it is." Stephanie leaned on the counter. "I have enough money now to go and fetch Rosalea. I'm leaving this weekend."

"Don't you have to wait for paperwork or something?" I moved to get the quilt then wrapped it in tissue paper.

"Those papers are being processed as we speak." She dug in her purse for her checkbook. "And further more, the paperwork on my new daughter has been in the works for a very long time. I just needed the money for the legal side of it."

"How old is the girl now? Ten?"

Stephanie giggled. "You are such a kidder. It didn't take *that* long. She's almost three. Mark is ecstatic. We're decorating her room this week. That's why I need the quilt. Nothing but the best for my daughter."

I glanced at her feet. "What size shoe do you wear?"

"A ten, why?"

"Just wondering." I smiled up at her. "I'm happy for you, Stephanie. Really. You've worked hard to become a mother."

"I'd do anything." She wrote the check, handed it to me and watched while I printed her receipt.

"Let me know if we can get anything else for you."

"Oh, I will." She wrapped her arms around the quilt and left.

Huh. All three of my suspects suddenly had the money they needed. Very suspicious to me. I picked up the phone and dialed Bruce's number.

"What now?"

Drat that caller ID. "That's not a very nice way to answer the phone. Especially at work." I paced behind the counter. "I've been thinking."

"Dangerous."

"Ever the comedian. I had several names on my suspect list –"

"I thought I told you to stay out of this investigation."

"You can't stop somebody from writing down names. Anyway, I had Melvin Brown, Kyle Anderson, Marilyn Olsen, Billy Butler, and Stephanie Jackson. Kyle is dead, and Billy isn't guilty, so that leaves three. And guess which three suddenly have the money they've been needing?" Take that, Bruce.

"Don't forget Lindsey, and what makes you think Billy isn't guilty?"

"Come on! My daughter did nothing wrong, and you know it. You said so yourself. Can you honestly tell me you can imagine that boy holding up a convenience store?"

"Maybe the crimes aren't related."

Why did he have to be so dense? Of course the crimes were related. I'd bet my life on it. Most likely would. "Okay, fine. Disregard my suspicions. I wish you all the luck on solving the case."

"Marsha, look—"

I hung up on him. Solving the case was left up to me, Marsha Calloway Steele, who had no idea what to do next. The pile of cut fabric beckoned. The back door to the shop opened, and I heard Mom humming as she made a pot of coffee. Always the first thing on her list when she came to work. I needed something to show for the hour I'd been here. Scooting back behind the sewing machine, I pretended to be engrossed in my work.

My mind whirred as fast as the needle. Melvin, Marilyn, or Stephanie? All wanted something desperately. Money. And lots of it. How much did it cost to live in Hollywood for three months? Adopt a child? Start a landscape business? Quite a bit, I was sure.

271

Melvin could have faked his robbery. So could Stephanie. I still couldn't figure out the store being robbed with Lindsey and me not being the wiser. It would all click eventually. Then I remembered Sharon and her missing necklace.

There'd been a lapse of time with her too. She knew she'd seen Lindsey, then nothing for how long? Forty-five minutes to an hour? Could whatever have caused her forgetfulness contribute to her death?

I dialed Bruce again. "Did they do an autopsy on Sharon Weiss?"

"What?"

"I need to know if she had anything unusual in her system."

"She died from hitting her head. Accidental death. End of story. Leave it alone or I'm calling Duane." Click.

He wouldn't dare! Bruce really bugged me. Threatening to call my boyfriend. What a low blow. There'd been tension between me and Bruce since I turned him down for a date in high school. Talk about holding grudges.

"Mom," I called out as I grabbed my purse. "I've got to run home for a few minutes."

"No problem. I left something for you."

"Thanks!" I dashed for my car and sped home. After unlocking the door to the former guesthouse, I knelt beside my father's medical books. Disorientation, forgetfulness, a waking sleep; I'd find something relative inside those pages. If not, I'd check the internet. One way or another, I'd have some answers before I quit for the day.

"Hey, Marsha." Duane stood in the doorway. "I've got chocolate chip cookies."

"You baked?"

"No, I found them sitting on the porch."

"Let me take them. Mom said she left something for me." I stood on tip toes to give him a kiss and set the cookies on the coffee table. "Help yourself. I've got something to look up."

37

"What are you looking for?" Duane sat in the one arm chair I owned with a glass of milk in one of his hands and the plate of cookies on the end table beside him.

I sat cross-legged on the floor with my father's journals spread out in front of me. "A drug that makes people forget things for a while."

Duane frowned and leaned forward. "Do you want to talk about what's bothering you? Drugs are never the answer."

"Nothing's bothering me, silly. It has to do with the case." I flipped open the first book. "With myself and Lindsey, money was stolen from the store while we were there, yet neither of us remember a thing. Then, if you recall, I stumbled home afterward with drunk-like symptoms."

"I remember." He winked. "I wanted to carry you to your room." Duane ate a cookie then downed some milk.

"Mom would have had a coronary." I giggled.

"Do you want me to help you look?"

I shook my head. "Go ahead and eat. I'm not sure what I'm looking for anyway. You can help when you're finished."

Half an hour later, I found what I'd been looking for. "Duane, listen to this. I think this might be it. I won't read it word for word, just the interesting parts. There's a lot of medical mumbo-jumbo, but here goes. Versed, or Midazoliam, is a clear, red or purplish cherry-flavored syrup. It's used for relaxing someone before a surgery. Hey, they sometimes use it to relax prisoners who are about to be executed." I ran my finger down the page. "Listen, this is interesting.

"Symptoms include loss of short term memory, 'waking up' again and again, but not remembering what happened a minute before. Oh, don't take it if you're doing opiates. Not a good thing. Some people wake up angry, but that's rare. You have total amnesia while under the influence. Do you think dentists use it? Would sure make having your teeth drilled easier to suffer through. The drug makes you groggy and disoriented. I bet that's what happened to Sharon Weiss. She fell and hit her head. That would make the suspect a murderer times two." I glanced up. "Duane?"

His eyes had a glazed effect, and he grinned with one side of his mouth. "Why are you wearing a hat?"

"I'm not." I put a hand to my head. "I had my hair cut, remember?"

"Oh, yeah. Why are you wearing a hat?" His words slurred and the glass of milk shattered to the floor.

I leaped to my feet. The book fell with a thud to the floor. "Duane!" I shook him. His head lolled back and forth as he tried to focus his gaze on me.

"You're beautiful. What's your name?"

The plate of cookies on the end table screamed at me. It all suddenly fell into place. That's how the suspect administered the drug. "How many cookies did you eat?"

"About a million."

"Good grief." I dashed for the phone and called nine-one-one. Bags of groceries sat on the kitchen counter. That's what Mom had dropped off; not the cookies. I almost dropped the phone. I'd eaten cookies at the store. So had Lindsey, and Sharon had rattled on about me sending her cookies that tasted funny. Oh, Lord, help us.

I carried the phone with me to the living room. I should have noted how many cookies had been on the plate. Eight sat there now. Could it be safe to say a dozen?

"Hey, beautiful. What's your name?"

"It's Marsha." Oh, Lord, he doesn't know me! "The ambulance is on its way. It'll take ten minutes. Hold on, sweetheart."

"That's my name? Funny name for a guy." Duane tried to stand and wobbled.

I dropped the phone and propped a shoulder beneath his arm. Heavy! With knees buckling, I eased him back into the chair. "You stay there."

"Okay." He grabbed me and pulled me onto his lap. His hands roamed in places they shouldn't. Wrestling him was like fighting an octopus. "Mars Bar, I love you." His eyes closed, and his head fell against the back of the chair

I felt for a pulse. Steady and strong. When I got my hands on whoever was poisoning the residents of this town, I'd make sure I had my Tazer ready, and I'd zap them more then once. I hadn't finished reading about Versed, but I was pretty sure if Duane was allergic to it he'd have stopped breathing by now. Worst case scenario; he'd wake up with a great big headache.

By sheer willpower I held myself together and avoided the now awake but groggy Duane's groping hands until the paramedics arrived. They nodded as I explained my suspicions and said they'd pass the information on to the doctors. They could determine with a blood test whether Duane had Versed in his symptom. Fortunately, an antidote existed.

As they wheeled my beloved out on a gurney, I grabbed my purse, made sure my cell phone was inside, locked the front door, then dashed out to my car. I'd call Bruce on the way. With one hand, I started the ignition and with the other punched in his number.

"Not again."

"Hush. This is important. Duane's being taken to the hospital. I think he ate cookies laced with Versed. I also think that's what happened to me and Lindsey. The leftover cookies are in my house. Get the spare key from the flower pot beside the door."

"Whoa, slow down."

"I can't talk anymore, Bruce. Didn't you hear me? The ambulance is taking Duane to the hospital!"

"Okay. I'll get the cookies from your house, drop them at the station, then meet you there."

I phoned Mom. "I won't be back at work. The paramedics are taking Duane to the hospital." Tears clogged my throat. "He ate poison cookies."

"Cookies! Where'd he get them?"

"He said someone left them on the front porch."

"Why would you let him eat something you had no idea where it came from?"

"I thought you left them."

"I wouldn't give him poison cookies! Gracious, Marsha. The groceries I left are clean."

"I didn't . . .oh, never mind. Can you close the store and come to the hospital?" A sob ripped from my throat. "I need you."

"I'll beat you there, sweetie."

What if something happened to Duane? What if I was wrong about him having an allergic reaction? Maybe it took longer than a few minutes for the body to react. I coaxed the Prius to a faster speed.

Life without him would be unbearable. Robert's death had been tragic enough. I'd loved him in my own way, but not the soul-encompassing, heart-wrenching love I felt for his brother Duane. The tears flowed unchecked, running down my cheeks and soaking the neckline of the tee shirt I wore under my faithful overalls.

The thirteen miles to the county hospital might as well have been a hundred. The road stretched before me like an unending asphalt ribbon. Maybe I could've asked Bruce for a police escort. I pressed harder on the gas.

Red and blue lights flashed in my rearview mirror. I contemplated speeding ahead and suffer the consequences later, but couldn't stomach one more thing going wrong. Gravel crunched as I pulled to the shoulder of the road.

I watched as the officer marched to my window, one hand on the weapon at his belt.

"Ma'am, do you know how fast you were going?"

"About seventy-five."

He stuck his tongue in his cheek. "Are you all right? You've been crying and that, coupled with speeding, is not a good combination."

"My boyfriend was just taken to the hospital." I wiped my eyes on my sleeve. "Can you call Bruce Barnett? He should be enroute as we speak."

"Why should I call him?"

"Please. I'm in a hurry, and I've already explained everything to him." My voice rose to near hysteria level.

"Settle down. I'll make the call." He stepped away and unclipped a phone from his belt. His gaze stayed on me as he spoke. "Roger. Follow me, ma'am."

The officer roared away with me hot on his tail. Bless you, Bruce. I'd try not to think ill of him ever again.

Mom, Leroy, and Lindsey waited in the parking lot. "Cool, mom. An escort!"

"Are you okay, sweetie?" Mom wrapped her arms around me after I slid from the car.

"They've taken Duane inside. The doctor said to wait in the visitor's room, and he'll let us know when he has news."

I nodded and swallowed against the fresh threat of tears. As we turned to leave, I caught a glimpse of the side of my car where Melvin had hit it with his lawnmower. A thin scratch ran near the rear bumper. Light blue paint flashed like a beacon. Lunging into the front seat, I withdrew the envelope containing the title and opened it. A blank sheet of paper fell out. Why hadn't I checked sooner?

I knew the name of our thief and murderer.

38

"Marsha, are you coming?" Mom laid a hand on my arm.

"Is Bruce here?" Withdrawing from the car, I left the fake title on the seat and faced my mother.

"He left about ten minutes ago, and said he'd be back in an hour." She peered in my face. "Are you all right?"

I nodded. Checking on Duane took first priority. I could give Bruce my information when he came back. As long as the suspect didn't know I'd figured anything out, we still had time. "I want to see Duane."

As soon as I sat in one of the green striped chairs in the waiting room, a doctor in scrubs entered. "Marsha Steele?"

I popped up. "That's me."

He smiled. "Mr. Steele can see you now. He'll be fine. We're keeping him overnight for observation. The tip you gave us was right on. He digested a rather large dose of a medication commonly known as Versed. We've administered an antecdote."

"Thank you." I tore down the hall as the doctor called out Duane's room number.

Duane sat up and grinned as I burst into his room. I wrapped my arms around him and sobbed into his shoulder. He rubbed my back. "Sweetheart, I'm going to be fine. I'm still a little dopey, but that'll pass."

"You scared me. When you didn't know my name, well, what if your memory loss would've been permanent?"

He tilted my face so I'd look at him. "Then I would've fallen in love with you all over again."

After planting a kiss on his lips, I moved to recline beside him. Within seconds, his breathing slowed, and I realized he'd fallen asleep. With the utmost care, I slid from beneath his arm and stared down at his face. The dark shadow of whiskers colored his face. Lashes a woman would die for rested against rugged cheeks. Full hair, showing a few strands of silver, topped off the beautiful picture. Mrs. Duane Steele. Yep, I liked the sound of that, and if he didn't propose soon, I'd do the asking myself.

Guilt over not loving Robert as he'd deserved almost caused me to double over in pain. How could I have married him and born his child, knowing I'd still loved Duane? Sobs shuddered through me. I was a horrible person.

In his way, Robert had known. That explained his staying out late more and more often as the years progressed. The reason he hadn't wanted to seek out his brother. Their separation had been my fault. *Forgive me, Robert.* My soul cried out for peace. Fear clogged my throat. What if I couldn't love Duane as he deserved? Maybe I was incapable of a love that deep.

No, I knew God loved me and forgave me of my selfishness the moment I asked. The best thing to do would be to move forward and be the best person I could.

I slid from the bed, planted a kiss on Duane's forehead, and made my way to the restroom. After washing my face and patting my hair into place, I shuffled back to the waiting room.

Mom hugged me. "Bruce is in inside. I mentioned you wanted to speak with him."

I took a deep breath and stepped in to deliver my news. "Bruce, I want you to sit down and not interrupt until I'm finished. When I'm done, if you still think I'm off my rocker, then I'll step aside and not interfere in your investigation again. Agreed?"

"You're always off your rocker."

I cocked my head and raised an eyebrow in what I hoped was the perfect imitation of my mom's intimidating 'mother' look. "Agreed?"

"Fine." He crossed his arms.

Beginning with Sharon Weiss's death, and counting off every one of the robberies that followed, plus The Corner Store and Kyle Anderson's death, then moving on to the paint on my Prius and the blank sheet of paper, I squared my shoulders.

"By now you know Duane was poisoned by Versed. All the times we'd eaten cookies, dropped off by a so-called, well-meaning friend, we'd been eating the medicine. Out of stupidity. . ." I held up a finger to stop his comment.

"We didn't check to see where the cookies came from. We assumed they came from well-meaning people. Also, I believe Sharon Weiss ate Versed, grew disoriented, thus falling to her death. Plus, Stephanie Jackson's husband is a pharmacist. Super easy for her to get her hands on drugs.

"Now, are you going to arrest her for the thefts in this town and the murder of Kyle Anderson?"

Bruce whipped his cell phone from his belt and phoned in the order to pick up Stephanie for questioning. He glanced up at me. "You did good." With those words, he marched from the room, his shoes clicking against the tiled floor.

Duane was awake again and held his arms open. I slid into the place I most wanted to be in the world. "You, my love, are an amazing woman."

"I did pretty well for myself, didn't I?" I closed my eyes against the knowledge I'd be in the market for a new car again. Maybe there'd be some way I could keep the Prius.

The ringing of the bedside phone woke me. After several fumbling attempts to grasp the handset, I succeeded. "Duane Steele's room."

"Marsha?"

"Bruce?"

"Stephanie has vanished. Her husband has no idea where she is. A suitcase is missing, along with the money they'd saved for the adoption. Don't go home alone."

39

"You think she's going to come after me?" I bolted to a sitting position. Duane stiffened beside me.

"Just a precaution. There's no way she can know we've figured it out."

We? Marsha Calloway Steele solved the crime with no support from River Valley's finest. Stephanie had to know I would check the title eventually, even being the procrastinator I am. I chewed the inside of my cheek. Everyone knew I'd been nosing around. It wouldn't be hard. That's why the two night-time visits to my home. "Okay, I'll stay here until she's caught." I hung up.

"What?"

"Stephanie wasn't home. It appears she's skipped town. Her husband had no idea she'd been stealing." I swung my legs over the side of the bed. "He thought she was really good at saving."

Duane grabbed for my hand. "Where are you going?"

"To let my mom know the latest and to grab a bite to eat from the cafeteria." I bent and delivered a kiss to his forehead and grabbed my purse. "Go back to sleep. I'll be here when you wake up."

Mom listened with a grim expression while I recounted my conversation with Bruce. Leroy laid an arm around her shoulder. "I'll watch out for your mother and daughter. You stay here with Duane."

"Thank you, Leroy." I gave him an impulsive peck on the cheek. "I couldn't trust them in better hands. Y'all go home. I'm getting something to eat. Duane and I should be able to join you in the morning."

I watched the three of them leave then turned to find my way to the cafeteria. A hand reached out of the women's restroom and yanked me inside. I stared into the barrel of Stephanie Jackson's gun. My heart skipped a beat. "Hello, Stephanie. Bruce is looking for you."

"He won't find me." She motioned for me to walk ahead of her. "Let's go."

"Where?" The first stirrings of anger simmered within me. How dare she do all the horrible things she'd done, then accost me in the hospital?

"None of your business. You won't be around long enough to care. There's a lot of places in these hills to leave you. By the time someone stumbles across your body, I'll be in Mexico and the proud mother of a beautiful little girl."

The saliva dried in my mouth. "Do you actually think they'll let you adopt a child after this?"

"They'll see the color of my money and won't ask too many questions."

"You won't be able to bring the child back to the states." I hoped she would like Mexico.

Stephanie poked me in the spine all the way to the parking lot and beside a dark green Toyota. If I looked closer, I knew I'd locate a smear of white paint on the bumper. The knowledge the woman had tried to run a couple of innocent kids off the road raised my blood pressure.

"Get in."

I slid in the driver side door and climbed over the gear shift to the passenger side, dropping my purse on the floorboard. My brain spun trying to figure out where we'd go that the others could find me. Keeping her gun trained on me, Stephanie backed from the parking lot and headed east on Interstate 40.

"Since you're going to kill me anyway, can I ask a couple of questions?"

She shrugged. "Sure. I don't like killing you, Marsha. I'd hoped we could be great friends. We'd share parenting stories, have play dates. That sort of thing."

As if. Didn't she realize my child was fifteen? "Why the stealing? If you were meant to be a parent, there are other ways."

She chuckled. "I thought you'd want to know how I figured out you knew it was me."

"Okay." That would've been my next question.

"I went to your place today after hearing Duane ate the cookies meant for you. Mark has a police scanner, so it's easy to keep up on what's going on. I'd suspected for a while that you were getting close to figuring things out, and I put enough medicine in those cookies to knock out a horse. Having a pharmacist for a husband comes in handy, doesn't it?" She giggled. "Anyway, it worried me. I don't have anything against that handsome man. Thought I might have put in too much. I broke in, saw the medical journals turned to a compromising page, and put two and two together. Brilliant, aren't I?"

"What did you do with Cleo?"

"Locked her in the shed. She's got a big bark, but still caved under a handful of dog biscuits." Stephanie whipped the wheel to take us down Highway 64. "I should've poisoned those too, but I've got nothing against animals."

"Why did you kill Kyle?"

"That man was too smart for his own good, and even nosier than you. He was in the pharmacy filling a prescription and saw me in the back filching drugs right under my dear husband's nose. He was going to blackmail me."

I nodded. "How much did you put in Sharon's cookies? The way I figure, she ate them, then fell and hit her head."

"Good guess. That woman really ought to learn to lock her front door. It's too easy to waltz in and drop something off."

Stephanie Jackson was officially crazy. My stomach growled. "Any chance we can get something to eat?"

"I'm finished talking, and you won't need food much longer."

I clicked my seatbelt into place, thankful she hadn't worn hers. Desperate times relied on desperate measures, or so the saying went. I leaned over and yanked the steering wheel from her hands. The gun went off, sending a bullet into my thigh. Oh, sweet heaven!

The pain burned worse than the Tazer. Nausea rose and spots swam in front of my eyes. Blood soaked the denim of my overalls. I blinked against the threatening dizziness and screamed as we sailed over the embankment.

We skid and bashed into a tree. My seatbelt locked into place. Stephanie wasn't so lucky. Her head bounced off the side window, knocking her unconscious. The airbags deployed, almost choking me on their powder.

After I fought my way free, I fumbled on the floor for my purse and zapped her with my Tazer for good measure. Acid rose in my throat as the pain in my leg worsened. I wanted to zap her again

The door was crinkled past the point of opening so I crawled through the window, whimpering like a wounded puppy, and fell into a heap on the ground. My breath came in gasps. How was I going to get home with a hole in my leg?

Stephanie groaned, spurring me to action. I pulled to my feet, scrambled to the driver's side, then succumbed to the temptation of the Tazer again, and pressed it against her lily-white skin. So what if she had a heart attack from the electricity. It would serve her right.

She jerked and glared at me. "Fair's fair, sweetie. And I do *not* want to be your friend." I palmed her in the side of the head. "That's for running my daughter off the road. This," I slapped her harder. "Is for shooting me." I doubled my fist and laid a good one along her jaw. "And this is for poisoning the man I love." Her eyes closed, and I slid to the ground, shaking the pain from my hand.

The world spun around me, and I swallowed back the bile rising in my throat. Anger could only spur a person so far, and now the pain overcame the infuriation roaring through me.

"Marsha!" I peered around the front of the car and tried to focus. Mom and Leroy slid down the embankment. Lindsey's face stared through the window of Mom's Cadillac.

"I'm over here." Mom slipped getting to my side. "How did you find me?"

"We followed you." She ran her hands over my leg. I winced. "Sorry. We were still in the parking lot trying to decide where to go for dinner. When Stephanie walked out of the hospital behind you, I wished I'd had a gun myself." She grinned. "Leroy drove worthy of a race car driver trying to keep up with that crazy woman."

Darkness threatened. "My purse is on the ground. Use my cell phone to call the police and an ambulance. I've been shot." I laid my head back and closed my eyes.

###

When I woke, Duane leaned over me. "Why aren't you in bed?"

He brushed his lips across mine. "They couldn't keep me down once I found out you'd been brought in." He stepped aside to let Bruce step up.

"Stephanie said you zapped her and hit her. Twice on the zap, three slaps to the head." He grinned. "She wants to press charges."

"Let her go for it." I returned his smile. "I did hit and zap. And I'd do it again."

"Good thing I took away your gun. You might've shot her."

"Good deduction."

He patted my shoulder. "I'm very impressed, Marsha. But you could've been killed. Next time, let the police handle it."

Did he honestly think there'd be a next time? "Sure thing." From now on, I'd stick to stuffing bunnies and Time-Out Babies.

Once Bruce left, Duane leaned over and smoothed my hair away from my face. "Woman, I love you so much it scares me to death."

"There's only one thing to do then."

"What's that?" The corner of his mouth quirked.

"Marry me."

40

The wedding march played over the stereo speakers set up in the back yard. With a deep breath, I smoothed the skirt of the embroidered floral dress I wore then stepped into the early evening light. Crickets sang while bull frogs provided the bass. We'd never taken down the decorations from Mom's party and twinkling lights gave a cheery glow to the faces of wedding guests. A light breeze stirred my curls.

Lindsey followed, the hem of her skirt rasping against the pebble walkway. She hadn't even balked at wearing a gown. Dressed in a summer suit of baby blue, Mom beamed at me when I glanced at her over my shoulder. I told her she looked beautiful. Her happiness almost made me forget the twinge still left in my thigh from Stephanie's bullet. I took another step and focused on Duane's face.

He and Leroy waited beneath a rose threaded arch. Leroy's ruddy face glowed brighter then the moon that would rise later that night. I couldn't think of a better man for a stepfather or a grandfather to my daughter.

Duane had said yes to my hospital proposal. All we needed now was a date.

Mom had suggested we have a double wedding, but I'd said no, not wanting to infringe on her day. She deserved it, and I wanted time to revel in the fact I'd be marrying the man of my dreams.

I took my position across from Duane. He mouthed, "I love you." My face heated and I glanced heavenward. What a gift I'd been given.

Mom took her place beside Leroy and handed me her bouquet.

"Dearly Beloved, we are gathered here together to join Leroy Bohan and Gertie Calloway in holy matrimony."

I lifted a hand to wipe away my happy tears and met Duane's gaze across the rose petal strewn aisle runner.

The second book in the River Valley mystery series is now available…Advance Notice.

Check out Cynthia's other books at www.cynthiahickey.com

ABOUT THE AUTHOR

Multi-published author Cynthia Hickey's first mystery, Fudge-Laced Felonies, won first place in the inspirational category of the Great Expectations contest in 2007. Her third cozy, Chocolate-Covered Crime, received a four-star review from Romantic Times. All three cozies have been re-released as ebooks through the MacGregor Literary Agency, along with a new cozy series. She has several historical romances releasing in 2013 and 2014 through Harlequin's Heartsong Presents. She lives in Arizona with her husband, one of their seven children, two dogs and two cats. She has five grandchildren who keep her busy and tell everyone they know that "Nana is a writer". Visit her website at www.cynthiahickey.com

OU

39291219R00172

Made in the USA
Lexington, KY
14 February 2015